CW01668436

Porter's Lodge

Book One: Sins of the Father

L T Brady

Sins of the Father: Book one — Porter's Lodge
Copyright © 2018 by L T Brady. All rights reserved.
First Edition: August 2018

978-1-9997185-2-7 - Paperback
978-1-9997185-3-4 - E-Book

All rights reserved. No portion of this book may be reproduced, stored in a retrieval system or transmitted at any time or by any means of mechanical, electronic, photocopying, recording or otherwise without the prior permission of L T Brady.

Acknowledgements

For Maxine who has dragged me to more horror films than I would like to remember and to those that have rekindled my love of Gothic and mystery.

And thank you to Alex for the beautiful drawing and to Jo, as ever, for helping me avoid embarrassing errors and enjoy editing.

The Ambros Family Tree in 1500s

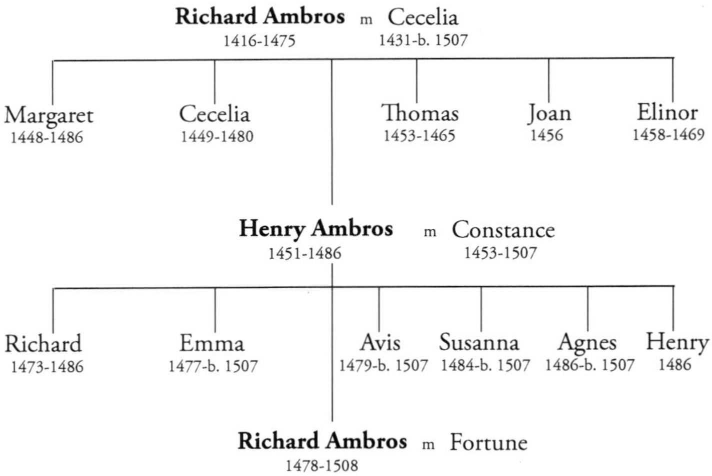

The Ambros Family Tree in 2021

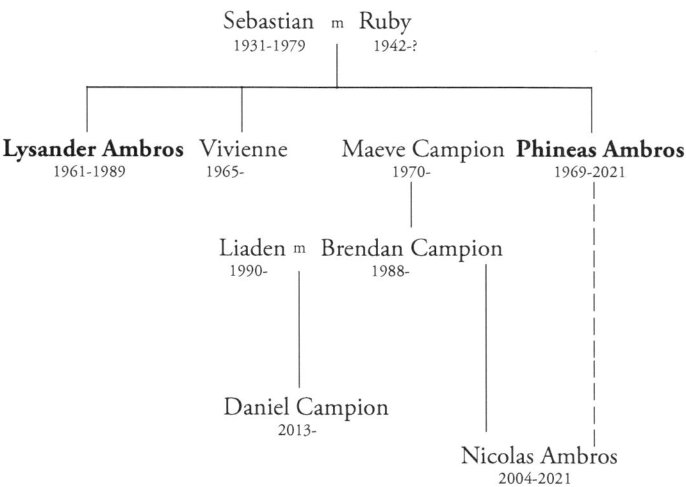

Porter's Lodge

Prologue

DISTANTLY, HE COULD HEAR THE sounds of shouts and screams from the battle. As he had done that day, he ignored it as best he could, heading forward and towards the tower instead. Smoke curled around the stone walls, so thick and dense it could have been tangible; something that Brendan could touch and use to climb.

But even in his dreams the smoke would not hold him. Somehow, he knew that even as he reached a hand out, hoping that this time, maybe this time...

As always, the smoke faltered, revealing the never-ending stare from the bodies underneath. Accusing and fixed, their eyes always seemed to find him no matter where he stood.

Failed. You failed us.

You failed him.

No.

He needed to climb. Not the stairs, Brendan already knew what would happen if he took that route. It always happened. Spiral staircases were unforgiving, they allowed no room to manoeuvre, no chance to quicken the desperate pace he had used the first time.

Yet somehow it always happened the same way. Somehow, without conscious will, no matter how much he screamed, he ended up on those stairs. His legs burning with effort, banging his shins on the stairs with graceless speed.

The worst thing was the hope. A minute earlier would be all he needed. One single minute. No matter the screams downstairs, no matter the fact that he had left friends downstairs to face hell on earth-

Just one more minute.

Please. Just one more minute.

The sound of glass smashing rang out as he flipped up the latch. The door creaked in protest at being yanked open. And, in the corner of the room, always the same, just the impression of a body already dropping, falling out of the shattered window.

It was all he had of his son.

Chapter One

September 2021

GETTING OUT OF BED AT seven minutes past five on a Monday morning was never a pleasant experience. Brendan had found that when it was combined with alcohol and an eight-year-old, matters didn't exactly improve.

Even less pleasant were angry wives who were trying not to be angry.

"You shouldn't go," Liaden said, tightening her dressing gown around her, hair a matted mess that he would usually tease her for.

Christ, those days seemed like a million years ago now. "It's work, not a battlefield," Brendan muttered, running the tap for some water.

"You're on leave-"

"To do what?" he asked, turning to her as he popped the paracetamol from the packet. "Cry?"

Steely grey eyes met his blue ones unflinchingly. "That would be preferable to you drowning yourself with vodka every night."

"We're out of vodka," Brendan muttered, as he knocked back the pills then the water.

"Wonder why."

Slamming the glass down, Brendan stared at his fingers, pressing the tips into the glass, idly wondering how long they would last before they faded away, vanished as if they had never been there in the first place.

"I am..." he took a deep breath, trying to focus. "I am working through it. Just give me time-"

"It's been three months."

"Yeah," he said bitterly, looking up to catch her gaze. "Three months."

Liaden studied him, her gaze wavering between sorrow and frustration. "I am not saying you should be over it, Brendan," she said, keeping her gaze on him and speaking with such care that he found himself being even more frustrated by it all. "I am saying that you should be doing something else other than trying to find an answer at the bottom of a glass-"

"Like what?" he snapped.

"I don't-"

"What's the magic cure for grief over losing a-" he cut himself off and looked away and out the window, eyes sweeping the garden to try and avoid the conversation.

And the pity he could see on her face.

"You can't even say it," Liaden said gently. "For losing a child, Brendan. For losing your son."

Losing...he'd lost him for years.

He'd just fucking failed to get him back.

"I'm going to work," he muttered, reaching out for his coat.

"Brendan-"

Whatever it was that she'd been about to say, he managed to cut off by slamming the front door closed between them.

On the other side of the city, Jake Atkins nearly screamed into his pillow when his bloody alarm went off. Reaching out, he fumbled with his phone and then tossed it back, barely caring when he heard the familiar crash of the phone not quite landing on his bedside table.

He'd get it later. Even the hazy knowledge that this was about to be his first day training in the Elites wasn't quite enough to sweep away the comforting fuzziness of sleep or make him leave the warmth of his bed.

"Are you up yet?" his mum shouted up the stairs, jolting him. Twenty-four years of the woman and her bellowing up the stairs worked like a charm as he scrambled up in a panic and then collapsed back down into his pillow, groaning and wide awake now.

"Yes," he lied, kicking down the covers in the hopes that somehow that might help him roll out of bed.

"I'm making your sandwiches."

Torn between laughing and rolling his eyes in irritation, Jake glared at the alarm clock waiting for it to turn…5.46…5.47…

"Jake!"

With a loud, longing groan for sleep, Jake got out of bed and stumbled out onto the landing, almost bumping into his dad.

"She's too awake," Jake complained.

"She's too loud," his dad corrected, shaking his head. "You'd think it was her first day."

"Induction day," Jake corrected warily. "I have to be trained to actually have the job."

"First day," his dad said, looking pleased. "Go have a shower, before she comes up here to do it for you."

It was worryingly possible that his mum would do exactly that.

As far as Brendan was concerned, London at quarter to six was just about peaceful. Fresher, calmer and more relaxed.

Not to mention you could get a seat on the frigging tube.

It was, however, an odd experience to walk down streets and know that he was seeing something entirely different to eighty percent of the population.

The percent without magic.

Granted, there were a fuck load of office blocks in London, of buildings that had no discernible use even to him. But it was utterly unfathomable that he could lean on the railings, having a strong coffee on the bridge and be staring straight at the Currock building's roof that rose up in the midst of all the other buildings while others merely saw endless offices. In fact, unless he was mistaken, he was the only one on the bridge currently able to see the great domed roof.

That was until someone leaned against the rails next to him and held out a muffin.

"Your missus will flay me alive if you don't shove that in your gob."

Brendan glanced at it and took the damned thing. "Does she think I've got an eating disorder now?" he asked, feeling his annoyance rise as Nate turned and leaned with his back against the rail of the bridge.

"I believe her exact words were 'shove some food in him to soak up that cheap vodka he was swigging last night'," Nate said with a careless shrug.

"She bought the damned stuff," Brendan muttered, turning the muffin around in his hand.

"I don't think she thought you'd stoop so low."

Yeah, whatever. Twisting his fingers, he felt his magic dart out, banishing the now empty coffee cup with ease. Brendan then used both hands to unwrap the muffin from the case, before banishing the paper too.

"Show off," Nate muttered, shaking his head as he stared out along the river with a strange expression on his face before he looked back. "They won't let you back on active duty," Nate said in a softer voice. "You do know that."

"I know it'll depend how desperate they are," Brendan corrected. "We've lost too many for them to keep being this picky."

"You know we have new recruits coming in?" Nate asked. "Little lambs, all ripe for us to train up and scare the shit out of."

"It'll take months before they're properly trained," Brendan muttered.

Nate nodded. "Probably, but they aren't the Hero of Ambros-"

With an annoyed snarl, Brendan turned and started walking along the bridge.

"You keep going towards work, you're gonna hear that a thousand times," Nate warned, following him. "That's what they're calling you, the Hero of Ambros-"

"Will you shut up?" Brendan muttered, stopping and turning to glare at Nate. "I get it. I don't need you saying it-"

"They won't let you in the building. It's one thing to have you drinking yourself to death at home, another to go to work and start spouting off at people-"

"I'm not spouting off at people, I'm spouting off to you," Brendan muttered as Nate caught up. "You don't count."

Nate flashed him a grin as they fell into step together and Nate slung an arm over his shoulder. "You really want to go to work?" he asked with a sigh.

"I can't sit at home," Brendan said frankly, wincing slightly at how that sounded.

"Yeah," Nate said with a last squeeze as he dropped his arm. "I know," he nodded and then glanced at him. "But work? You couldn't just go to the pub and watch the match?"

"You've got everything?" Jake's dad asked as he turned off the engine and settled back in the car seat.

Jake nodded as he let out an almost whistling breath. "Yeah," he said, drumming his fingers on the new bag his parents had bought him as a celebration present when he'd passed the interview stage.

"And you know where you're going?"

"I did survive for three years at uni without you sending me directions," Jake muttered. "I looked it up last night."

"Relax," his dad suggested after a moment. "This is as much you inspecting them as them looking at you. Just go in and have a good day."

Eyes riveted on the platform board, counting down until the train arrived, Jake sighed. "I know," he said, feeling a bit bad for being such a brat. "I just...I really wish Mum hadn't announced this to everyone she's ever met."

His dad laughed, looking slightly sheepish and Jake almost groaned.

Apparently, his mum hadn't been the only one.

"She's excited," his dad argued, looking at the platform. "And proud. We both are."

Torn between feeling pleased and feeling desperately awkward, Jake wriggled to get out of his seat belt. "Thanks," he said, not really sure what else to say.

"Here." His dad reached out and slid a twenty into Jake's coat pocket.

"Dad-"

"Buy some beers or something after you finish," his dad said, clapping Jake on the shoulder. "Go on, or you'll miss the train."

With an awkward half hug, Jake took a deep breath and opened the door.

Duncan, the guard on the staff gate for the Currock Building, raised an eyebrow at Brendan's appearance.

"Don't," Nate said with a sigh. "I've pointed out he's a saddo for coming into work. He ain't listening."

"Freak," Duncan said with a half-hearted teasing grin, even as his eyes narrowed a little as if scanning Brendan for something. "You could always take my shift if you fancy."

"Not got the patience," Brendan said, letting Duncan scan his staff pass.

"You ready for the newbies?" Nate asked, handing his own over.

The worried glances vanished in the wake of genuine annoyance. "Why can you lot not stagger these things? I've got new healers, the political interns and baby Elites coming in today."

"Nurses?" Nate asked eagerly. "Young nurses?"

Brendan shoved him forward. "Perv," he teased, shaking his head at Duncan.

Nate laughed, stumbling as they walked down the gravel and towards the grand steps. "Thank God for early starts," he said, looking around at the quiet grounds. "I fucking hate tourist season," he muttered.

"It'll calm soon," Brendan said, trying not to focus on the fact that he hadn't seen any tourists due to his 'leave'. Usually the summer months were spent dodging any time at the office due to the influx of visitors to the gardens and tours of the official Council rooms.

"It had better. It's amazing how interested people are since…" Nate's mouth tightened.

"Yeah," Brendan shook his head. "Well…to be expected I guess."

"Mm," Nate said and, for the first time, Brendan saw a shadow cross his friend's face at the memory of Ambros and the losses they'd experienced there. Uncomfortable with the reminder that there were other people grieving, Brendan left it.

He was hardly in the position to be an emotional rock for anyone at the moment.

The wards that he had passed through for the past fifteen years were barely an issue anymore as he trotted up the grand stairs and through the heavily spelled doors. The opening to the Currock building was quiet, only a scattered few were coming up and through the massive doors and into the imposing entrance.

"Boss know you're coming in?" Nate asked as they turned left and through one of the almost hidden doors within the first darkened arch. In the middle, the four at the reception desk were getting ready for a busy day as they worked underneath a woven, glass tree that was the symbol of the Council.

"No," Brendan said, heading for the lift. "Thought I'd surprise him," he added, pressing the button to call it.

Nate snorted. "Oh, yeah. He'll love that."

"I'd heard he'd mellowed this summer," Brendan flashed Nate a grin as he stepped into the lift and pressed for the third floor.

"Like saying a bishop is slightly less Catholic than the Pope," Nate shook his head. "He'll throw you out by the scruff of your neck."

"He's been threatening that since I was seventeen," Brendan sighed, leaning back against the mirrored wall of the lift. "He ain't done it yet."

Being back in the office was almost like coming home. After the grandeur of the rest of the building the office always looked run down and messy. It was good though; it didn't look like a museum like the rest of the building. Instead the room, with its stacks of paper work and ancient looking computers, chipped desks and ugly carpet, looked familiar and easy, Brendan thought as he sat at his desk. Functional.

He had a few pictures wedged into the lining of his notice board – one from a date he and Liaden had been on, a cheap Kodak one from their wedding and one of their son Danny on his fifth birthday which he should probably replace now, given that the photograph was three years old.

There was also one of his eldest, hideously out of date as the toddler peered up curiously at the camera and squinted in the summer sun. It had been taken a few months after Nicolas' first birthday. Brendan had been looking after him in the garden (in the shade because at the grand old age of seventeen he'd been attempting to be responsible and shit), but the baby had to have had a different plan and had crawled out into the sun then looked annoyed at being called back...

Tentatively, Brendan dragged a finger down the picture, wishing that just for a second-

"You shouldn't be here," Boss said behind him, shattering the memory.

"I can't be at home," Brendan said quietly as he dropped his finger from the picture and turned.

As if being weighed and measured, Brendan waited patiently while Boss stared at him, cold blue eyes almost shocking in his weathered face. "You can be the fucking secretary then," Boss decided, turning on his heel, large bulk weaving through the desks without hunching or seeming to manoeuvre. Instead, the desks looked as if, over time, they'd simply moved to safe places to avoid being in his way as he patrolled the area.

Brendan met Nate's eyes as he sat across from him. "Teacher's pet," Nate muttered and threw him a file. "Be a dear and make that look pretty for a review meeting, would ya?"

The file was dog-eared, falling apart, and most of the papers were scrunched and had tea stains.

"It's a miracle you manage to get anything through a trial," Brendan sighed, pulling the folder across the desk to start ordering it.

"Funny, it's one of yours that I took."

Bugger. Brendan winced when he saw his own scribbles on some of the earlier forms and collected research. Avoiding Nate's gaze, he started to attempt to sort it out. Paperwork really was dull.

Which was why he was almost relieved when Boss came stomping through the office ten minutes later. "Poppy's gone fucking ill," Boss snarled to them all.

"Labour," Eleanor corrected, sounding almost bored as she called out from the booth behind Brendan. "It's called labour, not illness. And she did warn you."

Nate caught Brendan's eye with a grin and shook his head. Amused, Brendan continued to sort through the folder that he must have put together half asleep or while severely pissed.

A shadow fell over his desk and Brendan paused, feeling a strange sense of impending doom.

"You wanna be useful?" Boss asked.

It was tempting to say no but, knowing Boss, he would just throw Brendan out and demand that he return home to the silence, to thinking and remembering and-

"What do you need?" Brendan asked with a wince, turning to face Boss properly.

"Induction lecture. There's a power-point and everything."

No.

"You want *me* to give a lecture to those kids?" Brendan asked in horror. "You do it: you're their bloody future Boss."

Boss folded his arms. "I'm your current Boss. Do as I say or I'll be your future ex-Boss."

Nate sniggered.

"You volunteering, Summers?" Boss snapped, gaze snapping to Nate.

"No Boss," Nate said quickly. "Was just impressed by your quick wit."

"Get out of my arse, Summers," Boss muttered as he refocused his attention on Brendan. "I can't put you on active duty and I need someone to give the lecture. Just... treat them like morons. Explain anything and everything. Hold a fucking Q and A session for all I care."

Brendan leaned back in the seat, trying to think of-

"Or," Boss added thoughtfully. "You could go home."

Bastard.

Smiling tightly, Brendan nodded. "Where is it?" he asked, pained.

It was probably embarrassing that Jake found leaving the tube station to be a little daunting. At that time of the morning there was no pause or patience given to anyone new to the city who had no idea of where they were going. All Jake could do was follow the crowd and hope they all knew where they were going. Eventually, he found the exit and stepped straight into rain which cascaded down like a curtain, trapped by the neat, modern pavement and splashed up by the almost marching pace of morning commuters.

Great.

There was a certain amount of skill involved in trying to concentrate on a dry spell and weave in and out of the almost motionless traffic. After a few drops fell onto his face, the spell kicked in and dried the rain as soon as it hit his skin and clothes.

On the bright side, the weather blew away any sleepiness he'd been feeling. It was so fresh that it calmed the nerves that had been building on the train and stole the nausea from his chest.

Swinging his bag forward he opened the front while walking. The Asda's bag his mother had put his lunch into that morning was pretty easy to find, tug out and stare at for a second when he saw the tempting outline of the freshly baked cake slice. Still, after a momentary hesitation and a muttered plea that his mother never found out what he'd done, the lunch went in the nearest bin.

He noted, with some satisfaction, the bars, and places to eat as he walked. A few even looked pretty decent. Then, above the shops and trees, rose a looming building that he couldn't help but recognise.

The Currock Building.

It was strange to think of how some of the people on the pavement saw the view. The most fundamental spell upheld by ancient magic was at work, ensuring that those without magic only saw the huge office buildings that they expected to see.

Those who do not know cannot see.

When he'd asked Amanda, a girl he'd lived next door to for years, what she saw on Google maps she had replied with disinterest that all she could spot were what looked like glass office buildings. How she and others like her couldn't see the tall trees from the sweeping grounds or the impressive domed glass roof rising up from the middle, he'd never really understand.

He could have screamed it at the top of his lungs or explained to Amanda in minute detail what he'd seen and it wouldn't make the blindest bit of difference.

Those who cannot know cannot be told.

Well…he'd probably have to deal with a few pissed off Guardians if he shouted it in the streets.

That would probably bring his career with the Elites to an abrupt stop.

As he neared, the security pass that had been sent with his acceptance letter burned in his back pocket. He hastily fumbled about behind him as a guard eyed him from the employee gate. Flashing a nervous smile, and the pass, Jake went on through, pretty sure that he was being glared at as he continued down the path.

The employee's gate took him to the side instead of through the tall iron gates that had made him shudder when he'd seen them in the online pictures. Jake could still clearly remember his dad and uncle Jeff in the healing centre after their accident with iron and magic. Even now the thought of the impervious metal made him shudder.

Despite going through the side entrance of the grounds, it was the employees and officials who walked through the main entrance to the Currock Building. Jake made his way along the path to the wide, grey stone steps and columned fronts. Beyond these, the entrance was a masterpiece of glass. As Jake got closer he could almost feel the number of spells woven into the glass walls and door. At a certain angle, and when the light was right, he could see the engravings and the colours of multiple spells layered throughout the glass and shimmering like shot silk.

Somewhat awed at the amount of work and power that had gone into just the front of the building, Jake made his way to the base of the stone steps and felt the protection wards for the first time. The two guards, dressed in Council Guard regalia and standing to either side of the stair base, paid absolutely no attention to him as he passed by.

At the top of the stairs, more guards stood at the base of each of the four columns. This time when Jake went through the wards he felt magic shiver through him, as if receiving a continuous static shock. The guard closest eyed him with an unreadable expression, then looked away, leaving Jake to wonder exactly what they were looking for.

The huge doubled door glass entrance was heavily etched and threaded with what looked like silver in some sort of intricate pattern, but the other workers' pace didn't allow him time to pause to study it in detail.

In the lobby, the Council tree was engraved onto the polished stone floor and ahead were small glass doors surrounded by twisted silver, gold and bronze. To either side, stairs led off to different floors and departments; quite a few of the people surrounding Jake went up them and (he'd guess) off to work.

Through the second double doors and wards that felt like treacle, was the grand reception area. Above them, huge etched panes of glass were held together with silver, letting in light that illuminated the entire area. A majestic staircase was opposite him, made of the same almost white stone as the rest of the building. They split halfway up and the carved tree of the Council lined the back wall: each branch there to represent the seven lords and ladies of the Council and their various departments. The runes etched into the branches detailed the seven different areas of focus: Strength, Wisdom, Light magic, Dark magic, Sight, Health and then Leadership at the top. Staring at it, Jake felt a thrumming pulse of nerves that maybe, one day, he'd have to interact with the famed seven.

The room itself was a huge semi-circle. Leading off from the room were huge archways to different parts of the building. Nervously, Jake stepped in; all too aware that, apart from him, there were ten other people, all of whom seemed to have a specific purpose for being in the grand reception room.

Slowly, Jake walked down the edge of the room that had about five gigantic arches leading off into different areas of the building, wincing as his shoes made an awful amount of noise in the eerie quiet of the room. As he walked, he found himself peering into the arched corridors before he approached the large, circular reception desk in the centre of the room.

It was 6.54.

If he signed in now, even if he got himself lost in the huge building, at least they'd know he was in the building on time.

Five people worked at the daunting reception desk that was sunken slightly into the floor. In the middle, once again, the Council symbol was replicated in a sculpted version: the inscriptions twisting up the carefully carved branches of the tree and Jake glanced at the Strength branch and the way it split into three departments. Those at the desk all seemed busy, despite it being before seven. Jake approached, unable to see an obvious cue or person to go to.

Did he just push in or-

The brunette closest to him glanced up and frowned when she saw him. Covering the phone with one hand, she asked, "Are you lost, hon?"

On automatic, Jake shook his head, winced and then nodded. Feeling daft, Jake grinned in hopeful embarrassment as she quirked an amused eye at him.

"Sorry…I'm meant to report to reception," he said in a questioning tone. "I'm here for the Induction Day."

The woman nodded and then turned her attention back to the person on the phone, answering some question about a deadline. All Jake could do was stand awkwardly, looking around as she typed away with sharp taps on the keyboard in front of her, fully focussed on her conversation.

It startled him when she just as suddenly covered the phone again and caught his attention with a glance. "Which department?"

His mind raced in panic; there were departments within the Elites? Was he meant to know that?

Seeing his blank look, the receptionist huffed a sigh and flapped a hand at him. "Is it with the healers? The Diplomats? The-"

"Oh!" Jake winced, "Yeah, the Elites."

"And your name?" she asked, a smile tugging on her perfectly painted lips.

"Jake Atkins."

She reached down fractionally, talking once again to the person on the phone.

"Card," she mouthed at Jake as she listened to the person on the other line.

Once again, Jake pulled out the security clearance card and flashed it at her. Waving an impatient hand, she gestured at him to actually give her the card. Somewhat reluctantly, he passed it over, watching as it disappeared forever behind her desk. Then with a confident slap, the receptionist placed another card on the polished reception top.

As Jake picked it up he felt something warm go through him and watched like a fascinated child as the card changed before his eyes.

In his hand was the official identity card of a trainee Elite. The plastic was firm and a light blue. It had his name, picture and some choice details as well as the Council emblem of the glass tree embossed on the bottom right corner. On the reverse was a black strip to swipe the card with.

Unbidden, a stupid smile crossed his face as he stared at it, then the receptionist.

"Put it in your wallet," she advised with some fondness.

As Jake fiddled about with his card and wallet, she finished her conversation and rooted about the desk for some forms.

"The card's keyed to you," she explained. "If anyone but you touches it, the card will simply return to its blank state. That said, do not start waving it about. The card stays out of sight unless you need it when on duty." Passing him a clipboard she continued. "Today's schedule is on the top. Underneath are just a few last-minute pieces of paperwork. You need to read them carefully and closely; they're important."

"Right." Jake nodded, accepting the clipboard.

"Go back the way you came and into the grand

reception hall," she instructed. "You need to go through the third archway as you turn left out of this one. Go up to the second floor and there will be directions from there to the Elite reception area. You need to hand those forms in there. The presentation will begin in under ten minutes."

Concentrating on the directions, Jake waved his clipboard in acknowledgement. "Thanks."

The receptionist gave him a polite smile before answering another phone call.

Almost sure he'd found the right archway, Jake stepped into the lift alone. There hadn't been any obvious sign of any others for the Induction Talk; either he was much earlier or much later than everyone else.

Once on the second floor, he found the directions... if they could be called directions. Hand scrawled, lettering written in thick, fading marker pen over lined paper which was blue tacked to the wall. In some cases, they hadn't even bothered with words, instead using arrows to sort of indicate which way to go. It definitely wasn't what he'd expected after the ease and elegance downstairs but it made him relax a little because it was probably exactly what he'd have done.

The Elites' reception area, found after a few wrong turns, matched the directions. The walls were faded and stained, the chairs mismatched and the plant in the corner had definitely seen better days. An aging, scruffy man in jeans and a battered jacket sat, leaning back in his chair with his face buried in his newspaper. When he turned the page, Jake saw a square face and squat nose with a faded scar running down the side of his face.

Running on automatic, Jake went for the easiest and

closest seat he could manage. Balancing the clipboard precariously on his lap, he glanced around. Most of the seats in the worn reception area were taken by about fifteen others who seemed to be around his age, the eldest maybe just short of twenty-five. Many were dressed as he, in suits. Though privately he thought that the others looked a lot less like a kid playing dress up than he did. One or two of them were dressed a bit too casually in Jake's opinion, and one guy in the corner looked as if he was frankly taking the piss. He was wearing muddy trainers and ripped tracksuit bottoms with a stained white, ill-fitting t-shirt, lounging in the chair and glaring at the desk.

Surely, Jake thought, he had a better chance than that guy.

Once he'd read the forms carefully and signed them, he handed them to the guy at the reception desk...or rather, he gingerly placed them on top of the as of yet unacknowledged pile and sped back to his seat.

In the time that had taken, a few more trainees had arrived, most noticeably the lad now occupying the seat next to Jake's.

Flashing an uncomfortable smile, Jake sat down, wishing he hadn't finished the forms as quickly as he had. Trying to relax himself again, he glanced around at the others, feeling all too aware of the silence pressing in on the group.

It was weird to think that these were the people he'd be training with, that in time would become familiar, even friends. They all seemed deep in thought and nervous. In fact, in Jake's line of vision, the only person that seemed at ease was the gruff old guy reading his newspaper.

Bored, Jake tilted his head, trying to read the football article on the back page. After about three minutes, he became suddenly aware of being watched.

The lad next to him was dressed smartly, maybe not quite a suit and tie, but with some effort. He was blond and tanned and his hazel eyes were narrowed as if he was perplexed as to what Jake was doing.

"Football page on the back. He's got a human paper," Jake explained in a muted whisper, not too sure if he should bother to explain. "I was trying to read it." There was no way he was going to mention that his mum had actually taken his phone and laptop last night, claiming that he'd not sleep if he did any late-night scrolling.

His dad had simply sniggered into his beer.

The guy's forehead creased for a moment and then he leaned in, suddenly intruding into Jake's personal space, but seemingly unaware of it. After a moment, he sat back with a nod. "Good eyesight," was all he said, eyes now on the newspaper, but more focused on the front page.

"I'm Jake," he said, feeling oddly amused by the exchange.

"Cole," the guy said, still staring at the paper before seeming to suddenly collect himself. Shifting a little, he glanced over at Jake. "Good to meet you," he added as if suddenly remembering to try and wrap himself in manners. He held out a hand for Jake to shake, the light catching on a ring on his smallest finger.

It was a little awkward to shake hands in the chair, but Jake supposed that was the kind of thing you did on a ridiculously long job interview. "Not a football fan, I take it?" Jake asked as they let go of each other's hand.

Cole glanced back over at the newspaper and shrugged a little, seemingly unwilling to commit to a comment that might be unpopular. Weirdly though, his hesitation bolstered Jake a little and he continued on. "My dad's a bit obsessed. Used to check all the sports scores before I got home to guess his mood. Especially if it was mum's team versus dad's."

Cole's expression was oddly inscrutable for a moment and then he shifted, turning his attention to Jake. "I take it that they're both sporting fans?" he asked.

"Just competitive." Jake grinned, thinking of Jamaica versus England in netball last year. "And your parents?"

"Uh…grandparents," Cole excused. "My grandfather is a bit obsessed with books so not so much…" he nodded in the direction of the newspaper.

"Grandma not into them either?"

"Never really came up. I guess not?" Cole seemed to mull it over.

"You know we're gonna have to do active stuff?" a boy asked on the other side of Cole, leaning in, having apparently heard the conversation. "This is the Elites. Won't all be sitting around reading."

Cole didn't seem to realise that was directed at him at first. When he did, he looked genuinely tickled. "I just… team sports. Not my…" he seemed to struggle for a way to phrase it, perhaps remembering they were still kinda in an interview situation. "I don't have a problem with 'active stuff'," he said finally.

"Can't wait," the boy said, shifting the chair over to them a little so that they were more in a mini semi-circle than part of a line. His dark hair was styled in a way that made him look like some ad campaign and he looked the part; like some Latin heartthrob had dropped down in front of them. "Seriously, this is gonna be fucking brilliant." He stuck out his hand towards Jake. "AJ," he said as Cole leaned back in his chair so that Jake could shake AJ's hand.

"Yeah," Jake said, trying not to let nerves threaten again. "Hope so."

Chapter Two

THE LECTURE ROOM WAS QUIET; a big open space with cool blue walls and rows upon rows leading down to the sunken centre which housed a desk and a projector screen.

It wouldn't be full; it wouldn't even be close to being full. They liked to keep the Elites selective; it was in the bloody title after all. Someone, probably Poppy, had been in at some point to distribute leaflets across the desks-

No. Not leaflets. Newspaper clippings. Different cases, different battles all the way back to the founding of the Council-

Brendan paused when he spotted a recent one about the Battle of Ambros.

The Hero of Ambros, Brendan Campion, was unavailable for comment after the grievous loss of his ex-partner and mentor Griffith Fallon. It is believed that he will attend the public funerals held for those that lost their lives.

And higher up, earlier in the article.

We have had confirmation that it was Brendan Campion who struck the killing blow, ending the evil that Phineas Ambros had wrecked upon his people, upon the Coven Lands and upon our own-

Without conscious thought, his magic screwed the paper up and tossed it across the room as he tried to control his breathing.

Fucking media.

At seven-o-four he had still, somehow, resisted the urge to open up the lecture room. Instead, Brendan sat, slumped in the chair with his feet dirtying the desk, childishly temped to kick the remote off where it rested on the wooden surface.

"You're five minutes late," Boss muttered as he made his way down the staired-aisle.

"Am I?" Brendan asked, not even bothering to hide his lack of concern. Boss made almost no sound as he came towards Brendan, face tight with suppressed temper.

"Stop sulking," Boss snapped when he got close enough to clearly read the expression on Brendan's face.

"I'm not sulking," Brendan replied in a monotone voice.

Ignoring him, Boss came to a halt, folded his arms and squared himself firmly in front of Brendan.

"You can sulk at home if you like," Boss continued, clearly ignoring Brendan, "I'm doing you a favour-"

"A favour?" Sudden fury snapped Brendan from his deliberately lazy pose. "What favour?" he hissed, muddy boots hitting the floor and ready to spring forward. "I'm lecturing a bunch of kids. No-one wants this job-"

"You're not meant to even be here," Boss exploded. "You haven't been cleared for duty yet; you shouldn't technically be in the building." Boss' eyes bored into Brendan's for a second, his thin mouth tightening at whatever it was he saw. "You're not being put back on active duty, not this soon, I don't care what you say. You can do this and suck it up or piss off home."

Brendan just about managed to contain his sneer at hearing that. "I shouldn't have been taken off in the first place," he muttered, staring determinedly at the remote. Out of the corner of his eye, Brendan saw Boss soften ever so slightly.

The sight simultaneously annoyed and exhausted him.

"I will not have this argument with you again," Boss begun, voice firm yet weary at the repeated topic. "You needed time to grieve-"

A fierce tide of emotion Brendan didn't even want to try and identify reared up as if a child had prodded a stick at a wound. Blind with it, he somehow found the remote in his hand and threw it violently in the direction of Boss' voice.

Anything to get him to shut up.

The remote hit the stairs with an unsatisfyingly dull thud as Boss straightened from his duck. Feeling haggard, Brendan slumped back in his chair and stared up at the ceiling, trying to pull his emotions back into something vaguely resembling normal.

"I need to be on duty," he said softly, examining a rather long crack in the ceiling. When Boss said nothing, Brendan glanced over at him. "For fuck's sake, you need me on duty; we're short as it is-"

"What I need is for these kids to be trained," Boss cut him off, equally quietly. "And for you to clear your head-" Boss held up a hand when Brendan moved to interrupt. "Regardless of my thoughts on the issue, the Council won't budge on this; you have to see a grief therapist before you can be fully reinstated. And if you're skulking around, I'm not sparing someone on active duty to do this."

Brendan let out a deep sigh and gave a barely imperceptible nod. Eyes trained on him, Boss summoned the remote from where it lay on the floor and turned on the screen. A quickly muttered spell under his breath (Boss had never been good when it came to mixing magic and technology) and the presentation screen, when Brendan turned to look at it, showed the surveillance camera footage of the kids in the waiting room.

He'd expected them to be silent, looking nervous and inept. Instead they were in groups, chatting away to each other and looking eager, apart from one sulking kid at the back. They looked bright, active, real and far, far too young for the job.

Fragile.

And, of course, there was Patrick at the desk, who had volunteered for the job after being injured months before. Poor Patrick looked frustrated as the growing noise level interrupted his reading, shooting the occasional glare about the room.

"They're too young," Brendan said eventually, sounding petulant even to his own ears.

Snorting, Boss walked up onto the slightly raised stage area and stared at the screen. "Strange; that's exactly what I thought about that snotty seventeen-year-old kid that came barging through my door all those years ago. Look at how that turned out."

For what felt like the first time in an age, a small, half smile grew on Brendan's face, "I'm not sure if that was meant to be encouraging or not."

"Youngest is twenty-two." Boss shook his head, scanning the faces before him. "It makes you feel old when you think twenty-two is still too young." He put the remote down on the desk for Brendan. "All I ask is that they come out of here with a clear idea of the job they're going to be doing. If there's one thing I can't stand it's answering the same bloody questions over and over again."

Brendan nodded and reached for the notes, flicking through them with some distaste.

"Anything else?" he asked, his tone just shy of mocking as Boss started to make his way to the side door.

"You might want to watch out for Goodman's son. The arrogant prick dropped the boy off this morning. Kid looks like he'd kill to get out of here. He'll either pout and sulk like you or he'll bugger off pretty quickly."

Brendan glared at Boss' retreating form. "'m not sulking," he muttered at the desk.

"Just try not to throttle the brat," Boss added as he opened the door.

"That's helpful," Brendan called back, shuffling the papers as the door closed with a firm click.

Craning his neck, he turned once more to look at the screen behind. With a nudge of magic, he opened the main doors and indulged his warped humour as he watched the kids suddenly look over towards the door as if he'd just summoned them all to their deaths. His hand reached out to turn the screen off, but the same warped humour demanded that he keep the screen on, just to let them think he'd been watching them all this time.

As if he had nothing better to do.

He returned to his notes as the first kid walked into the room and watched them over the top of the page.

It wasn't the best impression to have the first recruit to walk through the door be a scruffy unwashed boy who practically seemed to be screaming for someone to throw him out of the room. Brendan wouldn't have given a damn what the boy was wearing, but the general 'I don't give a toss' attitude exuding from the boy got his back up.

That had to be Goodman's son, Brendan decided.

For a second that feeling was back again. That strangled, sick feeling that made him want to curl up and stop. Closing his eyes, he shoved that feeling down and determinedly tried to ignore it.

When he felt calmer, he opened his eyes and lowered the page of notes. All the kids had come into the room, remaining roughly in the same groups they'd been talking in out in the waiting room.

The sea of faces staring at him were mostly nervous, though there were a few puzzled expressions as if the recruits were trying to work out where they'd seen him before.

A quick glance at the screen confirmed that all the kids were in. Another nudge of his magic closed the door once more and he sat back, rubbing his mouth with the back of his forefinger. Some were getting out things to take notes with, annoying him for some reason. He waited until all eyes were focused on him, not really caring how long it took.

Besides, the longer he waited, the longer he was out the house.

The noise died down and suddenly he found himself to be the centre of attention. Not that it would usually bother him but recently he'd found that such looks made him prickle slightly, struggle to focus.

Boss owed him big time for this.

Swallowing a sudden insane impulse to snap at them all to stop staring, he instead took a deep breath.

"You all ready?" he asked.

Silence.

Fantastic.

This was going to be an uncomfortable hour then.

About three of them nodded, while the rest looked like deer caught in headlights, as if this was the strangest question he could possibly ask them. Under the table he squeezed his fist, wishing for the stupid stress ball that Nate had up in the office.

Taking the three nods as a general consensus, he continued.

"Right." He summoned the remote to his hand and switched the screen off without looking. "Who knows what the Elites do?"

As he'd quickly come to expect, no-one seemed eager to answer. All of them looked expectantly at each other until one blessed girl hesitantly raised her hand.

"They're one of the three magical law enforcers for the Council and deal with what the Protectors and Guardians can't."

"Basically yeah," Brendan shifted. "That's the official line, but it's a little unclear. So, can anyone tell me what the Protectors do?"

Thankfully, as if bolstered by the fact that he hadn't tortured the girl, others started to raise their hands. He nodded at one of the lads closest to him.

"They patrol," the boy replied looking desperately nervous.

Brendan waited a moment to see if the boy was going to add anything. The silence stretched on and on and the kid started to look as if he might throw up.

"Yeah," Brendan finally relented and saved the boy who slumped in relief. "They patrol, deal with theft, and disturbances. Years ago, they were the Council's army, now they keep the peace and are the most recognised of all the departments. You call 990, humans call 999."

Deciding not to risk the painful silence once more with another question, Brendan moved on. "The Guardians tend to be the least visible. They uphold the three ancient spells: Those who do not know, cannot see; those who cannot know cannot be told and those who have no magic will never know. You all know that in recent times we have had to change this slightly. Human ministers and such have been told and the Guardians ensure that these people are monitored and deal with any intentional breech of these spells and laws. They also work closely with the diplomatic department to liaise with the rest of the magical community. It is imperative that we keep them informed with what we do to help them. No-one wants exposure."

Scanning their faces, he was relatively sure that no-one was lost or confused by the explanation.

"Right, if everyone's got that, can anyone tell me what the Elites deal with?" Brendan asked, praying for raised hands.

Surprisingly it didn't take long for a hand to go up; a lad in plain clothes who was sitting in the middle and couldn't seem to look him in the eye.

"Yes?"

"They deal with the Coven issues and with more time-consuming crimes such as murder," the boy replied simply.

There was a ripple as Brendan nodded. "Right. Now this may bore some of you but we need to ensure that you all have a proper foundation of knowledge."

As much as he hated the tense silence that came when he asked a question, it was probably the best way of getting the information through to them.

"What can you tell me about the Coven?"

The lovely girl from earlier saved him by raising her hand straight away.

"They...the Coven was the first form of government for witches. Originally it was a group that came together and then the Coven continued through the ensuing bloodlines. The families became more and more powerful," she hesitated, her eyes darting about nervously as if waiting for someone to make a scorning remark. When none came she continued after an encouraging nod from Brendan. "The Coven became dictatorial and corrupt. A group of freedom fighters fought them in the late fifteenth century and won. Those freedom fighters became the first elected leaders of the Council."

Brendan nodded, pleasantly surprised. "What's your name?"

"Daphne Groening," she replied looking both embarrassed and delighted.

"Okay," Brendan continued, "Daphne's right. By the late 1400s, the Coven was cruel and out of control. The Council rose in opposition and, when they won, it was agreed the Council would rule democratically. However, the Coven was never fully dismantled. To do so would have involved killing children and eradicating whole families. Because of this, Coven rules still survive today, subservient to the Council laws but those who remain under Coven law or living in pockets of land controlled by Coven families have since become experts at loopholes.

"Worryingly the Coven's power seems to be growing once more; more and more people are being born into Coven law again, there is a growing divide between the Coven ruling families as some want to dismantle the Coven and others will not give up their power.

"Can anyone tell me the biggest problem this creates?"

He'd thrown them, he could tell. They'd obviously expected that the question and answer part of the lecture was done.

A suited lad in the middle raised his hand.

"Well…there are two governing bodies; two sets of laws and rules. Surely it blurs the lines of what's acceptable and what's legal."

"Exactly." Brendan smiled at him, pleased. "Elites deal with the problems that occur from having two opposing governments. It's difficult; you'll often come across people who don't want you there. You'll see much more extreme versions of dark magic, people pushing the natural allowances of magic and creating spells much more complex than our ancestors ever dreamed of. There are frictions that occur due to old rivalries-"

A red headed kid slowly raised his hand, "You're gonna train us to deal with that, right?"

Somehow, Brendan managed to swallow the sarcastic

retort that automatically rose to his lips. "Yeah, I think we can stretch to that."

A few faces grinned up at him.

"You'll get your training schedules at some point today. Magical and physical training tends to be in the afternoons while the political stuff is in the mornings. Once you get to a certain point, we'll start getting you to sit in on interviews, train you up through experience. By that time, I'd imagine there won't be so many of you. You then get a chance to carry out your own investigation, using the skills you've learnt. It's pass or fail.

"It'll be long days, those will be even longer if you're lucky enough to be asked into a meeting. I'll warn you now that your shifts are guidelines only. If you have other considerable commitments you may need to have a serious think about your priorities."

A lump lodged itself in his throat.

By the time he'd started this job properly all his other priorities had been snatched away-

He stopped that thought before it went anywhere.

"Your social life will take a big hit," he continued on, determined to make them aware of the reality of their choice. "Some people will quit; it's hard work and it's dangerous and it's not for everyone. Now more than ever you must be aware of exactly the risk you will face in this job. We're entering a new era after Ambros. The Coven is more fractured than it's ever been and the Council structures are..." he debated how to phrase it to newbies, "under review. It's not going to be an easy ride."

God, he needed a drink.

How old were they again?

Twenty-two? Wasn't that how young the youngest was?

Too young. Too young for this.

His son had been even younger.

You were never too young to die.

"Now if you go back out to the waiting room your tour guides are probably waiting," he said quickly as he gripped the side of the desk, suddenly wanting them out. He couldn't....

They had to leave.

"Off you go," he ordered in a tone that sounded strange to his ears.

They all rose, quiet and shaken. He watched them go, glared at the ones that looked like they were going to come over and talk to him.

Go away.

Now.

Please.

Only when he was alone and had firmly locked the doors and set up a silencing ward did he throw the desk across the room with a good hard push of magic and slide down the wall.

Christ, he needed a drink.

Chapter Three

Life for Jake settled into something like a routine. Within a week there were thirty-six of them, whittled down already from the two groups that had come in. Quickly, he became stunned that he'd once struggled to organise his time at university – suddenly he was getting up at five and not getting back until ten at night some days. Exhausted, he'd fall into bed, only to get up and do the exact same thing the next day.

"Who are you?" his mum asked one Sunday morning in October when he stumbled downstairs, bleary eyed and aching. "You look like a son I used to have."

"You're not as funny as you think you are," he mumbled, almost collapsing over the coffee she was making.

"Well then," she said, and reached to take his mug away from him, then laughed when he groaned and wrapped himself around it protectively. Shaking her head, she took a deep sip of her own drink and watched him.

"What?"

"You look thin," she chided and turned to the fridge.

"Mum, I don't need-" He broke off as his dad came stomping back in, trying to get rid of the mud on his shoes. "Dad, tell her I don't need feeding."

His dad glared at him as if Jake had just begged for money. He toed off his shoes and placed the herbs on the counter, then blew into his hands to warm them up.

"You need gloves," his mum said, turning from the fridge with a pile of food in her hands.

"I need them kissed to warm them up," his dad said, and then reached to put his hands on her, causing his mum to shriek and Jake's sister Grace to complain from the table as she tried to study.

Trying to ignore them, Jake turned away and sat down at the table by Grace, glancing over at the book she was reading. "Politics?" he asked.

"You said that it was your gap," she replied smartly. "I don't want it to be mine when I apply." She turned the page and shot him an arrogant look, "I'm gonna be better than you."

He stuck his tongue out at her. "We just discussed that book in a seminar," he said, reaching for the biscuit tin that sat suspiciously close to her. "It's a pile of-"

"Language," his mum called.

"Rubbish," Jake said smoothly and then mouthed 'utter shite' at Grace.

Her bright brown eyes glared at him for about seven seconds before she slammed the book shut and then slammed the lid closed on the biscuit tin and stormed out with it.

"Mum," he said, trying to keep his tone sweet as he turned towards her. "You know how I'm your only son-"

She threw a packet of crumpets at him. "You know where the oven is."

Sunday mornings with Danny were something that Brendan had always seen as being quite precious. Liaden's odd hours had meant that they'd often been his time with his son, time that had often been spent playing around when Danny had been very little and was quickly becoming a games afternoon with his son sulking for part of it, because Danny was never the best loser.

It dimly surprised him to realise that he'd let it slip. It was stupid; of course he had, but the past few months had felt like a never-ending bad day and he felt almost baffled when he sat down with the calendar to realise that he'd turned thirty-three.

"Dad?" Danny asked hesitantly, creeping close to where Brendan sat on the sofa. His blond hair was tousled all over the place because the boy never sat still, even in sleep, and he had on some superhero pyjamas that made him look so very young.

"Yeah?" he asked, reaching to curl an arm around his son and bring him up over the arm of the sofa to sit cosily in his lap, smiling when Danny dug his feet into the gap between the sofa cushions for warmth.

"Are you busy?" Danny asked, his voice…nervous? Brendan lifted his head to almost place it on Danny's head, not wanting his son to see his expression.

"No," he said, pushing the calendar away. "What shall we play?"

He'd guessed right, but it was still a kick in the gut when Danny slumped with some relief as if he'd expected to be told off. Fuck, he was awful at this. One kid convinced he didn't want to spend time with him, the other…

Who knew what Nicolas had been told.

He tried to push the thought away as Danny scampered to put some game in and pick up the controllers, scarily adept at setting it all up. A little wariness crossed his face when he turned back, but Brendan forced his face to smooth out and appear as normal as possible, even as his usual taunts towards his son died in his throat.

He lost himself in the game for a little while. Tried to focus on the joy of spending time with Danny, of laughing at how dramatic an eight-year-old boy could be when faced with the chance of beating his father at something. Tried to push through the urge to flee when Liaden came home and sat in the armchair, apparently amused by Danny's commentary. But he could feel Liaden's gaze on him, knew that he wasn't fooling her and twenty minutes later found himself exiting the game and silently leaving the room.

He made it about as far as the dining room table, running a hand along the back of a chair not sure if he wanted to picture it or not. A dark-haired boy, probably better than both him and Danny at the game. Brendan could remember desperately wanting a brother growing up, especially when he'd been faced with a step-sister that his younger self had found sorely disappointing as a concept.

His sons had never even been in the same room at the same time.

"Thank you," Liaden said quietly from the doorway.

"For spending time with my own son?" he snapped.

"For pushing through," she said, voice cracking out like a whip. "I… fine." Then she was gone and he felt a warring confusion of relief and anger over her not being in the room anymore. Everything felt too much. Too much to cope with, to explain, to apologise for...a mountain of shit that made him want to curl up and collapse every time he even thought about attempting to shovel his way through it.

He needed air.

And a drink.

It was probably kinda sad that Jake ended up back at the Currock building on his day off, but his sister was right; the political side of the job was already seriously starting to trip him up.

It was also probably kinda sad that he felt an odd thrill at going in on a day off. Being able to head in, scan his way through and head up to the grand library without feeling rushed or double checking where he needed to be made him feel like he was actually...grown-up. Finally.

They'd been introduced to the library on the second day in smaller groups. The centre of the building, behind the grand reception hall and the huge staircase, was home to a terrifyingly massive circular room completely filled with records, documents and books. Different levels, sections with work stations and some truly terrifyingly effective librarians, all specialising in their own areas, and a small army of researchers in the vaults below.

There was something about working there that felt more focused though. Almost a reverence and a respect for the knowledge that must have taken so long to accumulate. And the books were stacked high, almost too high for Jake to reach up, yet it never felt dark or oppressive. The glass roof above let in a good degree of natural light and magic seemed to keep the light filtering through the levels so that it never felt like he was walking into shadowy gloom.

As far as Jake was concerned, he'd make the most of it while he could. He took up a seat in the politics section and was piled up with about seven books from a sleek, stylish woman who smiled at him with something between amusement and approval when he explained his problem.

The next problem was that trying to read the books was boring as fuck. There were times when he could read the same passage about four times and still not get it.

Shit. Shit, shit, shit.

Frustrated, he groaned and banged his head down on the open pages, half desperately hoping that it might somehow push the information into his head that way.

Didn't work.

He took a long, deep breath and then sat up, idly wondering if he should take a break when he spotted Cole Lorcan sitting in the corner, clearly trying not to make eye contact.

They'd not really seen much of each other since the first day. They'd all been split into smaller groups with a maximum of six as they were trained by Elites. Something to do with skill sets and Jake was pretty sure that Cole was what was affectionately (maybe?) termed the geek squad. Which probably meant that Cole knew half of this stuff backwards.

As if sensing Jake had come to a plan, Cole glanced over and then frowned when he saw that Jake was still looking in his direction. "What?" he mouthed, looking a little confused.

Eh, why not?

Standing, Jake picked up the book and walked over to Cole's table, slightly emboldened when Cole leaned back from his books and didn't seem to be giving a 'fuck off' vibe. A glance down at the books on Cole's desk made Jake wince because it wasn't even in English and Cole was a good way through the ancient looking tome.

"I…" Jake smiled self-deprecatingly, "Do you get this stuff?"

Cole blinked at him and then tilted his head to see what Jake had been reading. "That's… probably not the best one," he said eventually, glancing between the book and Jake as if trying to gauge something.

"Laila gave it to me," Jake whispered, glancing around as if Laila might suddenly pop up at hearing such remarks about her recommendations.

Cole almost looked confused by his reply, but seemed to blow past it. "What is it exactly that you need?" he asked. Something in Jake's expression must have changed because he looked taken aback and then sighed. "From the books," he clarified. "Why are you reading them?"

There was a momentary war inside, the necessity of help battling the desperation to impress. But he barrelled through. "It's my… I find this stuff difficult. The politics, the history, the cases."

"You're not training to be a lawyer," Cole pointed out quietly.

"I'm training to be effective," Jake argued. "Look, I get if you're busy but-"

Cole rolled his eyes. "Pick a case a day," he said after a moment. "Read it, look into what you don't understand and what interests you. Even a case every two days. It needs to be practical and useful to your mind. Doing that," he said, angling his head towards the pile on the desk that Jake had been using, "will just bore you and make it into an ordeal."

Oh. Surprised (pleasantly surprised), Jake nodded. "Thanks, that-"

He broke off when Cole reached for Jake's notebook and started to scribble some cases down. "Cover these," he said, writing down three. "They're ones that have come up for me a few times. Then...I dunno. Ask the Elites training us."

Huh. "Is that what you do?"

"Sometimes," Cole admitted, glancing around the library. "I..." he looked back. "My schooling was very focused on this stuff. I... I get it." When he looked up, he was wincing apologetically.

Fair enough. "Figured. You're with Daphne, Jemma and Sam, right?"

Cole nodded. "Jemma's dropped out," he said after a moment. "She loved the research stuff and they loved her. Full job and everything."

"Tempted?"

Cole smiled in a quiet, almost amused way. "Not really. Same as you. I like to know that what I'm doing is being used effectively."

"Not sure it's quite the same, but sure," Jake said, fingers curling around the edge of the book he'd brought over. It would be easy to end the conversation there, for them to part ways and go about their day.

"Fancy lunch?" he heard himself asking and felt a wobble of confidence when Cole looked genuinely surprised. There was even a glance around, as if Cole was silently checking that Jake wasn't speaking to anyone else.

"Oh. I...Yeah," Cole said, sounding surprised but pleased. "Sure."

"You found him then," Liaden stated as she watched Nate arrange Brendan on the sofa.

"Human bar," Nate said with a sigh as he tried to keep Brendan's arm balanced upon his chest. "Makes it harder to get the attention of the staff and ask questions."

Brilliant, Liaden thought as she sunk down into the armchair opposite.

"He'll sleep it off," Nate decided, giving up with Brendan's arm. Instead, he turned and sat with his back to the sofa to look up at Liaden. "He'll be fine in the morning."

She couldn't help the snort. "He'll be sober in the morning," she corrected. "He's far from fine."

As expected, no magical fix came from Nate. Instead he ducked his head, a sorrowful expression on his face. "How is he with Danny?"

"You can see it in his face," Liaden closed her eyes, wishing she could forget the look that sometimes lurked in her husband's eyes. "He looks at Danny and sees Nicolas. And the second it happens, he turns from Danny and finds something to distract him. Danny's too young to understand but..." she winced at the thought, "he's starting to pick up on it."

"Have you talked to him?"

Really? Glaring at him and insulted, Liaden sat up properly. "Of course I have. But...I didn't know Nicolas. He was this...possibility. Important to Brendan, so important but...he was just an idea to me. I used to imagine it sometimes, me being a brilliant step-mother and helping him adjust or worried about how he would be with Danny but...and Brendan won't talk to anyone, not even his mother about any of it."

"God, I hadn't even considered Maeve," Nate winced. "How's she-"

"Devastated. But she's talking about it...she buried the box of birthday and Christmas cards she'd kept for him." It had been so sad, so utterly pathetically sad that it was all they'd had. Both Maeve and Brendan's step father, Owen, had cried silently as they created the small hole by the weeping willow tree that apparently Nicolas had loved as a baby.

Brendan had refused to go.

Stubborn, stubborn idiot. Angry, and not entirely sure who with, Liaden looked away, drumming her fingers on the arm of the sofa.

"At least that's healthy," Nate sighed turning his head slightly to regard his friend.

"If I can get him into therapy can you get him to stay away from alcohol?"

Nate's face softened a little in sympathy. "Yeah...yeah I can do that. But you know what he's like with the idea of therapy-"

"If I don't put my foot down now..." Liaden shook her head. "I need to do it before we dig ourselves into too deep a hole. For Danny if nothing else."

Nate sighed and pushed himself up to stand. "You call me if you need-"

Grateful, Liaden nodded with a tight smile as she tried to hold the tears back. It was stupid, she thought as she stared at her husband's sleeping face. The moment someone was nice it made you want to cry your eyes out.

As he passed, Nate squeezed her shoulder. "Promise me you'll call. I'll take Danny or babysit that dickhead-"

She laughed weakly. "Go home and get some rest, Nate."

It was only after a night of smoking that Brendan remembered with crystal clear clarity why it was such a bastard of an idea.

His mouth tasted like an ashtray – dry, bitter and fucking foul.

Groaning at the situation, Brendan turned deeper into his-

Cushion?

Baffled, Brendan risked opening his eyes once more and studied the back of his sofa.

Oh.

He had no memory of getting home which probably meant he'd been found and dragged home.

What time was it?

Sitting up was the mother of all mistakes. His head swum and his stomach rebelled fiercely. Suddenly hit with the smell of old alcohol, Brendan turned into the sofa as if to find an escape from the sensation.

"'lo," a little voice murmured.

It was too early. Or possibly not too early but he was too hungover to work out what the time was, let alone play with Danny.

"You all right, kiddo?" he asked, dangling a clumsy hand down to find his son's soft hair.

Unfortunately, his son took that as permission to clamber up. Pressing his lips together to avoid throwing up, Brendan turned to let Danny settle on his stomach.

The soft blond hair was in need of a cut, Brendan thought as he smoothed Danny's head once more. "You're getting a bit shaggy, kid," he said.

Danny grinned at him. "So are you, Dad," Danny said, leaning forward to touch Brendan's hair. Brendan reached a hand up automatically to steady the child, comforted by the weight of the boy under his hands, the warmth of him reassuring.

It still hit him sometimes, how much Danny looked like him, was like him. So different from Nicolas who had been much quieter and more reserved; the shy grin that had to be pried out of him but was the most rewarding-

Had been the most rewarding thing. Had been.

Brendan studied Danny, his hand moving down to cup his son's cheek as his thumb absently stroked soothingly.

"Dad's awake," Danny declared suddenly, peering over Brendan's head.

This was unlikely to be pleasant.

"So I see," Liaden said as she reached over, her arms appearing in Brendan's line of sight as she summoned their son with a glance. "What are we having for lunch?" she asked Danny.

Lunch?

Sitting up (and slightly regretting the speed that he used to do so) Brendan sat on the edge of the sofa and ducked his head down to wait for the nausea to pass. "Who found me?" he asked.

"Nate," Liaden said in a short tone.

When no more information came, Brendan winced and ran his fingers through his hair to try and wake up and become coherent enough for the argument that was brewing. Slowly he looked back up and then to the left, watching his wife start to make a sandwich while Danny followed her like a duckling, peering at everything she was doing.

"I shouldn't have done it," Brendan said slowly.

"It?" Liaden asked in far too breezy a tone. "Which it?"

Danny stared between them both, suddenly quiet and wary. After a moment, Liaden sighed and stroked a hand across his head and bent down a little to talk to him quietly before she got on with her task.

She didn't so much as look at Brendan until Danny flashed a grin again and started patting at the bread.

"I won't do this," Liaden said quietly. "I won't...I want to help you. But you don't want to be helped at the moment and I don't know how long I can let you stay that way. Not with..." she bent to kiss Danny's hair and met Brendan's eyes.

Anger bubbled and brewed, hot and tight. "It's been three months," he snarled, dimly aware that he was starting to use the phrase far too often.

The only thing that the tone succeeded in doing was making his son look up with frightened eyes. Liaden continued with the lunch and then stopped abruptly to look at him properly.

"You'll never stop mourning," she said, her voice shaking with what he assumed might either be nerves or anger. "I'm not asking you to. I am asking you to realise that while you lost something huge it doesn't mean that life is over. It doesn't mean you lock yourself away from us."

It made him look away and stare at his hands. And all he could see was the way they had reached for that damned latch a minute too late.

"Talk to me," his wife begged, sounding closer. "Anything. I don't...I have no idea how to help-"

"You can't," Brendan muttered, determined not to look at her.

The sigh echoed over him and he hated how much worse it made him feel. There was a flicker of anger again but he shoved it down.

It was all so fucking pointless.

"And a therapist-"

He stood, as if to put physical distance between himself and the idea. "No," he snapped, wincing at the urge to hurl.

"Pick," Liaden said in a dangerous tone. "Me, Nate or a therapist."

Pick?

Slowly, Brendan turned back to her. "Or?"

"Or you won't have a choice left," Liaden said, as she put the sandwich on a plastic plate for Danny and walked out of the room. Danny hovered and then a flicker of uncertainty crossed his face as he stared at Brendan.

His son shouldn't look at him like that. Christ, Brendan thought as he buried his head in his knees, hearing Danny scamper out the room after Liaden, his son shouldn't ever feel wary of him.

What the fuck was he doing?

He managed to walk out the backdoor before he simply threw his magic at the wall. The raw, unfocused power smashed into the bricks and burnt through them with an almighty cracking noise.

The debris he crushed to dust.

Chapter Four

FRANKLY THE ESSAY WAS NOT going well.

The blank piece of paper had been glaring up at Jake for almost forty minutes; it was all he could do not to throw the damn thing across the room.

Still, they were two months in and down to twenty-six of them. Most that had left had been shipped off to other parts of the Council. Training, as Jake had known it, was almost over.

Just this poxy essay left.

Pursing his lips, he raised his gaze up to look along the table to glare at Cole who looked annoyingly relaxed, reading what appeared to be an ancient tome on Coven custom.

Jake knew for a fact that Cole had finished his essay ages ago so the freak was just reading it out of some perverse sense of interest. And reading it with ease apparently. Given that it took Jake twenty minutes to understand the first page of one of those books, the sight of Cole reading did not help his mood.

Frustrated, he shoved the paper away from him. The paper just skidded an inch across the table making Jake feel even more pathetic. Watching it, Jake cracked his jaw and rapped his hand on the table, startling Cole.

"Just let me copy your introduction," Jake all but whined. "All I need is something to give me a boost, just to get me started-"

"No," Cole said without inflection, returning his attention to his book.

Pulling the paper back, Jake studied the doodles he'd scribbled into the margin. Shockingly, they did little to improve his understanding or his interest. Flicking a glance back up, Jake frowned at how peaceful the jammy bastard looked.

"Can you do something more helpful than just sitting there and reading?"

"No." Flipping a few pages, Cole shook his head. "This book is ridiculous."

Jake started to absently colour in one of the patterns. "I have a genuine fear that I'll walk into the research room one day and discover you've had all the books revised."

Cole glared over the top of the book. "Not all of them," he said, as if that were the daft part. "You out tonight?"

Jake shook his head, "Not if I can't get some of this written," he tapped his pen viciously onto the pad. "You and AJ seem to have flown through it."

Cole hummed at that. "Fine." Jake could almost hear Cole rolling his eyes as the book snapped shut, finally. "What've you got so far?"

Picking up the paper, Jake stood it up facing Cole. "That."

A look of pained amusement tugged at Cole's mouth. "I meant the research. Tell me you've done some."

"Yeah…and then you read the same books and told me they were crap."

"Oh for..." Cole stood up with more effort than was needed. "Give me a minute."

As Cole disappeared into the extensive library, Jake leant back slightly in his chair and drummed his palms softly on the polished mahogany table top. Across from him, slightly hidden from view, Daphne looked up and glared. Mollified, he raised his hands from the table and shot her an apologetic look.

He figured he was forgiven when she returned her attention and accusing gaze back to her work.

Bored, Jake glanced back down at his paper. The title was written nicely enough even if he had to read it three times over every time he glanced at it.

"Study and describe the contract of the Tittensor and Vauvile alliance, detailing any potential loopholes for either party and the ways these could be dealt with."

And if he'd thought the question was bad the first time he'd read it, being faced with the original contract had sent him into palpitations. The damned thing had been written hundreds of years ago back when expressions such as hitherto and all that archaic mumbo jumbo had been used. In his experience, legal contracts were hard enough to read without the added bonus of being barely able to understand the language it was written in.

To be fair though, he was doing far better with it since following Cole's advice. A pile of books banging down onto the table startled Jake out of his thoughts. Staring in trepidation, he watched Cole return to his chair.

"And these don't have condensed versions?" Jake asked hopefully.

"You could always try Wikipedia." Cole suggested snidely.

Letting out a calming breath, Jake twisted his head at an angle to read the titles on the spines of the pile in front of him. "And I really need to read them all?"

"One on the treaty, one on Council law, one on Coven law, one on Coven history and one on successful cases against Coven attempts at loopholes," Cole listed as he settled himself back. "Stop being lazy."

"Okay." Jake reached out and picked up the first book on top of the pile. "Okay, so if I finish my notes on this book by ten, we go to the pub to celebrate?"

"Seriously? You think you can get through that in…" Cole checked his watch, "three and a half hours?"

"Shush," Jake opened up the thick, heavy cover and flipped to the page he guessed was the start of the actual text, "You're interrupting study time."

For the first time since they'd entered the library, Cole flashed a full grin, "If you manage that I will buy for you all night."

On the other side of the building, Brendan sat in a quiet room. Far too quiet and irritatingly calm. And cream. Cream walls, cream flowers, cream sofa, cream cushions.

It made him squirm and shift, looking away from the woman in the cool blue suit and towards the fish tank that bubbled away in the corner.

Jesus, even the pebbles in that were cream.

"How are you this evening?"

Turning his attention back to the psychiatrist the Council had…suggested he go to, Brendan drummed his fingers on the arm of the sofa.

Five weeks he'd managed it: not drinking, trying to make an effort with Liaden and Danny. Five fucking weeks until the pressure mounted in his head again until he'd struggled to breathe and he could see out of the corner of his eye the way everyone started to glance at him, worried again. He'd paced the house for hours; nothing managed to cut through the mind-numbing fuzz that stretched out like a yawning chasm in his head. The feeling that made him want to find something strong and alcoholic to cut through it.

He'd had one drink. One. And it screamed its way through his head in a feeling so addictive he couldn't give it up.

Then he'd woken up on the sofa again with a hangover that faded into that same fucking numbness far too quickly.

"I'm…." he hesitated and then let out an annoyed breath. Small talk had never really been his thing. "I drank," he said eventually, knowing that Doctor Anna Barnes probably already knew. The gossip mill at the Council was surprisingly advanced.

"Why?" The question was asked in a calm, deceptively relaxed manner.

Bristling at it, Brendan shot her a disbelieving look. "I have no idea," he hissed out, voice laced with sarcasm.

Annoyingly, she didn't rise to the bait. "From what I understand, you've been sober for a number of weeks now. What changed?"

Brendan shook his head, shrugging his shoulders a little, his gaze dropping away and focussing on a spot on the wall just over her shoulder.

"Your wife, Liaden, told me that she'd attempted to move some things out of your spare room-"

"It's not a spare room," Brendan snapped and then caught himself with a wince. "It happened days ago, it doesn't matter."

"Some strong emotions can take days to build, especially," Doctor Barnes narrowed her eyes, clearly assessing him, "especially when one is attempting to ignore such emotions."

"Is that what I'm doing?"

"Yes." The answer was so calm and thankfully direct, which was a relief from the usual tip-toeing, but unusual enough that he had no tools to deal with it.

Doctor Barnes leaned back, crossing shapely legs that were definitely one of her most attractive features. "Why do you think you're being ordered to attend sessions with me, Brendan?"

"I'm here for my wife, to save my marriage," Brendan muttered, still avoiding eye contact.

"Because you're grieving."

His heart thudded at the mere mention of it. Clicking his tongue in frustration he stared determinedly at the place where wall and ceiling met.

"Many Elites found it difficult to cope with the death count at Ambros-"

Shock had him snapping his eyes to hers. His mouth gaped open to correct her but god help him he couldn't even touch the subject, let alone talk about it.

"Or should I ignore the official Council statements and assume it is not Griffith Fallon you grieve but your dead son?"

The severity of the phrase 'dead son' stole his breath as if someone had just stabbed him through the chest.

That room filled with blood, the sword soaked with it and the almost manic laughter taunting him.

He felt like he was about to vomit.

The silence stretched on and on as Brendan tried to swallow back whatever the hell it was that was trying to crawl out of him and rip him apart. There was no way his mind could work under that assault, let alone form a coherent reply.

The good doctor just waited.

Eventually the ache ebbed away a little. Faded into something that he could shut away and ignore.

"I..." he shook his head and stared at the condensation that was growing on the window against the blurred lights outside.

"You seem taken aback," she said as Brendan tried to collect himself. "What is more unsettling; the grief or the shock of hearing me raise the subject?"

Talking about it made it hard to ignore and shove away. "It's Council policy not to...they asked me to..."

"That seems...senseless?" She said, as if she were some journalist commenting on their latest policy. She used such an unconcerned tone that Brendan had to clench his teeth. "The fact that you're Phineas Ambros' unacknowledged son is public knowledge as is the fact that Nicolas Ambros was your son-"

"Is," Brendan snarled. "Dead or alive he is still my-" he broke himself off as that tight feeling in his throat threatened again.

"Your son," she finished for him. "Why is it so hard for you to say?"

The carpet was short and rough, almost a blueish cream as opposed to the slightly pinkish cream of the sofa. "It's not good for propaganda," he said, pointedly ignoring the last question. "People don't need to be reminded that the current poster boy technically committed patricide."

"But you aren't talking to the papers or to the public; this is a private conversation. And it seems to go further than that. Everyone close to you has noted your reluctance to even remotely mention anything related to what happened at Ambros in July."

Leaning back, Brendan raised a challenging eyebrow at her and clamped his lips shut.

"Do you think your son is dead?"

"He was stabbed through the chest and thrown out of a tower window," Brendan snapped, not allowing his mind to focus on the words coming out of his mouth.

"I read the report. But you haven't answered my question. Do you think your son is dead?"

Frustrated beyond belief, Brendan shook his head, grinding his teeth together.

"Was that a no?"

"That's…I…" Brendan suddenly couldn't swallow. "I can't think about it," he hissed. "That night I… I can't-"

"Why not?" she sounded so distant, hardly even there. He shut his eyes against it, as if he could block out the conversation and try to remember why people being overly cautious about the topic had annoyed him so much.

"Brendan?"

"I just…" he breathed out, trying to catch himself again.

"Okay." Her voice suddenly was soft, soothing and had him opening his eyes to stare at her. Doctor Barnes' soft brown eyes were sympathetic, warm and calm and for some reason, he found himself unable to look at them for too long.

"Okay?" he asked, his voice sounding as if it had been shredded.

"Yes."

Feeling confused and almost bereft at the loss of the topic, Brendan frowned at her rug, trying to reorder his thoughts.

"Can you tell me about him?" she asked, maintaining the gentle tone. It should have grated, being treated like he was fragile, but instead he felt a strange sense of relief. His mind automatically brought up the answers for him, too scant for his liking. He should have known his eldest son inside out, had a thousand memories to bore people with of his teenage boy. For a brief second, he met her eyes and opened his mouth and then dismissed the idea; the memories too precious to offer up to the world. He could see it now, the nodding and questions, but all the while someone inwardly deciding he was biased, unaware of his son's true nature.

Somehow, by speaking, it felt as if he was offering the baby up for scrutiny.

"It can be common," the doctor said in that same coaxing tone as he remained silent, "For parents that lost their children at a young age to-"

"He was seventeen," Brendan said dully.

"When he died, yes. But not when you lost him. For all intents and purposes, your son was lost to you at the age of three," she corrected. "And when a parent experiences that loss after such a relatively short time with their child they can feel the need to…store up the memories. As if sharing them would dilute their parental claim."

He wasn't even sure what the fuck that meant. Instead, Brendan raised an eyebrow at her, unimpressed by the theory.

"Then tell me something about him," she dared.

It was manipulation (and hardly subtle at that) but it bloody well worked. Bristling, he frowned at the idea that…that what? That he was worried he didn't know enough about his son to be considered his father?

Bitch.

"He was shy," Brendan said slowly. "The moment anyone new came over he would come over to one of us and just hold a hand or jeans…anything. Wouldn't hide though," he added with a smile, remembering how his son had fought ever so slightly when they'd try to pick him up. "Just…needed that reassurance."

Nicolas had always come to him first as well. Leaned his nut-brown hair into Brendan's jeans and watched with wide green eyes.

"Danny isn't," Brendan added, without much thought. "The bugger will run up to anyone. Can't tell you how often I've considered putting tracking spells on the kid." His words caught up to him and he found himself frowning. "Shouldn't…" he shook his head.

"It's natural to compare differences," she said calmly. "It doesn't mean one is better or worse in your eyes, just different."

He wasn't sure what to do with that.

"What was his favourite food?" she asked again, cutting through his thoughts.

"Peanut butter," Brendan answered, not needing to even think about it. "Once gave him a tablespoon of the stuff for dessert..." he hesitated, not entirely sure that was something he should admit to. "Used to call it 'not butter'."

"Favourite place?"

"That bloody willow tree out in the-"

They'd put a grave stone there.

Brendan swallowed it all back and turned his head to the window, hating what his mother had done. Putting up a fucking slab of unyielding stone and ruining the place his son had loved seemed so wrong.

Doctor Barnes let him be silent for a time, but he could feel her gaze resting upon him.

"That night," she said slowly, "the one where your son was taken-"

Brendan shifted uncomfortably, still not looking back at her.

"-do you wish to talk about that instead?"

It surprised Brendan that his immediate response wasn't to tell her to just fuck off. Instead, he sat, not entirely sure how he was feeling as his thoughts twisted into tangled knots, struggling against each other.

"I went out to celebrate," he said softly. The image of the restaurant, of his mother and Owen toasting to him and Rachel rolling her eyes at him flashed before him as did the constant question: what exactly had he been doing at the moment that the Ambros team had broken through Matthew Hayden's door to steal Nicolas?

“I saw the report,” Doctor Barnes said softly. “This isn’t that. What do you want to talk about?”

“I…” his words trailed off, lost inside somewhere and he hesitated for a moment. “It’s a mess,” he admitted, waving to his head.

“That’s why you are here. We can try to…untangle some ideas. Even if it’s putting words to how you feel. Nothing you say will hurt me. That’s the joy of talking to someone who isn’t a relative or loved one.”

He knew that. But… turning back to her, he studied Doctor Barnes for an age, trying to work out how she might respond or what she might think.

“I didn’t get it,” he said after a while. “When they called. I…They knew who had him. In my mind it was like some crazy relative picking up your kid. Someone would go and get Nicolas and I’d be able to scream at Phineas Ambros and…” he trailed off with a bitter laugh. “I spent most of the ride there imagining what I’d say to him.”

“I think most would,” Doctor Barnes allowed quietly.

“And then…” Brendan sucked in a breath. “We got there and the…there were healers and Elites and everyone was quiet. And they kept telling me not to go in and I didn’t give a shit about going in. I kept…I wanted to go and arrest Ambros with the Elites. And they kept looking at Owen and Mum and…” He shook his head. “And then I realised that the…that there were bodies being brought out of the house.”

The grief always surprised him. Not because he’d cared deeply for the family, but because they were his son’s family. That sudden moment when he’d realised that he’d have to watch his son learn about this moment one day.

That Nicolas wouldn't have any real lasting memories of his own mother.

"When did you realise?" Doctor Barnes asked softly. "That it wasn't a simple process to get Nicolas back?"

Silent as the room was, he could almost hear himself shouting. Screaming. "I don't...they took us to the Currock Building. To the Dark Lord's room back when it was Jonah Myers. And...Owen wasn't there. He was meeting with the legal teams, with the Elites and I was...I dunno. Giving mum hell. As I do." Staring down at his hands seemed easier than meeting Doctor Barnes' sympathetic eyes. "It must have been early morning by the time he came in. There's...they'd claimed him. Phineas, I mean. Claimed Nicolas as heir apparent. Claimed he wasn't with the group that attacked the house. Said it was some splinter group so he couldn't be charged..." Brendan shook his head, more to try and shake away the feelings that reared up at the memory. "And Owen said we'd fight it but...it's ancient magic. Protection of the line. And the Coven saw it as a rallying point..." Brendan touched a finger to his wedding ring, stroking the white gold. "Couldn't get so much as a picture." He looked up. "Thought it would change a few years ago. Nicolas' status should have changed to heir when he turned thirteen, but it never did. Didn't make the blindest bit of difference. The Council set up allowances to let the Coven families survive and they never managed to find a way out of their own magical laws."

"Did...did it occur to you that-"

He nearly snorted at the awkwardly worded question. "That Phineas could have claimed me instead?" he smiled bitterly. "Phineas Ambros...I'm not what he wanted."

"Why?" Doctor Barnes asked, then held up a hand. "Apologies, that was poorly worded. Why is that your answer, is what I meant to ask. You are powerful, successful, admired. Even when Nicolas was taken you were drawing interest. And you were only nineteen. Yes, you were a father, but there must have been some part of you that responded as befitted…a child who hasn't been claimed by his biological father."

Bitter laughter erupted from him. "That man isn't my…was never my father. In any shape of the word. And I told him what I thought of him months ago when I shoved that blade through his heart and tried to burn him inside out. I don't know why he didn't want me and I don't give a shit. He took my child from me. Twice."

"Do you believe that's why Phineas killed Nicolas? To take him from you once again?"

Yes.

"We're three minutes over," he said, looking at the clock, feeling suddenly flayed and raw. If it hadn't have looked like too much of a weakness, he would have swiped at his eyes, but as it was, he simply clenched his fists and tried not to move too much.

"So we are," she agreed without malice or frustration in her tone, apparently accepting that he wasn't ready for that conversation. "But you did well," she said, and then smiled at his snort. "I would suggest that you try to share a story or two about Nicolas. Perhaps with Danny."

As if he wasn't screwing up his son enough without wittering on about the mistakes he'd made with Nicolas.

"Or Lindsay."

The thought made him laugh again without humour.

"If Matthew Hayden ever catches me at his daughter's grave he'd kill me on the spot," he said, putting his coat on. "Still, viable option if it ever gets too much."

"She was the mother of your son-"

"Is," he snapped. "He's still my son and she's still his mother. And Matthew is still an unforgiving wanker."

He left before she could come up with anymore words of wisdom.

"Are you sure this is a good idea?" Brendan asked as they approached the pub. Outside, people gathered close against the wall in order to smoke and not get soaked. In the dim November light, the people almost blurred into lumped shadows with thin streams of smoke weaving into the heavy rain.

Enviously, he glanced at them. The need for a cigarette was causing his fingers to twitch restlessly as a whiff of smoke billowed towards him.

Nate shrugged. "We're on duty," he said, stepping up into the pub and ducking his head under the heavy doorframe. "If you can't sit in a pub and not have a drink then we really do have problems."

Like they didn't already.

"Why are we here?" Brendan asked as they slipped into a quiet booth that gave them a pretty good view of the bar.

"Recruits," Nate answered, taking a long sip of coffee. "Getting rowdy apparently," he added with a dismissive shrug.

"And what? They figured that if you classed it as rowdy then there'd be real trouble?"

"Something like that," Nate said, turning his attention back to Brendan. "How's therapy?"

"How's yours?" Brendan snapped back.

"Cried about Griffith for an hour," Nate answered, fiddling with the little biscuit the pub put on the side of their coffees. "Manly tears," he added with an attempt at a grin.

He was a shit friend.

"Kind of half expect him to haul me out over his shoulder sometimes," Brendan confessed.

"While finishing your pint," Nate decided with a weak laugh. "He'd be better at this than me."

"That's because he was a crotchety old bastard," Brendan said, taking a sip of his drink. "'Whatever you boys think you've done-'"

"'I've done it fucking better and more often so shut it'," Nate finished. "It was…it's good to talk about him honestly. None of this…I dunno. Feel like I'm giving his eulogy when most people ask."

Brendan smiled faintly at that and tapped the beer mat on its side a few times before tossing it back.

"I didn't want him," Brendan heard his voice say.

Nate blinked in shock, looking baffled for a moment before dawning comprehension hit. "Oh…" He wrinkled his nose clearly unsure what to do with the information.

"I was fifteen," Brendan said looking down at the table and pulling the beer mat close again. "I swore black is blue that it wasn't me that got Lindsey pregnant. Over and over and then when Nicolas was born…paternity spells are fucking easy to do," he said ruefully. "I ran away for two days before Owen came looking for me and dragged me back to my mother."

"It changed though," Nate prompted quietly.

"My mum would have him once a month. I'd...I'd practically flee the house. When he was five months my aunt got sick and mum went to help. Owen was meant to look after him. My step-father found me watching the end of the football match, put Nicolas on the sofa next to me and told me he had no idea when he'd be back."

The surprised laughter from Nate echoed his own feelings. He could remember being...appalled by Owen's idea.

"Had to pick him up. Bastard had put Nicolas close enough to the edge that...I'd never held him before. Managed to quieten him down and the baby just..." The memory was enough to make his fragile control wobble. "Looked at me. They have a way of doing it. They look at you like they can see all that you are and will be and...he snuggled in and went to sleep."

"You were hooked?" Nate asked.

"Never even looked at the TV," Brendan said, trying to lighten the mood. "Nor out the window. Owen was watching me the whole time."

"That's some good parenting," Nate murmured. "Sneaky," he added after a moment's thought. "But good."

"Owen's so sneaky that you don't expect that sort of thing from him," Brendan said, glancing over when a loud laugh came from one of the tables. "That them?"

Nate peered around. "Yeah, see that one? Dark haired lad? AJ? He's already had complaints."

The lad in question was already up at the bar, arm around a girl's shoulders as he knocked back a shot of something that was a vivid blue colour. Next to him a mixed-race lad was staring at his own shot with some degree of reluctance.

"They're up for six tomorrow, right?" Brendan asked as he watched.

"Oh yeah, Fred's planned some special music for class."

Brendan laughed.

It surprised him that he could do it without making a conscious effort. "Back in a sec," he said as AJ stumbled away from the bar and the girl, releasing her to clap a hand on the shoulder of another boy and shove a drink into his hand. Brendan made his way to the bar and placed the beer mat that he still held over the shot glass.

"Hey! What-" the kid's eyes widened. "I know what this looks like," he started to protest, "but I managed to get all the research for my essay paper done and my mate's offered to buy-"

"Project selections tomorrow," Brendan replied, catching the attention of the lad behind the bar. "Friendly advice? Those that are left are talented, but there are still a few weak links. Lazy, distracted, gifted and think they can skirt through," a small part of him winced when he realised he was paraphrasing some of a speech that Eun and Griffith had once given him back when he'd been an arrogant, self-destructive twenty-year-old mess. "Believe me, you want to get there when you have a chance of a good team."

"In other words, I should go home, get some sleep and turn up bright eyed tomorrow morning?"

"Something like that." Brendan glanced back at Nate who was texting with a frown on his face, forehead wrinkled and Brendan felt a flicker of something that might be suspicion…

When he turned back, the kid was staring at him. "Yeah," he said, looking as if the last thing in the world he wanted was to be sensible. "I'll just grab my mate?"

"What's your name?" Brendan asked.

"Uh..." the kid blinked as if he'd just been asked a difficult question. "Jake?"

Ignoring the questioning tone, Brendan scanned through the crowds, finding AJ again. "Not your problem," he said slowly.

"But-"

"You're training," Brendan dismissed, already knowing where that conversation was heading and, even if it showed some good character, proved the kid was a soft touch. "Your job is to focus on getting good. We're here for them," he said, nodding towards AJ who was leaning eagerly on the bar to get someone's attention.

The kid still hesitated, but as if seeing the growing crowd, he accepted the point. "I...thanks?" he asked.

"No problem," Brendan said, keeping his gaze on AJ before returning to Nate who was looking oddly amused.

"Haul him out or let him learn?" Nate asked with a small nod of his head in AJ's direction.

Brendan took a swig of coffee and sat back. "Give him another hour. He needs to be capable but suffering."

Nate shrugged and leaned back. "Okay, then. Gives us some entertainment tomorrow."

Chapter Five

It quickly became obvious why Brendan Campion (Brendan Campion!) had suggested that he didn't get utterly wasted the night before.

They were being sorted into groups based on their arrival time and the only person earlier than him and Cole was Daphne. Daphne who was like a frickin' encyclopaedia and a favourite of every trainer they'd ever endured.

She looked only mildly pleased to see them and that was probably only because Cole seemed to know every damned thing about the Coven and could translate pretty much anything. In comparison, Jake wasn't entirely sure what he brought to the table but the project was...well...everything.

"AJ isn't with you, is he?" Daphne asked Jake as they joined her on the table.

"No," Jake admitted, still feeling a little guilty about it. Still, he hadn't been sure as to how easy it would be to drag AJ away from the bar when he was in a party mood. "Have you narrowed down any ideas?"

Daphne shook her head but slid over the project pages. "They want to see certain skills from us. Research, strategy, team work, spell craft. Combat skill isn't a high priority at this stage."

"And we have complete free reign?" Jake asked, twisting the paper so he could read. The idea was kind of brilliant and terrifying; to have utter control of a cold case to show what they had learned. Rumour was they were rarely solved, but it gave them a real-life scenario that the Elites could measure their skills against.

And they had to do it around their training.

"Yes," Daphne replied. "I... I've been wracking my brains about which one to do."

"We get first call though? I mean there was that one two years ago. Dead body found by Whitechapel-"

"No," Cole said, still looking through the front sheets.

"Why not?" Daphne asked, pulling over the notepad that she never seemed to be without. "It's recent enough that we could have a chance of solving it. And if we solve it-"

"It was sensationalist enough that we all knew about it," Cole answered, putting down the papers. "And if we know about it, then that means they were under pressure to solve it. Trained Elites couldn't solve it. Unless you have a new angle then leave it alone."

Under the thrum of disappointment, Jake knew he was right. It was bloody annoying but he was right.

"So we go for something less known?" Daphne asked.

Jake opened his mouth and then restrained himself from groaning as Robert walked in. Robert who was practically marched to the Currock building every single day by his dad.

"How's that fair?" he muttered sharing a look with Daphne.

"Contacts," Cole muttered under his breath.

True. But still…they may as well have put them in threes, Jake thought as Robert took his seat.

The thing about parenting, Brendan had found, was that it was mainly just not freaking out when your kid was being gross. Brendan's mum had bought them some bowls that had different animals on the bottom and Danny had decided to scoop porridge out as quick as possible to see what he had. Which meant there was porridge like…everywhere.

Danny peered over at him, almost as if daring him to say something. Sighing, Brendan reached over and grabbed a damp cloth, chucking it at his son. Danny screeched as it hit his face and then obediently scrubbed the splodges off his face.

"What are you eating?" Danny asked curiously, head angling close. Brendan gestured with his hand to push the bowl away from the boy.

"Coffee."

"You don't eat coffee, you drink coffee."

Brendan stuck his tongue out at the kid who took it as an invitation to scramble off his seat and crawl up into Brendan's lap. Wrapping his arms around the boy, Brendan rested his head on the blond mop of hair and breathed him in. "You smell like porridge," he muttered. "Maybe I should just eat you." With that, he started to tickle the boy, mouthing playfully as if he might gobble the kid up which caused Danny to let out peals of laughter, his little body wriggling like a puppy's.

"Dad," he huffed. "Mum said you have to eat."

"Mum's fussing too much," Brendan dismissed, resettling him before reaching for another sip of coffee.

"Can I just have coffee tomorrow?" Danny asked and Brendan frowned because the kid sounded almost too earnest. Still, it was a stroke of genius, the little git. Brendan rolled his eyes and then admitted defeat, using magic to put some bread in the toaster.

"There," he said, pulling the bowl of porridge over. "Now we'll eat breakfast together."

His son nodded and shot him a triumphant smile that made some part of Brendan's heart sink because if the kid was actually being manipulative, then that meant he'd picked up enough that he felt the need to be manipulative.

"I'm sorry," he murmured gently, bringing up a hand to stroke the boy's hair. When Danny peered at him in curiosity, Brendan brought their faces closer together. "It's been a rubbish few months, hasn't it?"

Danny wriggled, as if a little unsure. "You've been sad," he whispered, as if nervous about how that statement would be taken. "Because of Nicolas."

Strange to wonder how Danny saw the concept of his older brother; a shadowed figure that had been mentioned, but that he'd never met. It was too complicated for an eight-year-old to fully understand so god knew what he had grasped.

"Yeah," Brendan said, unable to help the way he tightened his arms around his child. His only living child. The thought made him struggle to breath for a moment.

"I don't want you to be sad."

"I'm gonna try," Brendan promised. "But...I love your brother. It's gonna take some time."

Danny nodded, and Brendan guessed that he'd probably heard a few versions of that idea. Knowing Liaden, she and Danny had probably talked about it a number of times; conversations that Brendan probably should have been a part of.

"Danny," Liaden said as she appeared in the doorway. "Can you go and get dressed for school, please."

They both peered over at her because her tone was strange. Danny nodded wordlessly and slipped away in a move that both made Brendan feel a welling pride and a punch in the stomach. As soon as the kid was out the door, Liaden was throwing up a silencing ward.

"What-"

She stepped close, actual fear in her eyes as she handed him the newspaper. Frozen, he didn't take it. Instead, Brendan stared up at her as if he could find a clue from her expression. But she shook her head and instead shook the newspaper again to draw his attention to it.

Slowly, he reached for it, eyes remaining on his wife's. Dimly, he heard the toast pop and watched a flicker of regret cross her face.

The paper was a magical one. Magic in no other way than to a human it would appear to be an old metro copy. The fucking thing came to them whether they wanted it or not, though Liaden usually read it for her job.

When he saw the Ambros name, his heart nearly stopped and he practically snatched it from her grip.

Ambros: Training a killer?

His gaze darted down the page. Picked up the repeated use of his son's name, the word torture and the details of the Ted Grey case from May. The kid who had been tortured in such a brutal manner that both he and Nate had thrown up after dealing with the remains that had been found in a shallow grave, not far from the boundary lines of Ambros.

Investigation. Elites. Nathan Summers. Damien Redgrave training Nicolas Ambros to be…

Brendan stood, the chair scratching viciously against the floor.

"Brendan," Liaden started firmly. "Nate phoned me to tell me about the paper. Do not-"

"He phoned you?" Brendan yelled, not even knowing why the hell he was yelling at her, but needing in some way to relieve the building burning ache in his guts. "He fucking phoned you this morning? How about phoning me the minute he got this… He's been investigating my son?"

She stood her ground, chin tilting in that way that usually meant she was about to dig her heels in and fight to the bitter end. "Brendan," she snapped, "he's been continuing an investigation that you both started in May. He has done nothing-"

Done nothing? "Don't defend him," Brendan said, pointing his finger at her, "Don't fucking defend him! He's meant to be my friend and he hasn't even mentioned-"

"Put your finger down," Liaden ordered, battering his hand away as she stepped closer. "And when? When could he bring this up? When you were drinking yourself into oblivion? Avoiding everyone? You are grieving for your son. When the hell could your best friend mention 'oh, by the way, I think your son might have tortured someone to death'?"

The words made him want to be sick and completely knocked the righteous indignation out of him. "He was sixteen when that happened," he whispered, clinging to it, "Sixteen-year olds do not-"

"You were a father at fifteen," Liaden pointed out, still fierce, "Boss had killed a man at that age. Your great-aunt was one of the most respected seers of her generation at sixteen. Sixteen years olds are perfectly capable of doing everything that an adult can."

He stared at her and realised dimly that he'd stood up at some point, had even managed to get halfway to the door. Realised that her grey eyes were bright, her cheeks flushed and that she'd lost weight. Realised that he'd stood there and yelled at her for something that wasn't even her fault and-

"I couldn't," he whispered. "I could never...I don't know anyone who could torture a nineteen-year-old to death. That takes..."

Liaden said nothing, but he could see her softening again, the flushes of temper turning into the sad look she usually had at the moment when she looked towards him. She waited, wrapping her arms around herself a little.

"I know my son," he said...begged? He wasn't sure, only that he was holding on tightly to something that he couldn't quite put into words. "I knew... he was shy and nervous and sweet. That...that kid couldn't have grown up to do that. He-"

"Sweetheart," she whispered, taking a slow step forward, hands unfolding and starting to reach out. "You don't know how Nicolas was raised. Either he was taught such things were of no consequence, or the alternative to not doing it was worse."

It robbed him of breath, of the ability to stand. And

Liaden was there in seconds, holding him tightly and whispering comfort in his ear.

Jake wasn't ashamed to admit that they'd hightailed it out of the meeting room as soon as they could. He had no interest in seeing AJ at the moment or seeing any of the other recruits smirk at him because he'd been stuck with Robert.

Maybe the library wouldn't have been his first choice, but Daphne and Cole seemed to think it was their second bloody home at the moment. And watching the pair go back and forth over the issue of what to select was making Jake feel both utterly useless and beyond grateful that he'd been stuck with the two brainiacs.

"What about Porter's Lodge?" Cole suggested.

Jake exchanged a blank look with Daphne and started to look at Robert-

Robert who had followed them to the library table and sat, slumped, arms folded and glaring at anyone that so much as glanced hopefully in his direction. Not much point there.

"Porter's Lodge?" Jake asked.

"There was a body found there six years ago in twenty fifteen," Cole said. "Unidentified and death ruled as an accident."

"Thrilling," Robert muttered.

"And," Cole said shooting him a foul look. "A body was found there in ninety-ninety-six and another in the eighties."

"Three?" Daphne asked, typing it into the database. "No...just the one in twenty fifteen."

Cole shook his head. "Porter's Lodge was owned by the Ambros family. Fourteen years ago, Phineas Ambros gave up land to the Council. Those bodies aren't on the Council's database."

"How do you know about it?" Robert asked sounding, for what might be the first time in his life, like someone who gave a damn.

"My family is from the area. My grandfather told me about it."

"So..." Daphne sat back. "We'd have to petition the Coven for those records...that would show negotiation skills and...that's a whole new angle." She started to smile. "Not bad, Lorcan."

To Jake's amusement, Cole looked supremely unimpressed with the compliment.

It was shit of him that he'd begged Liaden to let him keep Danny at home. He was pretty sure that the only reason she'd agreed to it was because she wasn't sure who at the school would remember that Danny was Nicolas Ambros' little brother and might bring it up or be a little shit about it to their boy. All of which had led to Brendan sitting on the sofa watching some Disney film with the kid.

It didn't take a genius to work out who knocked on their door in the afternoon. Liaden silently rose from where she'd been working on the laptop and paused at the lounge door.

"Do you want to see him?"

No. But Brendan nodded and shifted because if they let it brew over, they'd probably just get more and more annoyed with each other. He lifted Danny up and then back down on the sofa before he crouched down in front of his son.

"Want a drink or anything?"

Danny shook his head and angled his chin, clearly simply concerned with seeing the TV screen. Ruffling his hair, Brendan took a breath and headed for the dining room that they never really used.

As he walked in, he spotted Nate instantly. His friend stood with his hands on the back of a chair and head hanging down, while Liaden stood opposite with her arms folded.

"I should have told you-" Nate started to say to the table before glancing up warily. He winced when he took in Brendan and he seemed to lose track of what he wanted to say.

A glance at Liaden had Brendan sighing and slipping into a chair. "Tell me," he said, not looking at either of them. "Lay out every fact."

There was a pause. He'd guess that the pair looked at each other, but he refused to glance up. Then Nate drew in a long breath and Brendan could hear Liaden taking a seat next to him.

"We swept Ambros before we withdrew. The amount of magic it took to keep us safe and operational in there was insane. But before we left, we managed to create blueprints and work out what rooms were which." Nate's fingers drummed softly on the wooden table. "We worked out which was Nicolas' room."

Oh.

It was stupid that hadn't occurred to him. He looked up and then over at Liaden who was watching him, beautiful grey eyes bright with some emotion.

"There was…I dunno. Text books, exercise books

from school. I'll get them back for you, once the Council officially releases the evidence. But yeah, there was a lot of stuff, including weapons. Lot of different blood sources on the blades despite them being wiped but there was a knife. Policy was to match any weapon found at Ambros to any wounds on bodies suspected of being killed at Ambros. The knife matched a lot of Grey's wounds.

"Which meant I had to check with the school. They confirmed that Nicolas had been withdrawn from school from April. Hadn't come back from the Easter break so he would have been around when Grey was captured."

Brenden finally glanced towards Nate who had fixed his gaze at a spot on the table, his shoulders hunched. "Last week…we…I don't know how, but we have Nicolas' magical signature on record. Matched it to a few of the spells on the body."

"Christ," Brendan hissed, leaning back in his chair and rubbing his hands over his face, half in attempt to shut out the fucking world for a second. Everything else was circumstantial, but that? Slowly, he dragged his hands together to meet in a prayer by his nose. "What spells?"

"Stamina, to keep someone awake. Some of the leftover ribbons of magic that would have burnt Grey from the inside were Nicolas' too. We matched more to Damien Redgrave, but Nicolas seems to have copied and matched. He was being trained. It's the only explanation to what we can see on the body."

Brendan shook his head, letting his hands drop to the table.

"So he was there and taking part," Liaden said

quietly. "That's undeniable. Do you know what the circumstances were?"

Nate threw her a look that was hard to read. Both grateful and annoyed almost. Throwing up his hands, Nate shrugged. "No," he said honestly. "I've been working on it since we matched the knife. School records are being a pain. Absences can be made public but internal pastoral issues not so much and they refuse to co-operate being an ancient school and not having a body to declare death. Tried to make contact with Vivienne Ozwald, she won't see me. But..." he shifted. "I did manage to interview a servant at Ambros." Nate shifted. "You're gonna like this less."

Bracing himself, Brendan gestured for him to continue even as Liaden moved to stand behind him, one hand on his shoulder. It was stupid, but the comfort helped. Somehow. Like someone could help him absorb whatever blow it was that Nate was about to deliver.

"She claimed that Nicolas did something. Made a power play or was plotting something. The week before we went in...he was locked up in the house. There were screeching arguments, Redgrave was summoned back. Phineas Ambros was blowing hot and cold like nothing she'd seen before. Apparently, at one point, Redgrave was yelling at Phineas. It was a mess the whole week before our attack." Nate shifted and then fixed Brendan with a look. "As far as she was aware, they weren't serving the kid food that week either."

He tried to bring up the image of the body that had been already half out the window as he'd walked in the tower room. Head already out, hands flailing to grab onto Phineas. Had he looked thin?

Liaden however must have spotted something and Nate winced when he glanced over at her.

"What?"

Nate shifted uncomfortably and looked away. It was Liaden who answered, voice pitching into something that sounded a little like a question. "The source for Ambros' treason came in a week before hand."

No.

Brendan glanced between them, shocked at how much it suddenly hurt to breathe as he kept his gaze on Nate who drew in a long breath and shook his head. "We don't know," Nate admitted. "Possibly. He'd have been well placed to gain the evidence. But again, if it was him, did he do it because he wanted an out or because he wanted to depose Phineas? Mate…I can go around in circles for days about the motivations and possibilities. The fact remains, we don't know enough."

But what if Nicolas had been the source? His mind instantly went to a terrified seventeen-year-old desperate to do the right thing, to find a way to escape…perhaps pushed into it because of what he'd been forced to do in May…

But another voice whispered. The one that had been nurtured by his training and experiences as an Elite. Any other Coven family and he'd suspect internal politics. Using loopholes to screw over family members and gain power…

"And this?" Liaden asked, tapping at the newspaper. "Where did this come from? I assume that the Council isn't releasing this as their official statement?"

"Fuck no," Nate hissed. "This is a shit show. I've been in about six meetings since this was released. Otherwise…" he trailed off as he seemed to weigh that up, "otherwise I still probably would have waited for you to tell me the coast was clear," he said with a hint of a smile at Liaden.

It annoyed him. Slumping down in the seat, he folded his arms and Nate immediately dropped the hopeful smile which made Brendan feel even more like a dick. Glancing between the two of them, Brendan reached for the newspaper again, summoning it to him to read properly.

"Any news on where Redgrave skulked off to?" he asked as he scanned through the article that seemed to imply that torture had been Nicolas' bonding session with Redgrave to become the next big serial killer. "Whatever you're finding, he's definitely been involved in it."

"Rumours are that he was injured and died of his wounds at Ambros. But, given that none of ours can verify that, seems more like they've planted that idea and are hoping we'll be thick enough to go for it." Nate hummed, "Though some are suggesting that maybe it was Damien Redgrave who killed Griffith. None of us saw who took him down."

"Griffith was burned out, magical exhaustion," Brendan said, shaking his head. "Redgrave usually leaves people in pieces-"

Nate shrugged. "We're keeping an ear out for him, but I'm not holding my breath. If he's out there, he's gonna be plotting."

"For what?" Liaden asked quietly. When they both looked over at her, she sighed. "Phineas Ambros is dead. Nicolas is dead. The family that Redgrave had devoted his life to has gone. All he can do now is save his own skin, surely?"

"I dunno," Nate huffed, "he's a piece of work. I can't

see him limping off into the sunset and accepting that he's been beaten."

"No," Brendan agreed. He stared down at the newspaper, scanning through again, hating where his mind jumped to. "So he's missing and so is Nicolas' body."

Liaden hissed at that while Nate nodded sadly. "Yeah, that had occurred to us. I mean… maybe…"

"Don't," Brendan snapped. "There is no good reason as to why he'd have taken the body. I can think of a hundred things he could do with…" he hesitated and then forced himself to say it, "the remains."

The remains. The remains that he should have buried somewhere safe and quiet so his son could actually rest in peace and not be diced up for Redgrave's schemes. Just another way in which he had failed his child.

Children, he thought glancing at the door and towards where Danny was sitting alone in a room. Again.

"We're flushing out the leak as best we can," Nate said slowly, obviously uncomfortable. "I…I'm sorry. This shouldn't have happened. We were gonna see if we could follow up on the lead that he might have been the informant so that you could have more answers…" He rocked back on the chair a little. "This wasn't the plan."

Yeah. It never was.

Chapter Six

IN THE WEEK SINCE THEY had declared their project, Jake was seriously starting to wonder if it was possible for your eyes to burn out from reading too much. Or you know, if that would be deemed as an acceptable reason to never again have to listen to Cole and Daphne argue about stupid nuances.

Because seriously. He was staring to consider it. Like...really seriously.

The female body that had been found in twenty fifteen had been the easiest file to find. Made even easier by the fact that Stuart McCafferty had been one of the Elites that had been called to the scene when a local had spotted the body. The local woman had since died so they only had her thrilling statement about walking the dog and spotting a body and her own bizarre concern that someone in the Elites would arrest her for trespassing.

Stuart himself had been assigned to them given his connection with the case and he was...interesting. They'd all sat in the room the day after declaring their project and sat in silence while Stuart had lectured them about the 'freakish house', how dangerous it had been and simultaneously implied that they wouldn't find anything of interest because he'd observed much of the property in a glance and was vastly experienced.

"And the two murders previous?" Cole had asked without a hint of a smirk on his face.

Stuart had blinked at them in confusion and then almost snatched up the two scant files that they'd complied for the murder in ninety-six and in eighty-one. To be somewhat fair to him, he'd sat and listened, flicking through and frowning at what he'd heard.

"But for it to be linked, the killer would have to be... in their sixties? Seventies?" he shook his head. "Not really the sensationalist enquiry that will build you a reputation."

Daphne had gaped at him. "But...it shows solid skills," she'd argued weakly, looking a little lost.

"Definitely," Stuart had allowed, almost sounding a bit apologetic. "And that's fine for you lot now. Just...you know...keep it in mind."

"Maybe it's the site of ritual killings by a local cult," Cole had deadpanned.

Stuart laughed as he stood, apparently missing Cole's tone. "That would be a headline," he allowed. "But unlikely."

The no-shit expression on Cole's face made Jake snigger the moment Stuart left the room. Even Rob had started to laugh as Cole had glared at the doorway.

"Mate, your face could turn honey sour," Jake had grinned. "He's a dick. We were always gonna meet some."

"Did he think I was being serious?" Cole demanded, turning to them all. Which was when Jake had spotted Daphne's almost devastated expression and softened a little, trying to catch her eye. But she had taken back the file and stared resolutely down at it all, lips almost white as she kept her thoughts to herself.

Still, Stuart had given them access to everything he'd had from twenty-fifteen and seemed to enjoy the narrative that he could create. Once or twice, Jake had even heard the spin that Stuart had suggested Porter's Lodge to them which pissed Cole off even more, to the point that the guy stomped around like a kid throwing a temper tantrum.

The other murder cases had meant that they'd had to make contact with the Coven and Jake had somehow found himself taking the lead on that. It had been weirdly fascinating to work out.

Even more fascinating was the reason why the murders had remained Coven domain. Ted Johnson, the man murdered in nineteen-eighty-one was on the Ambros family tree. As was Eric Redgrave, the body from the nineties.

"God, all the bodies previously found in Porter's Lodge were all members of the Ambros family?" Daphne had gasped reaching for the new files.

"Yup," Jake replied.

Which would have all been fine except that suddenly he found himself buried in documents for the Ambros family line and staring in bafflement at a family tree that had seen far too many murders and violent attacks in the past century. And the Coven archivists were particular about everything; they wanted exact references and pinpoint accuracy whenever Jake requested information. That meant, before anything could be gained, they had to know exactly what they wanted.

Jake was pretty sure that the novelty for the whole thing had faded away after the first forty minutes.

After a week, they'd sort of taken a victim each to research around their training. Jake had Eric Redgrave which had been a headache in the making because Eric Redgrave was like some second cousin or something to Damien Redgrave and literally every Coven contact and Council operative heard the word Redgrave and assumed it was for another investigation and then tied him up with bureaucracy because his clearance level was jack shit.

"So," Daphne said with a happy smile as she sat down and joined them for lunch. "Here's what I have about Ted Johnson. Body found in the fountain in ninety-eighty-one by Vivienne Ambros, now known as Lady Ozwald."

"What?" Jake asked, reaching for a packet of crisps. "Why was she there?"

"It was the family home," Daphne said, cutting up a sandwich into manageable fingers as she talked. "Ruby and Sebastian Ambros lived in Porter's Lodge for years with their children. By nineteen-eighty-one, Sebastian was two years dead, Lysander, their eldest, had moved to Ambros and Ruby was still living at Porter's Lodge with the youngest two: Vivienne and Phineas."

"Did we know this?" Jake asked, thudding down his papers. "That Porter's Lodge was the home of Ruby and Sebastian Ambros?"

Cole had peered over and then glanced at the others. "Rings a bell," he said quietly. "Cause of death?"

Daphne blinked at him almost in disappointment, "Uh...drowning?"

"That's on a file, right? Not just you guessing?" Cole asked.

"Oh, no, it's the cause of death on the death certificate,"

Daphne said, relaxing a little. "Uh and the scene was a mess. The family had been out for the evening. Vivienne Ambros came home in the morning to the body. The Ambros family took over the investigation…the assumed story is that Johnson confronted an intruder and died protecting the house." She slid the photographs over; and Jake glanced down briefly, taking in the fountain with the almost crushed edge.

It had surprised Jake the first time he'd seen a picture of the house. Only because the name had suggested that it might be some slightly bigger rustic house, not a massive country estate that looked like it was some grand Tudor place, albeit one that was in danger of falling apart.

"Okay so when Eric Redgrave was killed," Jake said cracking his neck, "the house was no longer occupied. The body was found in the entrance hall in ninety-seven, but had been murdered the year before. There was an official search that was led by his cousin, Jason Redgrave, who happens to be Damien Redgrave's uncle."

He was almost resigned to the shifting, awkward reaction that seemed to happen after the name was mentioned.

"Cause of death?" Rob asked.

"His head was caved in," Jake replied simply. "Someone had smashed it into the stone floor so forcefully that the floor was broken." He slid over a copy of the scene minus the body. "Scorch marks on the wall – either he fought back or was attacked and ducked which the attacker used to their advantage. Inner door was locked up, hadn't been disturbed so it seems unlikely that either Eric Redgrave or his attacker had gone inside."

"Theories?" Cole asked.

That was trickier. "No idea. Phineas was the Lord of Ambros by that point; his brother Lysander had died seven years earlier. Ruby Ambros isn't mentioned at all and Vivienne Ambros had become Lady Ozwald via her marriage. Almost seems as if the entire Redgrave family rallied round and there was a Coven investigation carried out by Ambros followers who answered to Phineas Ambros. There are no further records."

"Knowing the Redgraves, you'd assume that they'd tracked down the killer and pulled the skin from their bones," Rob muttered. When they all looked at him, he sneered a little. "Come on. Damien Redgrave trained people in torture; we've all seen the headlines this week."

Yeah, there was no denying that.

"Mine," Cole said, sitting forward and then looking deeply unimpressed when Rob muttered 'ours', "is unidentified. We went through Stuart's old files. They went through the house but said half of it had been bricked up and clearly hadn't been disturbed in centuries. The other side hadn't been disturbed in decades. They went through the rooms that had been opened and took out the body. Never identified her. She was in her early seventies, died of magical exhaustion and was spotted half out the window. By a trespasser," he added with the smallest hint of an amused grin like he was a cheeky kid.

Snorting at that, Jake shot him a look before he drew in breath. "There is something else," he said as they all looked over. "So, I'm calling the Ambros records keeper, the Council delegates and investigators and then, I was asking about Redgrave murder files. Which then means I'm bounced around because apparently no-one else in the history of the world has ever been called Redgrave other than Damien Redgrave. Anyway, I get to someone and ask about the Redgrave body at Porter's Lodge and this woman starts talking to me about a big investigation in the seventies."

"What?" Daphne breathed, leaning forward. "But Eric Redgrave was killed in the nineties."

"Yeah. Except that another Redgrave was killed at Porter's Lodge." Jake pulled out the folder. "So, in nineteen-seventy-six, the Council got a call from Sebastian Ambros. He claimed to have killed Tom Redgrave in defence of his family."

"Well..." Daphne tilted her head and glanced at the others. "I mean this is solved, right? If Sebastian Ambros admitted to it-"

"And refused an investigation?" Jake asked. "I mean, I guess why would you investigate if you knew you'd killed someone? But by law, he should have been investigated. The Coven voted against the investigation. Narrow margin, but they voted against it. The Council got involved and then withdrew."

"Withdrew?" Cole asked. "Is that explained?"

"Sebastian Redgrave and his oldest son had defensive wounds. His wife, Ruby, was exhausted, as in she was in a magical coma for about a month. Seems that Sebastian Ambros had a well-documented drug problem when you start to look through the records. He basically had no magic. Everything pointed to the family being attacked and defending themselves. But...same family attacked, same house and same family line as a victim. I...that seems like a lot to be excused as a coincidence."

Cole sat back thoughtfully as Rob shrugged, looking far more refreshed than the rest of them. "Guess we have only one thing to do," Rob suggested. "We need to go to Porter's Lodge."

"You sound far too excited about that," Jake muttered. "We're literally going to a fricking murder house from the sounds of it."

"They say that the family is cursed," Daphne said softly, eyes fixed on the final folder that Jake had brought to the table.

"With schizophrenia," Jake argued. "This is…maybe someone was trying to pick them off, or maybe they were having some internal battle with each other. But something happened in that thirty-year span and yet Damien Redgrave and Phineas Ambros were as thick as thieves up until Phineas Ambros' death. Seems more likely that the family was attacked."

"Which makes the body in twenty fifteen seem like the anomaly," Daphne murmured.

"Not if it's Ruby Ambros," Cole said suddenly.

They all snapped their attention to him, the air almost prickling with expectation. Cole glanced at them and then shrugged, "It's not that much of a leap," he argued. "She'd have been the right age. Ruby Ambros disappeared after Phineas became Lord Ambros, but this was her home. She died around the right time too, but there's never been a grave or a burial or anything. If it is her, she links all the murders."

Daphne reached for the folder again. "We can do a test on the remains," she said.

"With who as the comparison?" Cole demanded.

"Vivienne Ozwald."

"Jesus, good luck getting that to happen," Jake yawned.

"It could be her mother. You don't think she'd want to know, or at least rule it out for us?" Daphne asked sincerely.

"I don't think you'll get the message to her," Jake said. "I can't even start to tell you how many times I had to nag and beg and bargain just to get an investigator on the phone. Fuck only knows how you'd get to Lady Ozwald."

"Is that where Stuart might help us?" Rob asked.

"There is no way he would risk his reputation with the Coven for this investigation," Cole dismissed. "He'd have to argue and deal and..." Cole tilted his head. "He won't," he finished simply.

"At the moment," Daphne said, drawing in breath. "We'll go to Porter's Lodge and see what we can compile to convince him..." she seemed to be mentally compiling the list in her head. "Maybe we can try to convince him when some other Elites are present too to make sure he actually listens properly."

Cole raised an eyebrow at her and grinned approvingly.

"Can't believe you're happy about going to that place," Jake whined, slumping on the table. "You're all fucking mad."

They'd agreed to go painfully early in the morning so that they could get in more time at the house. Still, that had been easy enough to decide in the warmth of an afternoon spent in the Currock's coffee shop, and quite another thing to experience in the ice and darkness of a November morning.

Jake walked over to Cole who was sitting on the wall at the edge of the Currock grounds. The weather was cooler now and Cole's breath fogged up looking like a dragon's breath as Jake handed over the cup of coffee he'd brought.

"Any sign of Rob?"

"I phoned his house," Cole said with a wicked grin as he wrapped his hands around the coffee. "His dad was so understanding."

"That's slightly evil," Jake murmured as he sat down next to Cole.

"If we're freezing our backsides off out here at this time then so is he," Cole said, leaning forward. "You don't drive then?"

"I do," Jake said. "I just spent all my money on a lads' holiday after my second year of uni. You ever been to Ibiza?"

He could swear that Cole looked startled at the question. "No," his friend answered, frowning at his coffee.

"We should go. When we pass as Elites. It's brilliant," Jake said, thinking back to endless nights of not worrying about anything but having fun. "Better than a car at least," he said with a smile. "How about you? Did you pass your test?"

"No," Cole said, shifting. "Never..." He seemed to squirm uncomfortably and seemed to be struggling for a moment. "You know, it's just living in London? Everyone says that there's no real reason to drive." He straightened, eyes resting with some relief on Rob as he appeared, walking over. Sans father.

"Did you...did you come here on your own?" Jake asked peering around, sure he must have missed him.

"Screw you," Rob hissed as he took a seat on Cole's other side. "Besides, my brother said it was fucking hilarious. Apparently, my dad still reckons I'm out clubbing," he said flashing up a series of messages. "He's gone driving around to find me."

Jake blinked at him and leaned to catch Cole's eyes. "You are seriously evil," he said admiringly.

"Should make up cards," Rob added, shifting to get comfortable. "Never occurred to me that I could screw with him by pretending to be interested in this."

"Should see if you can make money out of it as well," Cole added with a hint of a smile, slowly seeming to adjust to the praise.

Rob nodded with approval.

God almighty, it was worse when he was enthusiastic. Not sure whether to admire the pair or be disgusted, Jake kept an eye out on the almost empty road.

There was a mini driving over.

"What car does Daphne have?" he asked with a sudden sinking horror as he glanced at Cole and Rob. Rob who was six-foot with inches to spare, Cole who must be just shy and he was-

"No," Rob murmured in distant horror. "You know a traveling spell?"

"You know a way to avoid making your brain ooze out of your ear without having a pre-established transportation spell?" Cole asked with a sigh as he stood.

"You're just saying that 'cause you're the short shit," Rob huffed.

"Remind me, the last time you got one up on your dad was...?" Cole asked as he strode forward.

"Shotgun," Jake said as he watched Cole approach the car.

He received identical looks of irritation.

It wasn't often that Brendan went to visit Lindsey's grave; he hadn't been exaggerating when he'd said Matthew Hayden would kill him. And, if Brendan were honest with himself, he and Lindsey probably wouldn't have continued to communicate had she not have ended up pregnant. If he'd found out that she'd died when he was nineteen and she twenty, he'd have had a flicker of sorrow and moved on.

But that hadn't been the way that life had gone. Instead, he found himself visiting her every so often because, of all the people in the world, perhaps she would have understood how he felt. And because, through that, it had become a refuge of sort, despite what he'd claimed with Doctor Barnes.

The November day had turned everything crisp and icy as he crouched down to brush the morning frost off the engraved letters with gloved hands. His touch lingered for a moment, thumb curling around the edge of the stone.

"The stuff they're saying," he whispered and then shook his head, dropping his hand as he felt a sudden wave of stupidity hit him. Talking to a grave was fucking useless and he knew it. Instead, he turned his head and watched the family that was in the distance, close enough that he could make out hair colour and clothes and probably guess at the relationship between them all, but far enough away that he felt somewhat safe.

One of the kids was about four or five, unaware of what they were doing at the graveyard and obviously bored, dancing away slightly from the group to kick at the grass with their feet in little yellow wellington boots.

"He was three," Brendan whispered to no-one. "He knew the difference between wrong and right. He used to snuggle close when people were sad. He cried when the dog died and hid at a scary part of some shitty cartoon on TV. He..." Brendan trailed off and shook his head, turning his attention back to the silent grave. "We weren't perfect parents, I know that. But he was good."

The grave didn't move, didn't respond, didn't give him a signal, did nothing but remain a stone marker in the ground.

It was a hateful sight. He let his gaze slide by and rest on the trees nestled in the slight dip of the hills, before reluctantly glancing back at the fresh grave at the far side of the hill, piled high with flowers and teddies. His hands fisted into the ground, fingers clenching uselessly on the grass that was scattered over the slight heap that covered Lindsey's body.

"I'd have lain him here, with you," he whispered. "They ripped him from your arms...I wanted to bring him here. Fuck knows why, not exactly a happy day out. But this is it now, isn't it? After me... after your father...no-one will remember that you fought back, that you died for our son. And I don't know if he even knew your name before he died. If he knew that both of us fought for him. Young as we were, dumb as we were..." He shook his head. "I haven't got a clue what they told him. And I don't know if he knew I was coming. How close I was. One minute, Lindsey. Maybe two-"

He stopped. Could almost see her, forever twenty, folding her arms and shaking her head because that was the kind of relationship they had been getting to; two people who loved their son and had different ideas about how to raise him. In his mind, Lindsey would be forever twenty and becoming someone he wasn't sure he liked as she went off to university and he had full custody of their son. He'd put up with her comments when she'd come back with new haircuts and new ideas, started to suspect that she was beginning to use Nicolas as some sort of accessory…

But she'd been his son's mother. And she had fought for their son when it had mattered. And she'd been dead by the time he'd arrived at her parents' house, body spread as she'd crawled after the boy.

She'd died for their son and he hadn't.

The thought made him gasp for breath, agony slicing through his guts. His hand spasmed, reaching out for the stone. It took him a few minutes to get himself under control.

"They're saying he deserved it," Brendan whispered. "That he deserved to be…" he shook his head, unable to say the words. "That…"

His phone went off and he ignored it. Once. Twice.

By the third time, he'd recovered enough to answer it blindly. "What?"

There was a second of hesitation and then the sound of a phone fumbling before he heard Boss's voice. "Campion?"

"Yeah," Brendan said, standing so that he was slightly away from the grave, though why he felt the need to bother, he had no idea. "What is it?"

"Are you free to come in?"

Frustrated, he restrained the urge to kick out at the grass given where he was. "Thought you wanted me to stay away?" he asked petulantly.

"I did." Boss didn't sound the slightest bit ashamed of it. "But Summers has a proposition for you if he's finished being a pathetic little shit."

There was the distant sound of Nate muttering something in the background, but it was too faint for Brendan to really work out what was being said.

He must have been silent for too long. It was long enough apparently that even Boss (who was emotionally stunted) seemed to hesitate. "Liaden said you went to the graveyard."

They were not having this conversation. They were not even going near this conversation. "You want me to go to the office or meet Nate somewhere?" Brendan asked, keeping his voice firm.

"Office." Boss sounded slightly relieved. "Try not to punch someone on your way in."

"Send the dickheads out then," Brendan suggested as he started to head down the hill and towards the exit.

"Campion, I haven't got time to work out who that would include and I'm short staffed as it is. Just get in, keep your head down and attempt to be something of an adult about it."

Daphne had been the perfect driver as they'd made their way down to Sussex and deep into the south downs. The countryside wasn't exactly Jake's cup-of-tea, but the sweeping hills and clumps of forest were beautiful in their own way. To his surprise, Jake found himself peering out of the window rather than studying his phone.

Eventually, they turned into a thick patch of woodland

and further into darkened lanes where trees seemed to reach across the road above, threading together and blocking the sunlight. Something about it seemed to change the atmosphere in the car and Jake could see both Rob and Cole staring out the windows in the back.

Another turn and a narrowly winding lane brought them to the old gates of Porter's Lodge. They almost hung off the crumbling stone pillars which looked as if they were struggling to hold the weight of the heavy gate.

The heavy *iron* gate.

Jake was so busy staring that he missed the moment that Daphne got out the car and unhooked the latch of the monstrous five barred gate, using her Elites training card to release the Council wards and open it up. As she moved away, he could see the engraved metal sign that was rusting and warping; the name Porter's Lodge still visible.

"Fucking creepy," was Rob's thoughtful judgement as he peered up at the trees and the steep mud banks that felt overwhelmingly claustrophobic.

It was hard to disagree. Once Daphne was back in the car, she drove at a crawling pace as they made their way up the uneven drive. The trees on the bank seemed to be opening up a little, but it was still dark enough to cast shadows across the car.

The radio seemed suddenly very loud.

Reaching forward, Jake switched it off, momentarily amused as the change in perspective revealed a pack of cigarettes in the well in front of the gear stick.

Daphne smoked? He glanced over at her and met her slightly challenging brown eyes.

Bemused, he turned his attention back to the windscreen

as the lane suddenly opened up, the banks smoothing down to something that possibly had been landscaped once upon a time. Under the car, the lane became gravel and the trees became overgrown bushes covering long grass that danced in the wind.

Ahead of them was a house and in front of it was a broken fountain, one side of the rim smashed to crumbling chunks while the rest seemed strangled by plant life.

The house itself could have been pretty. It was one of those old Tudor buildings that had clearly been added to over the years but Christ only knew how it had been called a Lodge. The place was like a massive manor house. You could have easily fit a small school in the building. The parts of the house that he could see had some sections boarded up and seemed to be a hodgepodge of brick and stone work.

As the car moved further along, the other half of the house came into view. The right-hand side of the house was probably only still standing from ancient building spells that older Coven properties had woven into the fabric of the structure as it was being built.

"The fountain," Daphne said quietly. "That's where Ted Johnson's body was found."

Someone had been killed not five feet from where he sat. Stunned, he sat and stared at the fountain, and surely it was impossible to think of anything but what had happened forty years ago.

"Are we going in?" Cole asked.

And apparently, it wasn't impossible for all of them.

"Yeah," Daphne said, shaking herself as she turned off the engine and pulled out the keys. With a decisive move, she opened the car door and stood, staring up at the building, the wind tossing her hair into short dark streamers against the stone walls.

Rob kicked at the back of Jake's seat.

He could take a hint!

Getting out of the car, he flipped the seat forward so the other two could clamber out and folded his arms against the wind.

"Jesus," Rob muttered, "It looks like it's been abandoned for centuries."

"The nineteen-eighties," Cole corrected absently.

"That," Rob said, pointing up at the east wing of the house, "has not been touched for longer than that."

"We should get our bearings," Daphne decided, "do the grounds and then the inside. That way we can work out where we are when we're inside."

"So we came here to go for a walk?" Rob asked doubtfully.

"And your plan is?"

"I'm just here to annoy my dad," Rob answered honestly and Jake couldn't quite restrain the groan that bubbled from his lips.

"Come on," Daphne demanded. "None of us want to be here with each other longer than we need to be."

She strode off, walking towards a side gate.

No-one ever felt like being called into Boss' office was a good thing. There had been a time that Brendan could vaguely remember when it had been another man's office. The place had actually been tidy and welcoming and somewhere that an official could visit without gingerly stepping around the room. Within a month of Boss being made head of the Elites, he'd changed the office into something painfully functional, unwelcoming and uncomfortable.

The desk was always flooded with papers that Boss would defend like they were his young. No-one could move anything; disturb a pile to find a document and heaven help you. The chairs were uneven and unsteady and didn't even look like they were attempting to match each other, which was why both he and Nate stood as Boss settled himself in behind the desk; Nate looking tired and strangely wary.

"So?" Brendan glanced out of the office window to the bull pen beyond that looked quieter than he had expected it would. "What's the idea?" he asked, and immediately stifled the urge to complain that Boss seemed to be using their meeting as an opportunity to catch up on paperwork.

"Boss wants me to put Stuart McCafferty on the Ted Grey case," Nate said, launching straight into it, like he was charging headlong into an offensive spell.

"Stuart McCafferty is a dickhead," Brendan told Boss firmly.

"And you'll notice, not currently in the office," Boss muttered to his work, scratching some note across a file. He huffed and looked up. "We need someone on it that will cause difficulty for Nate."

"Why?"

"Because Boss hates me and enjoys making me cry," Nate replied, glaring at the ceiling. He shifted a little as if to sit on the edge of Boss' desk and then leaned away when Boss glanced at him.

"Because the press are starting to question the team looking into the Grey murder and don't even get me started on Lucas Grey's reaction," Boss said, refocusing his attention once Nate was fully upright. "McCafferty is a glory seeking little shit who seems to think you and he are locked in a bitter rivalry. He will look for every negative possibility as we connect Ambros to Grey. Especially as it will get him noticed by our fucking Lord of Strength." Boss scrubbed at his head. "Lucas isn't letting it go and Stuart is playing into his hands."

The very idea of it made him want to throw something. Instead, Brendan folded his arms and shifted his feet because there was no fucking way he was leaving the room until Boss admitted this was a stupid idea.

Boss raised an eyebrow as he studied Brendan. "Sorry, Campion. Did you think somehow that we lived in happy la-la land? That just because we don't look into your boy being a cold-blooded killer the whole world will accept that? To do this right, Nate needs to work every angle, including the one that suggests Ambros Junior was a vicious little-"

He broke off when Brendan surged forward, half intent on wrapping his fingers around the man's throat. The wards around the desk flared up and it took every ounce of ability Brendan had to avoid being thrown back across the wall.

All through it, Boss sat back in his chair and looked bored. Then looked at Nate. "See? Gonna assume you two want to still be friends at the end of this investigation. Let McCafferty ask those questions and piss Campion off because he'll enjoy it and because he won't be the only one to ask them. We need to do this right." He seemed to suddenly consider something. "Campion, if you could make sure that the pair of them still have their jobs at the end of it, I'd appreciate it. Had too many recruits drop out already," he added before glancing back down at the paperwork and glaring at it, as if the sheet of paper was somehow to blame.

Nate hadn't moved either, though his expression was a little more frustrated when Brendan looked over. "You know if it comes down to it, I'll help Brendan thump him one?"

A slight huff of bitter laughter came out of Boss as he put the paper to one side and started on the next. "You know if McCafferty is fired, I'll send both of you to the dinners and galas and social networking things that he does for us all-"

"Does for himself," Brendan corrected.

"Still does it. Swear to god, you two will be bowing and scraping and dancing with Council and Coven representatives until the day you die." Boss turned the paper over and then rolled his eyes. "The Teagues…" he shook his head. "Did Omar sort them out last time?" he asked, but looked down as if talking more to himself.

"Alix," Nate corrected absently. "All right, fine." He shook his head. "Can I at least give Brendan the carrot now that you've delivered the great big fucking stick?"

"I'm mostly convinced that you two give each other the carrot every other week," Boss said, scribbling Alix's name on a post-it. "Why stop now?"

"McCafferty is mentoring a group of trainees-"

Oh god. "This is the carrot?" Brendan asked in disbelief. "Are you fucking serious?"

"And," Nate continued, "One of his groups is looking at Porter's Lodge. Gotta say, never heard of it before last week. You?"

No. "Nate, get to the point," Brendan said, resisting the urge to slump. "Quickly."

"Porter's Lodge is an old Ambros property. One of a number of properties given to us in reparation for taking your kid-"

"What?" Brendan yelped, turning to look at Boss who seemed to be tuning them both out now. "They gave the Council a holiday house? What the hell was the Council thinking? How-"

"You can yell and leave or stay and listen," Boss said as if bored beyond words.

Brendan stared at him, swallowing back the words before he turned back to Nate. After a moment, he nodded, already longing for a drink.

"You would have justifiable free reign to look into the history of the Ambros family without getting in the way of our investigation," Nate said softly. "You say you want to know more about Nicolas? This...this might be a way of doing that. In a roundabout way," he said, looking a little uncertain.

Brendan glanced back at Boss who was now flicking through a document and then at Nate who was looking more and more nervous.

"Keep you busy," was all Boss said as the silence stretched and, for all that he looked uninterested in the conversation, Brendan had seen him do this too often to be fooled by it.

God, he fucking hated this. Feeling trapped and like he was on some balance board that would tip no matter what he wanted or the fact that he just wanted to stay still for five fucking seconds to work out his own mind. But he had to move now and god knew it was easier to move with Nate by his side than not.

"Who are the trainees?" he asked, as if that would make the slightest bit of difference. "And what, exactly, is the case?"

To Jake, the grounds of Porter's Lodge looked like they'd been created specifically to be used as the back drop to one of those horror films his oldest sister liked to watch and shriek at so that she could climb into her boyfriend's lap.

As they explored the grounds, it became clear that, buried in the bushes, were old iron railings that made him shudder. They surrounded the entire property in a threatening manner that made Jake want to stay far away from them. It was strange though – there was a boundary line being marked out by the iron and bushes. Within the grounds, there was another section of iron, but the spaces seemed to make no sense and didn't section anything off properly, but almost seemed to act like the walls of a maze.

"Did you know about the iron?"

They'd agreed to walk around together; all of them had seen enough of the aforementioned films to be cautious and they could hardly agree on a meeting place if none of them knew where anything was.

Cole shook his head, eyeing the railings hidden in the yew tree with the same distaste that Jake was feeling. Up ahead, Daphne and Rob walked together, though what the hell they had to talk about Jake had no clue. "They seemed to be trying to keep something out," Cole murmured.

"Or in," Jake added, not sure that helped at all.

Cole jolted a little, as if the idea hadn't occurred to him, which pleased Jake probably more than it should.

"Got graves," Rob called out, he and Daphne hurrying ahead. "And what might have been a chapel."

Right. Because they needed it to get creepier.

Jogging to catch up, Jake spotted the lumps and the scattered grey slab that rose out from the overgrown greenery.

"How many?" Cole asked as they joined the others.

"Uh…I dunno. About fifteen?" Rob said, glancing haphazardly across the area, as if Jake and Cole couldn't have done that.

The names were so faint that it was almost impossible to see them. Slightly wishing he had listened to his mum's attempts to teach him the different cleaning spells that he could use, Jake sighed.

"We need to look into this," Daphne said because… well…she was Daphne. "Maybe talk to someone who works with restoring graves."

"Another shit place to visit?" Rob asked. "Shall we make a list of the least fun places on earth to go?"

Christ, Rob really was a whining bastard at times. Turning to catch Cole's eye, Jake paused when he saw his friend had wandered off a little way and was staring at another grave, set slightly apart from the others…and bigger. It hadn't been in Jake's immediate eyeline when they'd come across the graveyard.

"Can you read that one?"

Cole didn't reply.

"You suck at trying to be dramatic," Rob muttered as if Cole was doing him some great harm. Walking over, Jake peered around the stone.

The writing was just as faded as the others, maybe more so. But Cole was staring at the symbol at the top that must have been deeply etched into the stone because it was still clear, if a little worn.

"You recognise it?" Daphne asked as she peered close too. "It's...it looks like...Is that the Ambros crest? But old?"

Ambros? Kind of made sense Jake supposed, given that the Ambros family had owned the house up until recently, but the idea that it was a grave of one of the Ambros family-

No, wait...

"It can't be," Jake said. "Coven family members are buried in the ancestral land. It's tradition and we all know how much they go gaga for that."

"It's not the Ambros crest," Cole said slowly. "It's a personal crest."

Daphne huffed and Jake had a sneaky suspicion that she was pissed off that they hadn't been impressed by her obscure knowledge. "It amounts to the same thing. But Jake is right-"

"That's Henry Ambros's crest," Cole leaned forward. "Twenty second Lord of Ambros."

"That can't be...Why would he be buried here?" Jake asked, baffled still.

Rob had gone still. He and Cole seemed to be exchanging the same awed looks. "Because..." Rob said stepping forward to stare at the grave with sheer reverence. "They didn't own the lands then. Not when the Council executed them."

When the Council...

No fucking way.

Chapter Seven

THE PUB THAT THEY'D ENDED up in was an old eleventh century thing that must have been updated so many times that Jake doubted the owners could still claim it was eleventh century, but whatever.

"The graves have no relevance in our investigation," Daphne said for the third time to Rob as he pulled apart the gigantic burger he'd ordered. "It's ridiculously unlikely that the murders are linked in any way to-"

"Who gives one?" Rob argued. "Henry Ambros is one of the lost Coven members, the executed twenty. It's a goldmine-"

"It's not a goldmine," Cole muttered. "You can't sell it, you idiot."

"It's Council property. The Coven families will fight to get these grounds back now-"

"Causing a diplomatic crisis?" Daphne snapped. "That'll hardly get us a pass. We're meant to prove we can solve cases, not that we can cause incidents between the Council and the Coven."

"Phineas Ambros is dead, anyway," Jake pointed out. "Would the other Coven families-"

"Yes," the other three snapped at him and wow, okay. Jake reached for his beer and fought the urge to sulk.

"Henry Ambros' grave would rekindle interest in how the lost twenty were treated," Daphne said with a sigh.

"I remember," Jake said, an ethics class suddenly coming back to him. "We did a lesson on it..." he winced at the thought of it, his mind racing to the story of Henry Ambros' son, the youngest to be executed out of the twenty Coven members. "Okay, I get the potential shit storm that could be raised, especially if his body was exhumed and there were signs of torture. Still...surely it would cause more of a problem to hide this?"

"We'd reveal it eventually," Daphne said, as if that were obvious. "But...you know what Stuart will do with this," she all but pleaded, "he'll want to use it to build up his name."

"Or be pissed that he missed this when he swept the grounds," Rob added. "How did they miss this?"

"Porter's Lodge is one of twenty-seven minor properties that were handed over in reparations thirteen years ago," Cole said absently. "I don't think the Council particularly gave a shit what the properties were, just that they could point to it and say 'look what we got'."

"Still. What about when they came to collect the last body. They must have swept the grounds."

That...that was a good point. That was a really good point. "Maybe they were hidden?"

"And we found it because we're already so fucking amazing at this job?" Rob asked, seemingly having decided to sit and sulk.

"All spells have an expiration," Cole murmured.

"Right," Daphne chimed, sitting up straight. "And..." she hummed as she flicked through the folder that may or may not have become surgically attached to her hand. "Look, no official visits have been made to the property since July."

"So?" Rob asked, taking the words out of Jake's mouth.

Cole finally looked up and at her, an odd look on his face as he sat back.

"The Ambros family," Daphne said, swallowing. "The line died in July. Phineas Ambros was killed, his heir, Phineas' grandson, was killed."

"Oh shit, yeah. Nicolas Ambros." Jake tilted his head, trying to remember what he'd read about the kid in the paper.

"Tosser," Rob muttered, and apparently that was all he felt he needed to say on that subject.

"And there's no-one else left?"

Daphne seemed to hesitate. "No-one that was claimed as his family, no."

Huh. "What about the father? Or the son..." Jake winced. "The middle guy?" he settled on and glared when Cole let out a snort at the phrase.

"Well..." Daphne shrugged. "That would be Brendan Campion."

What?

His bafflement must have shown because it made even Rob sigh and sit up properly. "The open secret of the Council. Phineas Ambros knocked up Maeve Campion after they left school. Rumour was he attacked her when she refused to have an abortion. Tried to do the job himself."

Christ. "But...the Coven is obsessed with family. It's how they survived the Council being created. Why wouldn't he-"

"It's the curse rumour again. That schizophrenia theory or something else," Daphne said with a shrug. "Brendan Campion is the first one in a few generations not to show signs. The other theory is that the family magic is poisoned in some way, a curse...either way the Ambros family were never exactly the picture of sanity. They may have tried to keep the blood line thin because of it."

Jake frowned and then stiffened. "Wait...Brendan Campion was the father of Nicolas Ambros and that's where he...wasn't Nicolas Ambros thrown out of a tower window? I'm sure I read that somewhere and all the...why was the kid even at Ambros-"

"Phineas Ambros claimed the kid when he was three. Stole him away one night, killed most of the mother's family and then..." Rob shrugged. "You said it was reparations?" Rob asked Cole. "Think it was probably part of the deal because of that? Time line matches up."

"The Council exchanged some houses in exchange for a free pass for murder?" Jake asked in disgust.

"Phineas Ambros always claimed he'd rescued the kid from the kidnappers and that he was stepping in as others had failed. Passed every truth spell in the book, but there still needed to be some smoothing over," Rob said. "My dad was always fascinated by it," he added at their surprised look. "The idea that someone could get around such a thing."

"Or that it was true," Cole said slowly.

They all looked at him in surprise.

"Depends on the definition of rescued," Cole added with a shrug. "And how easily he could twist the questions-"

"They grilled him," Rob defended. "Yes or no questions

only for a huge portion of it. No-one could ever figure out why the hell it was that he decided that he wanted a baby rather than a nineteen-year-old."

Huh? "What-"

"Campion was fifteen when he had his son," Rob explained, apparently preening at the gossip. "Pretty sure it was used a couple of times to dismiss Campion; reckless and lacking in responsibility. That and my dad says he has a vicious temper when he wants. But he's powerful so...you know. The Council are desperate to keep him on-side."

Not sure how to respond to that, Jake shook away the...slightly less than complimentary comments about the man he admired. "And the other one?" Jake asked. "He has another kid, right?"

"With Liaden Buan. The cousin of Patience Buan, a Lady of the Coven," Rob said. "She's...a writer of some kind. Like a journalist?"

"The Buan family would battle Ambros. Would have," Cole muttered, frowning at his slip. "The whole hereditary claim would go on for years without an outcome." He shifted and shook his head. "Point is," he said a little firmly, "that Ambros magic must be fading; there's no one left who can keep any of the spells going."

There was a long silence as the implications of that fully sunk in.

"We need to tell someone," Daphne said, her shoulders falling and looking strangely defeated. "Because that is important, we have no idea what might be left in the vacuum of those spells and there might be others that are failing too." She looked worried suddenly. "There could be a lot of people at risk..."

"So either way, we need another meeting with Stuart?" Jake asked doubtfully, then grinned as, across from him, Cole groaned and tried to press his head through the table.

Thankfully for Brendan, Nate had picked up the copies of the findings that the trainees had handed in each week. Apparently, Stuart McCafferty had been boasting like a peacock about the change of assignment.

Christ, he hoped that Boss knew what he was doing with this plan.

He'd taken the folders from a rather frenetic looking Nate and shoved them in a bag, told his friend to give him a day or two and stomped off home, firing off an apologetic text to Liaden asking that she leave him alone too.

There was a study at the back of the house that had been made from the tiny box room. Liaden had converted the loft when they'd first bought the house and had been young and naïve and imagined filling the house up with all their kids and friends, but Danny had been their only child together and people often had their own lives. Still, Brendan had always insisted that one of the rooms close to theirs be left for Nicolas.

He paused, glancing at the cramped study and then back at the larger room that his eldest son had never even seen. After a moment of debate, he opened the door slowly and stepped in.

It was clean and fresh. He'd guess that Liaden cleaned it or kept freshening spells on it because he never went in unless he was thinking about Nicolas and wanted to be alone. It was a weird mismatch; stuff left over from when his son had been three and a few things that Liaden had bought, knowing with more logic than he had allowed himself that they'd be dealing with a teenager instead.

It looked like such an innocuous room. For a normal kid.

He closed the door behind him, stepping close to the bedside table and skimming the tips of his fingers over the framed picture of him, Nicolas and Lindsey, taken at Nicolas' third birthday. Lindsey and Nicolas' dark hair blending together so much that you had to bring the photograph close and tilt it against the light to work out where the difference was. She'd been proud of her hair, he remembered. When they'd first met...had sex...she'd had long, long hair that was often plaited at school in a thick braid that he'd been oddly obsessed with.

He'd felt oddly...mournful when she'd cut it off. Like the girl he'd known and fancied was slowly fading away in front of his eyes. A visual representation as to how distant they were becoming. How unlikely it was that Nicolas would ever know those versions of them; the sweet, determined girl and the wild, idiotic boy.

His eyes jumped to his son's face, the serious expression that was just breaking into a delighted smile and he wondered, briefly, if he could genuinely remember the toddler's laugh or whether, somehow over the years, he'd gotten it confused with Danny's.

It was sickening to remember that he was the only living person in that photograph. The image jumped and became unsteady for a moment and he carefully replaced the photograph, brushing a thumb over the glass and wishing-

It seemed like he spent half his life wishing.

Turning away, he summoned over the desk chair and

used the bed as a desk, dumping the stuff on it, not sure why this felt fitting. The pictures of Porter's Lodge across the ages (which was in no fucking way a lodge!), he pinned in a line on the wall with magic before adding in the four different murders that had happened on the grounds. He took note of the names mentioned and then, without a trace of guilt, flicked through the files on the four trainees, slightly relieved that someone seemed to have removed the personal details because that stuff was always useless.

They were a diverse bunch, he thought as he tossed Goodman's file to one side as not really worth his time. Jake Atkins, the kid he'd chatted to a few times, seemed to have some potential even if he was in desperate need of some confidence. And seer tendencies...Jesus, the kid had pretty much a golden ticket to full time employment. Cole Lorcan who seemed to have been raised by some sort of archivist grandfather and flagged up as potentially going more into research; and also requiring drug testing every two weeks which made him snort. Daphne Groening had a glowing CV, recommendations and was also tipped for research though more recent additions to the file showed there had been a few emails to Boss about encouraging her to stay with the Elites.

Whomever had picked the case had done well. They'd already made contact with the Coven, successfully navigated the archives, which had taken Brendan about three years to get his head around. The team had played to their strengths and could now show off some magical prowess with the house.

He could work with that, he thought as he leaned back

in the chair, glancing between the four victims. And it was interesting.

A gentle knock at the door startled him and he glanced at the clock, stunned to realise that he'd been at it for about three hours.

"Come in," he called and then smiled when he saw Liaden had a plate of food in her hand. He said nothing as she came in, but watched, smiling when he realised that she was wearing one of his hoodies over her work wear and feeling, for the first time in a while, the stir of something that wasn't just a desperate need to lose himself in her.

"What?" she asked, tucking a blond strand behind her ear with a curious look at him.

"Just remembering how lucky I am," he said, leaning forward to pluck a sausage roll off the plate. "Did you warm these yourself?" he asked, somewhat impressed by the lack of raw pastry or charred remains.

"I did," she said, a teasing lilt in her voice. "And I didn't burn it. I feel I'm getting the hang of this cooking malarkey." She placed the plate on the desk and bent close to him to press a kiss to his lips.

He savoured it for a moment. "Then I shouldn't worry about-"

"Oh god no," she said, moving to straighten up. He slid an arm around her gently and then smiled when she took the hint and slid into his lap. Grinning, she settled herself before twisting and stealing one off the plate, "Start cooking again," she ordered after taking a bite and studying it. "Our son genuinely is starting to think that fish and chips that aren't still part frozen is a gourmet meal."

Snorting, Brendan reached for her hand and kissed it. "I'll pick some stuff up tomorrow," he promised.

She smiled, even as her eyes darted to the documents on the wall. "You seem…settled. I wasn't sure when you stayed in here."

"Sometimes," Brendan admitted, "Nate knows me too well. A case I can get stuck into that has just enough linking me to Nicolas' life? Full reign over it?" Brendan shrugged and lifted his hand to her face. "Finally feel as if I can do something. Even if it is to know a bit more about the family that ended up raising him."

"Technically, they're your family too," Liaden pointed out, twisting a little and leaning in to tuck her head under his chin.

"Technically, they're not," Brendan replied, not really allowing the sting to land this time. Then, when she let out a sigh, he relented and pressed a kiss to her forehead. "I don't want to be curious about them," he admitted in a whisper that ruffled some strands of her blond hair.

"Then be curious for him," she suggested, her hand coming up to his chest and thumb stroking soothing sweeps onto his jumper.

It made him smile and shift, gathering her a little tighter. "Okay," he said simply and rested his cheek on her hair.

As far as Jake was concerned, it was far too late to bother anyone at the office and everyone seemed to be buzzing about some visit from a Council operative earlier in the day which had frayed relations enough that even raising an issue that would need to be passed on seemed like a stupid idea.

Daphne opened her mouth a few times in-between Stuart's boasting claims but, in the end, sat back with a defeated air.

"Not looking forward to that part," Jake murmured to Cole who was leaning against the wall and texting.

"Hmm?"

"Office politics," Jake said, still a little taken aback by the way most of the Elites were talking. Actually finding out what had happened seemed to be a monumental task as none of them were forthcoming about what had actually happened. Apparently, newbie recruits still weren't to be trusted.

Made a certain kind of sense, Jake supposed. Didn't stop it from being as irritating as hell though.

Cole shrugged. "Everyone looks to blame someone else," he muttered, shoving his phone in his pocket. "Have you talked to AJ lately?"

No. Since getting their separate assignments last week he'd had little reason to and, bad as it sounded even in his head, Jake had to confess to being a bit relieved by that. Managing the work load and getting a decent review was way easier when he wasn't battling a hangover or spending his spare time creating that hangover. "Why?" Jake asked.

A pair of hazel eyes studied him and then Cole shrugged. "No real reason," he said. But he glanced at the Elites around them that were working on the files while bitching in the vaguest way possible.

Cole nodded and then shook his head. "He's...We went out a few days ago to celebrate doing the essay."

"Drinking?"

"Mm."

It was hard to tell what it was that seemed defensive about Cole's stance. It might have been the curl of his shoulders or the way he leaned away from Jake ever so slightly, fiddling with the ring on his smallest finger. Whatever it was, Jake felt himself brace for impact, but Cole just shook his head, clearly wanting to keep that information to himself. Or maybe he just didn't want to have that conversation in the middle of the office.

Jake glanced at Daphne and then grabbed Cole's elbow, propelling him back into the hall. It must have been a shock to Cole because he stumbled and followed without protest, as if baffled by what was happening.

Jake found a door to one of the old stock rooms that was a damned mess because no-one in their office gave a damn if the pencils, pens and 'shit' were organised correctly. Cole let out a sigh as Jake slammed the door shut.

"What is it with you two?" he asked. "Seriously? You've never really spoken and now you're going drinking together and you want to hear about him?" Jake ticked off his list in his head and then frowned. "Did you write his essay for him?"

"What?" Cole stared at Jake like he was mad. "Write the essay? No!" He looked so put-out by the idea that he'd helped someone cheat that it was if he'd eaten something sour. "I just…we just…he's…tricky."

"Tricky?"

"I dunno." Cole looked deeply uncomfortable. "I don't usually drink too much. I just…I might have mentioned…

he'd have said something if I had." He looked like he was reassuring himself.

"About?"

"I..." Cole winced and closed his eyes. "We were talking about keeping up with the pace. And..." he seemed to consider what he was saying very carefully. "I mentioned that I'd dabbled with some drugs. I'd taken stuff to..." Cole looked away, "I don't know. To fit in?" he said awkwardly. "Be accepted? I dunno. It...it got me what I needed," Cole said with a rueful shrug.

Oh. "When?"

"When I was seventeen," Cole admitted. "I... I can't remember if I told him...about a dealer. Or even if he would go for it."

Right. "So what did you do?"

Under any other circumstances it would have been funny to see the way that Cole's lips literally seemed to seal themselves together. It was like watching the shutters go down and the closed sign come up.

"I'm handling it," Cole snapped.

"Your issue or him?"

That, thankfully, seemed to surprise Cole. "My issue? I'm not..." he actually sighed. "I...I'm not getting high, Jake. Not with AJ or with anyone. Christ, the Council probably knows more about what goes into my body than I do."

Well, that was something. He'd successfully avoided any issue with drugs at university. They screwed up magic so spectacularly that no-one he'd known who was magical went near it and no-one that had been human had done anything stronger than weed with the occasional smattering of speed.

You'd think that both AJ and Cole would have more sense.

"Is AJ all right?"

Relief crossed Cole's face at being finally removed from the line of fire. "I dunno," Cole confessed. "I think he wanted a quick solution to the fact that he…well…he's-"

"Struggling?"

"Not cruising through as he thought he would," Cole corrected. "He's good, I think. Has to be to make it this far, but he's lazy too. I just… I don't know where we left it or what we agreed…"

"Right," Jake glared at the door and then at Cole, "Do you…" he glanced back at the door. "You want to go for a drink? Talk about it?"

The scrutiny for such a small question was weird. "Why?"

Jake shrugged.

It seemed as if Cole would turn his nose up at the request but in the end, after a truly strange amount of thought, Cole nodded.

Cole watched him with a weary air as Jake brought the drinks over. They'd found a quiet pub filled with sticky tables, tired bar staff and the strong smell of urine wafting from the toilet.

Kind of suited the mood.

"So," Jake said softly as he sat. "How come you stopped whatever it was that you did?"

His friend looked deeply uncomfortable with the

conversation and traced the rings that had taken off the varnish on the table. “No lecture?” he asked.

Jake shrugged. “You clearly aren’t doing it now,” he said, taking a sip. “Everyone does stupid things when they’re a teenager.”

Cole snorted and reached for his drink, staring at it for a moment before he took a sip. He’d requested a double whisky and Jake watched without comment as he took a slow mouthful and glanced at the bar as if to work out which bottle had been used. “Council knows,” Cole said eventually. “I’m tested regularly. If anything unusual or suspect comes up then I’m out.”

“They still took you knowing what you did?” Jake asked, curious at the idea. He’d kind of thought that it would be a huge barrier to working for the Elites but…if Cole had agreed to the tests then he’d probably remain the least likely to be taking anything while he worked.

The nod wasn’t really needed. “They liked my skill set,” Cole said slowly. “I just…if the Council thought I was trying to set up Elites and dealers-”

“And you really don’t remember what was said?”

“I,” Cole said, putting his head in his hands. “We were talking about managing time and he was admitting that he’d been struggling with all of this…” he waved a hand as if to indicate their job, “and he’d done the paper quickly so I don’t know how good it is. And he was… we were talking about how likely it was that we would have to continue doing the activities we were doing in training. And then there were shots-”

“Yeah, AJ is the king of shots,” Jake said sympathetically.

“So it seems,” Cole muttered. “I just…I can’t remember

the last part of the evening." He shook his head and rubbed a hand over his face. "I dunno. Maybe I should just avoid going drinking with him."

"Plan," Jake said with a grin. "Or at least until he learns to calm down. So what do you-"

He broke off as his phone rang. Startled, he dug it out of his pocket and saw Daphne's number on the screen. Mouthing her name to Cole, Jake answered the phone.

"Where are you?" she demanded.

"I...Cole and I went for a drink," Jake said, sitting back in his chair, immediately trying to work out if that was an acceptable thing to do or not.

"Why?"

Well, he could hardly answer that! "We're not far," he said, realising that didn't answer the question but unable to think of anything else to say.

"I finally managed to tell Stuart about our day and he laughed," she said, sounding beyond frustrated. "He actually thought I was playing a prank on him. He congratulated me for getting a sense of humour."

Ouch. And slightly funny. But mostly ouch. "Did you explain the theory we had as to why-"

"Of course I did," she snapped. "He barely listened. He kept laughing."

Okay, that was less funny. "We should go back," Jake said firmly. "Get some proof. Pictures," he said with a flash of inspiration.

Daphne was silent which he took to mean she disapproved with him coming up with a solution that she hadn't seen. "I'll go tonight," she decided.

Whoa. "No," Jake said firmly. "No. We're investigating

murders. Don't go there alone at dark. That's asking for trouble."

"Come with me then."

"Daphne..." Jake sighed. "You know going there at this time is..." he hesitated, looking at Cole who'd raised an eyebrow at what he said. "Not clever," he finished, feeling stupid, but also somehow sure that it was that comment that she would listen to.

And it seemed he was right; there was a really long pause as Daphne seemed to consider his words. "Stuart... he said that Brendan Campion was taking over as our supervisor for the case. What if he-" her voice wobbled as she trailed off.

Shit. Stunned, Jake sat back and stared at Cole who was watching him with interested, curious eyes. For a moment, Jake almost wanted to agree with her, to make sure that they impressed Campion when he looked through their work-

"If something goes wrong, that'll impress him a lot less," he heard himself say as he tried to shove down his own threatening panic.

There was a long silence as he could almost hear Daphne turning the idea over in her head before she let out a really long, frustrated sigh. "We're meeting Brendan Campion tomorrow at midday," she said eventually. "Just make sure that-"

"Yeah," Jake said. "We'll wrap it up here. Cole and I can go back to the office to check everything over."

"Right." She sounded doubtful, almost as if she wanted him to swear in blood or be there herself to supervise him. "We'll meet at ten."

Staring in annoyance at the ceiling, Jake sighed. "Fine. See you then."

She ended the call without saying anything more and Jake drew a deep breath before he looked down and met Cole's curious gaze.

"Not sure you're gonna like this," Jake started.

Chapter Eight

"It'll be better than McCafferty," Cole muttered as they walked through the main entrance and headed for the lift the following morning. He nodded and then looked away and muttered something indistinguishable.

"Do you even need me for this conversation?" Jake asked, "Genuinely think you've been answering yourself for the past ten minutes."

"Four minutes." Cole violently pressed the button to call the lift then folded his arms. "Are you still star struck by him?" he asked abruptly.

"I'm not fucking star struck," Jake muttered, a sudden yawning chasm of embarrassment threatening. "I was never star struck." He eyed up the two women closest to them, hoping to god that they hadn't heard.

Gossip spread around the Currock building like warm butter on toast.

The doubtful look that Cole shot him made Jake want to grin, despite it all. "And Daphne?" Cole asked. "She definitely-"

"Fancied him?"

"No, just...she wanted to impress him." Cole pressed for the lift again. "She didn't fancy him, right?"

Jake shrugged. "He's…an attractive man." An idea suddenly occurred. "Wait. Do you like-"

Cole blinked at him and then shook his head as the lift doors finally opened for them. "At least Rob's there," he said, his mind apparently moving on though god knew what to.

"Better than McCafferty," Jake reminded him, trying not to laugh.

"Yeah." Cole chewed at his lip, following him and pressing for the fourth floor. "Rob's gonna lead with the graves, isn't he?"

"Five seconds ago, you were relieved he was there."

"I just…"

"You want to impress him too," Jake grinned. "Knew you were full of it. I think you're a secret fan-boy."

The lift opened to an almost silent hallway, filled with small offices that were often used to store case information. "Better than McCafferty," Cole said, as if that was some sort of explanation. And, Jake guessed, it kinda was. To be trained by Brendan Campion was…well, it was something that he'd half day-dreamed about when he'd been invited to the first round of interviews.

Which was a nugget of information that he wasn't sharing with a single soul. And especially not someone who seemed to be more than happy to have a chat with himself as he walked through the building. In fact, Cole seemed so lost in his thoughts that he practically ran into Jake when he stopped dead at seeing the office was already occupied by the man himself.

Brendan Campion was sat on the table, arms folded and looking across the wall as Daphne started to pin things to it. She looked unnerved and tired, but determined with her lips pursed into a thoughtful frown. She glanced over at them and then returned her gaze silently to the task.

"It helps," Campion said without turning, "to see it all laid out. Frees up your mind to see connections." He turned and cast a gaze over the two of them, blond hair ruffled from the wind and the battered brown leather jacket that Jake had glimpsed before looked like it been with him for years. His blue gaze jumped to the clock that read half nine and he nodded to himself before turning back to Daphne. "What time did you tell them?"

"Ten," she said, pausing before she turned to face Jake and Cole fully.

"And Goodman?"

She hesitated. "Nine," she admitted.

Campion said nothing, but glanced at them again before he turned his attention back to the wall. "Crime scene photographs came in," he said softly.

Cole stepped forward. "We've had them for ages," he started to protest.

"With the bodies," Daphne said to Cole gently. It was surprising how much more relaxed she seemed already. "Come see," she invited.

Throwing something of a wary glance at Campion, Jake stepped forward and watched as she pinned the crime scene photographs. She seemed determined to keep to a certain format and, for the moment, he couldn't tell what the format was, but at the bottom was Ted Johnson, body face down in the fountain that was half smashed. Above him was Eric Redgrave whose legs were sticking out of the door, face down as well. A picture from another angle showed the spiderwebbed cracks in the stone flooring. Above him, there was an older photograph of a crumpled body on the stairs inside. Stairs so wide that you could have probably laid another two bodies in the same position on either side of what remained of Tom Redgrave. He was staring up at the ceiling as if in shock, the blood vessels in his face standing out in stark relief as if he'd suffered some poison. But it was the gaping hole in his chest that had clearly killed him.

"And the unidentified body?" Cole asked quietly.

Daphne smiled and reached for the edge of the wall then, with a glance back at Campion, pulled with her magic causing a second, transparent layer to form over the wall. Upon it, very vague blueprints suddenly revealed themselves, the ground floor and grounds of Porter's Lodge underneath where the bodies had been. Ted Johnson by the fountain, Eric Redgrave on the porch and Tom Redgrave on the staircase. To the left of it was another blueprint, this time of the second floor, and Daphne started to pin the pictures of the elderly woman to the windows overlooking the drive.

Cole stepped forward, fingers tracing the outline of the downstairs. "Can you tell the layout?" he asked. "The east wing was closed down centuries ago, I reckon. If we knew-"

"McCafferty's blueprints don't cover much," Campion said, tilting his head. "They examined the entrance way and where the body was. The rest was locked up. He did manage to look through some of the west wing, but he wasn't all that interested in the case." Campion looked for a moment like he'd say more, but then thought better of it.

"But you agree that we have something?" Cole asked suddenly. "Not just the graves."

Daphne sucked in a breath and winced, causing Cole's expression to falter a little before it smoothed out into an expressionless mask.

"Graves?" Campion asked, turning to look at Cole fully, then at Daphne.

"There are graves on the grounds," Daphne said, a little too loudly. "They're of little consequence to-" she stopped herself when Campion raised an eyebrow then let out a defeated sigh. With a not so subtle glare at Cole, she set her jaw. "Stuart laughed us off. I'd prefer to tell you when we have proof."

Campion turned to Jake expectantly.

"We saw Henry Ambros' grave-" Jake begun.

"We think it's revealed itself because there's no longer a Lord of Ambros or an heir alive to keep the magic..." Daphne's voice, which had started off so strong and annoyed trailed off into quiet mortification as if she suddenly realised exactly what she was saying and to whom she was saying it.

For a moment, Campion was silent and the atmosphere was...sharp? There was no other way that Jake could describe it. The breath that Campion let out after almost exactly ten seconds was audible and Jake almost braced for impact.

"Anything else?" Campion asked in a hard tone, surprising Jake. Campion didn't seem happy, but his reaction wasn't quite the explosion that Jake had been half expecting. "While we're on shitty conversations?" Campion added, shoulders tight.

Daphne shook her head, but Cole glared at her. "We suspect that the unidentified woman is Ruby Ambros.

Phineas' mother," he said firmly, and his eyes narrowed as if he was waiting to be scolded.

Surprisingly though, Campion seemed to take that a lot better. Brow furrowing, he pushed off the table and walked over to study the picture that Daphne had just put up. The body was sat at the window, looking like a terrifying wax work as she stared unseeingly out of the window across the grounds, and propped up well enough that it hadn't collapsed to the floor after death. "Huh," Campion muttered as he studied the picture. "What did she die of?"

"Exhaustion," Jake said quietly. "Magical exhaustion. It can happen with the elderly as their body fades and they misjudge the power they have left. Happened to my grandpa, he never accepted that he needed to slow down."

Campion turned to him and Jake nearly swallowed his own tongue. "But?" Campion pressed when Jake said nothing.

"She's…her life story is tricky to pin down," Cole answered, thankfully helping out. "I took the lead on her," he added when Campion turned to look in his direction. "After Phineas became Lord Ambros she sort of…vanishes from society, from common appearances. The house looks like it's been abandoned, but maybe she was living there? But that would then raise the question of why give it to the Council? Ruby would have lived there while it was under Council ownership."

Campion clicked his tongue before turning away from the board to face Cole properly. "So why do you think it's her?"

"I…" Cole looked at the others, as if forgetting it had

been his theory. "Right age, right place, fits the timeline. She was declared dead by Ambros around that time."

Campion's face showed little as he glanced back at the unidentified female. "And all of the other victims are also on the Ambros family tree?"

"Yeah," Daphne said as she stepped forward. "We had a look and all of them have Mary Ambros as an ancestor which links back into the tree. Her father, William, actually lived at Porter's Lodge too, apparently."

Campion nodded and then glanced at another wall. "Atkins, would you cast the tree on there?"

Nodding, Jake walked over, performing as he was told. "Who should I use as the root?"

"Go for Henry Ambros," Campion suggested, still staring at the woman's body before looking over at the other three.

It wasn't easy magic. Coven lines were public record, but revealing themselves to the eyes of strangers always made magic wobble and shake as if nervous or mistrustful. Henry Ambros' name bloomed at the top along with his wife Constance and then spread to his seven children, sole grandchild and then continued. Down and down the ornate writing and links went, surprisingly without many branches until William Ambros had three children and his daughter's line broke the mould. Her younger brother's family continued with one child until a man named Jeremy Ambros and then again until Sebastian Ambros married Ruby-

"Lorcan?" Jake asked, turning to Cole.

"Told you," Cole said, eyes fixed on the Grant branch of

the tree. "My family are from that area. Sure somehow we're related. Think her father was one of eight or something."

Huh.

The official line ended with Phineas Ambros. Nothing was underneath him and Jake studiously avoided looking in Campion's direction, really not too sure what the man's reaction to that would be. When he did risk it, Campion wasn't staring forlornly at the blank space where his name should be, but was instead glaring at Damien Redgrave as he appeared on the tree, fingers twitching, and Jake could swear that he saw the faintest shimmer of magic between the digits.

"Well," Daphne said as she reached forward and tapped at their three murder victims' names, turning them red, "We know that they died under violent circumstances." She glanced at the others and then over at Campion. "And obviously Henry Ambros was executed, as was his eldest son," she tapped on those names turning them yellow, then hesitated.

Campion carelessly flicked his fingers at the tree, turning Phineas Ambros red without comment. He stepped closer, eyes fixed on the bottom of the offshoot. "There are fourteen people still alive," he murmured as he studied the dates. "Or who haven't had official death confirmed… which means someone must have confirmed Ruby Ambros' death for it to have been updated on this."

Yeah. Jake glanced at the wealth of names and then jumped when Campion tapped the wall and then turned to them. "You'd best go out and find the rest of the family members."

What?

"Not the Redgrave line," Campion said, maybe reading the terror in their faces at that prospect. "The rest: the Grants, the Summers, the Johnsons. There are way too many lines that have been broken off at a young age," he said, glancing back.

"So you agree that someone might have been attacking the family?" Daphne asked and Jake winced because he got why she was pleased, but maybe she could remember who she was speaking to.

"Yeah," Campion agreed. "Maybe." He tilted his head. "Atkins, search the splinter line on the system. See how many you can contact. Lorcan, get historical on the splinter line. See if there's a reason for so many broken off-shoots. Groening, do the main Ambros family. Start with..." he hesitated, but so briefly that Jake wondered if he were reading too much into it, "those who would have had contact with Ruby Ambros in her lifetime."

Campion, it seemed, was taking the Redgrave line and Jake couldn't quite work out if he was relieved or slightly terrified by that.

Awkwardly, Rob walked in just after midday with such cautiousness that it was immediately obvious he was suffering from a hangover. Campion, by that point, was sprawled in a chair, searching for something on a precariously balanced laptop while the rest of them trawled through records that Campion had given them access to and Jake had a moment's hope that he actually hadn't noticed Rob practically creeping into the room.

Any hopes that Campion hadn't noticed him died when

the oldest box of folders magically slid in Rob's direction. "You like the graves?" Campion asked, not looking up, "Then you can go through those."

Rob's expression was hard to read given that he was wearing sunglasses indoors like some kind of twat, but he at least leaned forward to peer down. "You believe us?"

"He has to be buried somewhere," Campion said, shrugging and swiping his fingers across the laptop screen.

Rob's face fell when he lifted out the first leather bound book. "This is old as shit."

"And?" Campion finally looked up, his expression challenging, as if daring Rob to complain. For a moment, Jake thought he would, jaw clenching as Rob looked like he was losing a battle to keep his mouth shut and his thoughts to himself. Somehow, he ended up simply nodding sharply and sitting down, sulking like a kid as he started to unpack his box.

It was the most they'd gotten out of Rob in weeks.

They worked through their piles in silence, though fuck only knew what Campion was doing on the laptop. Every so often, someone would turn a name on the Ambros family tree red or declare someone missing or, in a few cases, find someone who had been violently attacked and irreparably injured.

After about one-o-clock, Campion finally picked up his folders, flicking through them as he continued to do something on the laptop. He'd spread out on one side of the conference table and everything seemed ordered in a way that made zero sense to Jake, but allowed Campion to dart between information with almost terrifying efficiency.

"We stopping for lunch?" Rob demanded about an hour after, slamming shut one of the thick old books in such a way that Cole actually winced and seemed to be eyeing up the book with some concern.

"Hmm?" Campion asked and then glanced at the clock that had been ticking away as if they'd all been trapped in an exam. "Sure. Fine. Go." He looked back down again as if he'd already lost interest in them.

"I can stay," Daphne said, looking torn, even as she slowly started to mark where she'd been up to with the folders. Jake blinked at her in surprise and then hid a smile as he realised her short hair was stuck up all over the place from where she'd been dragging her hand through it.

Campion shook his head as Cole silently rose. "Go. Goodman's paying."

"I-" Rob glared and then huffed. "Fine."

That man had some serious powers. Grinning at Cole as Rob turned to get his coat, Jake finally closed up the file he'd been reading and felt his stomach give a relieved sigh.

Once the kids had gone, it took about fifteen minutes for Nate to arrive, dumping down the KFC that he'd gone to get. "Fucking Stuart," he snapped. "One day of this and I've already had three rows with him."

Brendan sighed and put the laptop to one side, closing the lid and reaching out a hand to summon his burger to him. Spinning in the chair, he studied the family tree which was coming up with a worrying amount of colour coding for unnatural deaths. "Maybe it'll mellow," he suggested half-heartedly.

"Maybe he'll stop being such a prick," Nate suggested, sitting on the table, feet on Goodman's chair. "That ain't normal," he muttered, nodding towards the family tree as he took a massive bite of his burger.

"Nope," Brendan agreed, cricking his neck. "How the fuck has this happened? It's like the family's been attacked over generations. And the central line has done nothing to help or avenge." He gestured to the wall. "In 1872, Ivy and her two young children were involved in a shipwreck. Only it looks like the ship sunk because of tampering and the few survivors that were there recorded that there had been someone on board attacking passengers. Or here. Luca Hornby. Found in a well in the 1950s, starved to death, but the fucking well had been boarded up. Someone buried him down there. Here, mid-nineties, Alan Grant, his wife Eliza and their daughter Joy disappeared. House left like they'd just gone to the shops. Never seen again." He rubbed a hand over his mouth.

"The Redgraves?" Nate asked quietly.

"Less violence and disappearance historically, but in the past century..." Brendan gestured to the bottom of the tree. "Two murders, one suspicious death." He leaned back in the chair. "And Albert Redgrave vanished in the eighties. Guess who his fucking grandson is?"

Nate paused and studied the tree briefly. "You know you can't track him down," he said warily. "And not just because the Council say it's a bad idea. Taking down Damien Redgrave...you are no-where near your best at the moment."

He refused to admit that. "What did you and McCafferty argue about?" Brendan asked, mainly because he was sure that Nate wouldn't tell him.

Instead, his friend shrugged and took another bite.

"We agreed to call each other by our first names and then Boss thought we were being sarcastic."

"You weren't?"

"Oh, I was. He wasn't," Nate said easily. "But then he realised it and we yelled, then Boss cursed us so that we get a pain not unlike an electric shock if we call each other anything other than our names and in a tone anything less than sincere."

"HR will have a field day with that," Brendan muttered.

"Second row was because he implied I was being too cautious when interviewing. Apparently, we should go full steam ahead when talking to an abused child." Nate caught Brendan's look and shook his head. "This kid, Bonnie Roberts, was in Ambros for a time and examined by Lord Ambros about seven years ago, but didn't stay. Most of the abuse came from Mummy dearest, so not…" he hesitated suddenly.

"Not one of my son's potential victims?" Brendan asked, shaking his head, half-tempted to hit something.

"No." Nate looked down at his burger. "And the final row was because he implied you were glory seeking and playing at being the wounded hero." Nate drew in a breath. "I got sent here by Boss."

"You punched him," Brendan sighed, putting the food down.

"Only…a bit." Nate grinned and then rolled his eyes. "Fuck me, mate. You'd have had him through the wall."

Accepting that, Brendan traced the patterns in the packaging with his little finger. "Boss still think it's a good idea? You and McCafferty?"

"Says it's gonna be the most unbiased operation ever,"

Nate huffed. "Swear to god, the bastard is considering making us full partners."

"No, he's not," Brendan said, glancing up at his friend.

"No. But he must have been putting up with a lot of questions because even with all of this he seems relieved." Nate relented a little and twisted to Brendan. "I forget how much shit he takes for us all sometimes, especially with Grey being his boss."

Yeah. "I won't hunt him down. Damien Redgrave, I mean," Brendan said, a little reluctant. "You have no idea how much I want to."

"I think I do," Nate said, voice softening. "But that man…he'd turn everything we have on its end, put it all on Nicolas just to hurt you. You know that. Damien Redgrave wouldn't give us anything close to the truth."

"Probably shouldn't come in alive then," Brendan muttered.

Nate watched him steadily, "But either way," he said slowly lightening his tone, "you just promised not to so it's a moot point." He paused and hummed. "That is the word, right?"

Brendan shrugged. "Cross my heart," he said, trying to match the lighter tone.

It was worth it when Nate grinned, shoulders relaxing a little. He held out his fries. "Want some as a thank you?"

It made him smile and reach out. "You must be grateful if you're sharing food."

"You have no idea. So what are you going to do?" Nate asked, gesturing back at the wall. "About all of this?"

"Figure out if there is some…lunatic family out for revenge," Brendan reached for the ketchup, poured and dipped part of his burger, ignoring Nate's disgusted sigh. "I'm not sure if Danny and I would be exempt or not."

Nate's eyes widened at that idea. "Fuck," he breathed. "Mate, maybe you should-"

"I'm not fragile," Brendan murmured. "And there's no way I'm letting anything come for Danny. Not after…" He bit at his lip and shook his head.

"You in the right headspace for this?" Nate checked carefully.

"Yeah." Brendan glanced back over at the wall, at the four murders and at the woman who, in another life, another world, he might have called Grandma. "I really am."

Chapter Nine

GOING TO SEE HIS MOTHER these days was never what Brendan would call a fully comfortable experience. They grieved in such different ways that they seemed to rub against each other like two chips of flint; all they created was heat and pain.

She was out when he arrived at the house. Owen had mentioned that they were going to see Rachel, probably because his step-sister was going to finally confess that she'd gotten engaged. Why the hell she thought none of them would be pleased, he hadn't a frickin' clue.

Brendan stomped into the kitchen, moving more on muscle memory than anything else. It was only as he picked up the kettle that he glanced up and caught a glimpse of the tree. In the November weather, it looked skeletal and like something out of a nightmare, the lowest branch almost seemed to be reaching down to skim the top of the stone they'd erected for Nicolas. It looked barren and bleak and like the worst place on the planet.

It stopped him though. He stared out of the window at the grave and then slowly put the kettle back without filling it or switching it on. Instead, he gripped the edge of the sink so tightly he half expected it to crack.

He hated it.

Three summers his son had toddled around under that tree. His first steps with Brendan had been there. Their first really slow, tottering game of football had been played under that tree, and Brendan could remember boasting to anyone who was too stupid to stay and listen that his son would be a footballer one day.

"You're not even there," he whispered, the image blurring. No. His son's broken body was probably still in the lake, rotting somewhere or had been scooped up by some Coven dickheads to do who the fuck knew what with.

All he saw when he studied that grave was his failure to make sure something was actually buried beneath it.

A hand on his shoulder made him jump and scrub at his face, annoyed. Owen said nothing, but waited until Brendan turned to look at him.

"Your mum's still getting her things," Owen said softly. "Do you want to do this another time?"

Brendan shook his head. "I...it's more of an official visit."

"She'll love that," Owen sighed. He reached for the kettle, putting it on far more efficiently than Brendan had earlier. "Any way just you and I can do it?"

Brendan shook his head, wishing he could take Owen up on his offer. "How is she?"

"She?" his mother asked from the doorway. He turned and drew in a breath at the sight of her. Clearly, his mother hadn't been eating properly because she looked thinner than she had in years. Her blond hair was a little too long to be called a bob anymore but she had on make-up which was more than she'd done the past few times he'd seen her. In fact, she looked more together than she had for some months.

"How are you?" he remedied, still staying close to Owen who turned away a little, leaving them to it as he sorted out tea and coffee. Her assessing look reminded him far too much of the way that she'd checked him over before he went to school in the weeks after she'd found out he'd gotten Lindsey pregnant.

She opened her mouth and then glanced over at Owen and sighed. Instead of answering, she held open her arms and he stepped forward, a little relieved that they weren't gonna talk about it for a bit. Instead, he ducked his head into her shoulder and breathed in the familiar smell of her perfume. She let him hide for a few seconds and then pulled away, cupping his face.

"Liaden said you've gone back to work."

Brendan nodded.

To his surprise, she simply nodded. "You've always done better with goals and things to do when you're…" suddenly she faltered and then sighed and met his eyes ruefully, thankfully not finishing that sentence.

"Not sure you're gonna like why I'm here," Brendan admitted.

She nodded him towards the table. "Something to do with work?"

Pulling out a chair at the little table by the wall, Brendan sighed and sat with his back leaning against it, knowing the perfect place to sit to avoid the hanging tat on the wall and secretly amused that, no matter the fact he was a grown man, his mother still pressed her lips together in some annoyance at the fact he didn't sit square. "Boss still won't put me out in the field. I'm babysitting the recruits." Brendan watched her sit and get comfortable as Owen brought over his coffee and his mother's tea before going back for his own. "They have a cold case."

His mother frowned and then turned and smiled at Owen as he took the seat next to her, sitting square with a slightly wry look at Brendan. For a man who spent his career finding loopholes to exploit, he did so love pointing out the rules.

"Porter's Lodge?" Brendan asked, taking a sip and shifting a little to face them fully.

Her expression suddenly became still. Owen frowned at her, but said nothing as he blew on the liquid, instead fixing Brendan with a questioning glare.

"What of it?" his mother asked, her voice oddly hoarse.

Aside from her reaction? He bit back a retort when Owen slowly shook his head in warning. "There were four murders there; Eric and Tom Redgrave," Brendan said. "Ted Johnson and an unidentified elderly female." He hesitated. "The kids have a theory that the woman was Ruby Ambros, Phineas' mother."

His mother sipped her drink, fingers wrapping around the mug as she stared at something he couldn't see. "It was where they lived," she said softly. "Phineas and his family. His grandfather was at Ambros and they were at Porter's Lodge. He said...he implied that happened often in the family history." She took a long breath and turned her head towards the window. "The Lord would be at Ambros while the heirs would reside at Porter's Lodge."

"You grew up by it," Brendan said. And hadn't he felt stupid to realise it. In his mind, his mother and Phineas had met…well…he hadn't really given that much thought, nor had he ever wanted to. He knew they'd known each other as kids, but discovering Porter's Lodge was about a mile from where she'd grown up…

"Mm," she said softly. "I doubt it's Ruby though. She was…" his mother smiled, almost in admiration. "My god was she a force."

"In what way?"

His mother glanced back at him. "You've never asked about them," she said as if suddenly realising it. "The Ambros family. You asked about Phineas but never-"

"I assumed…" what had he assumed? "I dunno. I assumed they were what you'd expect. Arrogant, cold and half mad."

She shook her head. "Percival was. Lord Percival. Phineas' grandfather. Every time Phineas went he'd come back…" She shook her head and eyed him thoughtfully. "My aunt moved to the boundary between Ambros and Council lands to learn from a seer in the area. When my father died, my mother moved us all over so she'd have her sister's help. We used to play in the woods there, Council and Coven children alike. Phineas joined us most of the time."

Yeah, Brendan could picture a young, secretive boy who manipulated the children he played with. He had a feeling that probably wasn't what his mother saw or remembered when she talked.

"He had a brother as well as a sister?"

"Lysander." His mother placed the tea down. "Much older; we'd rarely see him. But Ruby would come into the woods to find us. Sometime she'd even tell us where to find berries in the summer or be the one we'd go to if one of us was injured or covered in mud. Your father once slipped in the river bed and was so covered in clay I'm amazed he didn't turn into a statue. My mother would have walloped me. Ruby just rolled her eyes and hosed him down."

"She died in violet circumstances." Brendan stirred his coffee, more for something to do than because it was needed. "As did his father and brother."

"Sebastian was…he was ill. He was addicted to heroin."

What?

He glanced over at Owen who looked equally surprised. "Heroin?" Owen asked, as if that couldn't possibly be right. "That destroys magic."

His mother nodded. "Apparently, Sebastian wanted to kill his magic. He…I know that people talk about the Ambros family having schizophrenia but this was…he would spend weeks in a dark room avoiding everyone and then have a day or two where he would be around. He was never…active or what I would call a strong man. I never really understood how he'd managed to get a woman like Ruby."

"And his death?"

His mother shook her head. "I was nine. He died in winter and we didn't really see much of the Ambros children in the winter. Phineas never really spoke of it. He was…he debated trying drugs when we were teenagers. That's the only reason I knew about his father's addiction."

"When did you move to the area?" Brendan asked.

His mother looked up and raised a fair eyebrow at him. "Am I being interviewed now?" she asked a little sharply.

"I'm not asking you because I care," Brendan snapped

back. "I'm asking you because there is a potential killer out there who might be targeting anyone with Ambros blood."

His mother sucked in a breath and exchanged a look with Owen who sat back thoughtfully.

"I moved when I was seven," she replied, looking a little shaken. His step-father looked away and Brendan could practically see the contingency plans starting to form in the man's head.

How much easier would everything be if the man in front of him had been his father in blood too? Dragging his attention back to his mother, he pushed. "Tom Redgrave was murdered in Ambros the year before," Brendan said slowly. "Any rumours?"

"If there were, they were kept from us." She looked distressed now and he felt momentary annoyance with himself for scaring her. "I never heard anything about any murders. Only Lysander's death." She chewed at her lip and drummed her fingers on the table in a jolting, staccato rhythm.

"Lysander's death?" he asked, watching her fingers. Usually when he did that it meant a cigarette wasn't far away. It wasn't quite the same for her; he'd almost bet that she'd make something tonight. Bake a cake or knit something.

Half of his son's jumpers over the years had probably been knitted because of Brendan.

The jarring beat stopped suddenly and his mother looked at him, long and hard and in such a way that he felt himself suddenly become more focused as she turned to Owen. "Would you give us a few minutes?" she asked softly.

What?

The surprise that Brendan felt was mirrored in Owen's

face. Never in his memory had his mother wanted Owen to leave the room. He'd been there for all discussions about Nicolas, about Phineas, even the gratingly embarrassing sex talk had seen Owen there too, squirming.

As if unsure he'd heard right, Owen gave a sharp nod and then stood up, almost ungainly as he left the room.

"Lysander died the year you were conceived," his mother said as Owen shut the door.

"The year Phineas tried to kill us both?" Brendan snapped.

His mother moved the tea to one side and leaned forward. "Lysander was vicious and cruel. Whenever I saw him as an adult he had no time for us. He'd berate and torment your father-"

"Do not call him that again."

The tone of his voice must have finally gotten through to her because his mother stopped and stuttered for a moment before nodding. "I loved Phineas," she whispered. "Had for years and he…he often said the same of me-" She reached out for him as Brendan pushed away, determined to end the conversation. "No," she pleaded. "Listen. I do not say this for nostalgia or because I want to you to think well of me or him. I chased your…I chased Phineas for years. He would verbally reciprocate but never physically. Ever."

"Mum-"

"Years, Brendan. Three years. You were conceived two nights after Lysander's death. I'd never seen him so…at ease. Hopeful. Within a month he was distant and within two…" she trailed off, bright green eyes shadowed with hurt.

He drew in a long breath. Part of him was tempted to follow up on her odd comment about him not thinking well of her, but he sensed it might push them further into an avenue of conversation that he didn't want to indulge in.

"And Lysander's death?"

Her lips curled a little in frustration. "I think your father killed him."

Brendan drummed his fingers on the table, pressing his lips together.

"Lysander was a monster. Phineas...I truly believe that whatever happened to him was some curse that Lysander left behind-"

"For Christ sakes," Brendan hissed as he stood up. "No wonder you wanted Owen out the room. Gonna tell me I should have helped him? Should have found out what it was that 'destroyed' him all those years ago?" he asked, fingers forming sarcastic air quotes as he shook his head in scorn.

"You weren't there. You didn't know him-"

"You know what I know? I know that he tortured people. I know that there were files and files on the man, all the things that were suspected-"

"Suspected," his mother argued, standing up.

"He stole my son and put a sword in him," Brendan yelled down at her. "He stabbed my son and threw him out a window. Defend that."

She couldn't. He could see the way her shoulders suddenly sunk and she looked away.

"He beat you, viciously. I've seen the report-"

Her head shot up in horror. "You've what?"

"I'm a Council Elite. You think I never looked?"

She surged forward grabbing onto his arm. "Then you

know. You know that he could have ended my pregnancy. That all of my injuries avoided harming you. You were safe-"

"That doesn't make any of it right." He shook her off, mindful of not hurting her, but desperately needing space from the woman. He turned his back to her and took a breath, pinching the bridge of his nose and trying to get them back to safer ground. "So you never heard any of the Ambros family mention that they were being hunted? Never saw them act in a way that would suggest it?"

There was a long pause and he couldn't look at her because he imagined his mother probably objected to the formal interview tone he was using. "I'd have mentioned it," his mother said tightly. "If there had been a threat to Ambros blood, then there would have been a threat to you, Nicolas and Danny."

Turning, he leaned back against the wall, needing the distance between them. His mother had sunk back down into her chair and was staring down into her mug.

Something about it...he couldn't put his finger on why he felt a sudden urge to push her.

"Thirty-three deaths," Brendan said slowly. "Since 1486 there have been thirty-three violent deaths in the Ambros family. Do you know what that is? That's twenty eight percent of people since 1486 who have died in violent circumstances. Twenty eight percent. You tell me that's coincidence."

She stared at him, green eyes shadowed as she drew in a breath.

"Or do you think that the Ambros family is so psychopathic that they've just been murdering each other all these years?" he pressed, pushing off the wall and glaring at her.

"Brendan-"

"It's crossed my mind. You know how many people theorise about the schizophrenia. The number of historians that want me tested?" He stared down at her and felt the words come out, the words that he never even wanted to think about, "Am I gonna turn into Phineas in a few years?"

She stared at him and the strange expression on her face made him bloody glad that she didn't say whatever was in her head. He closed his eyes and looked away before breathing out slowly.

The second he thought that was happening, he'd slice his own throat. And if Danny...

God, he needed to not think about it. There was nothing to be gained in doing so. Instead, he opened his eyes to stare down at the tiled floor and remembered trying to kick the grouting out once when Owen had been telling him off about deliberately kicking a football into Mr Pembroke's greenhouse while his mum had stayed on the doorstep, apologising profusely for his behaviour.

Why did he always do this to her?

"You doubt that the woman at Porter's Lodge would be Ruby Ambros?" he asked, needing to turn this away from their own shitty family history.

His mother allowed the diversion. "I...I have no idea what happened to her. I wish I did." She drew in a breath suddenly and looked up, as if something had occurred to her. "You...do you have a date of death?"

"No, but the body we suspect might be hers was found in twenty fifteen, so-"

His mother blinked and went pale.

“Down to the year?” Liaden asked, impressed as she brought over the pizza box. “That’s impressively straight forward of a seer.”

Brendan shrugged as he shifted Danny to his other knee and reached for a slice of pizza. “Doesn’t exactly help us. So what if she predicted the year of Ruby’s death?”

“Maybe there was more to it,” Liaden offered as she sat down on the other side of the sofa, leg curled under her. “Have you contacted your great-aunt?”

God. “Tempted to send the kids,” Brendan muttered. “I can’t manage that woman. She speaks in fucking riddles. Unless you want the year of death for the wife of a Coven heir apparently.”

Liaden glared at him and then ducked her head to rub her nose against Danny’s, forcing Brendan to manoeuvre his slice of pizza out of her way. “Isn’t Dad being rude,” she sing-songed down to their eight-year-old. “What word don’t we say to other children?”

“Fucking,” Danny replied with perfect boredom over the word and the question.

“Well done. Have some pizza.” Liaden reached up for Brendan’s slice and stole it for their child with a warning glare.

Yeah, all right. Shifting, Brendan looked down and tried to restrain a grin as Danny started to lick the top from his pizza like the little adorable odd-ball that he was. “They have something,” he sighed. “I don’t know what, but they have something.”

“And your mother says there was no gossip about the

bodies found there?" Liaden sighed as she tucked her feet under her and took a slice, flicking the channel to some cartoon. Danny immediately perked up and slid down from Brendan's lap, pizza dangling precariously as he shuffled closer to the TV.

Brendan sent the plastic plate towards his son who took it from the air and continued to stare at the TV.

"Doubt that," Brendan said. "There was my mum, her brother and sister. Aunt Eliza who died a few years ago and some boys that emigrated in the eighties. They'd have all been kids." He nodded towards Danny. "Adults only talk about boring things when you're that age. And it was official enough that there was a record of it."

His wife took his hand when he reached for another slice. Surprised, he looked over at her.

"I'm fine," he soothed when he saw her worried expression. Brendan tugged her close, grinning as she reached to save the pizza box and placed it on the cushions where she'd been sitting. "I am," he whispered to her hair as she settled in close. "Mum and I are never gonna agree about Phineas. I accepted that a while ago."

"Accepted it?"

"Acknowledged it," Brendan remedied. "Gave up arguing it. Don't know how Owen does it, but..." he shrugged. "I'll avoid questioning her about it in the future."

She hummed against his chest. Then tentatively: "Owen said he found you looking out at the tree." She paused. "The grave."

"It's not a grave."

"Closest thing."

He said nothing, staring at the cartoon for a bit. His

eyes dropped down from the screen to the little boy who sat staring up at it. Danny was so blond that the colours from the TV almost glinted against his hair.

"Would you want to create an official one?"

"Why? There'd be nothing buried there," Brendan snapped.

"For you. For Danny to visit when he's older and understands, for-" she broke off as Brendan shook his head. "Okay," she said, her tone soothing. "Okay."

It wasn't. But he pressed in close to her and tried to pretend that it was.

They were running late.

Jake was starting to hate being late. Maybe that was a sign of growing up?

Brendan was waiting for them when they arrived at the reception of the retirement home. He was leaning against the wall, arms folded and looking distinctly out of place against the floral patterns in his battered brown leather jacket and jeans. His eyes caught Jake's quickly, but he didn't move, waiting and glancing around every so often as they signed in.

"An old people's home?" Jake asked as they walked over. "Why?"

"My great-aunt Iris lives here," Brendan said, nodding at Cole. "You said you had another lead?"

"Yeah there's an Ambros descendent – he's in a healing ward. Daphne's taking Rob." Jake hesitated, not too sure if they should have run that by Brendan. But Brendan nodded and then peeled himself off the wall with such reluctance that Jake nearly wanted to double check how old he was.

"Why are we here?" Cole demanded as they followed him through the sitting room. There were a few people sitting around, eyes on them all as they strode forward.

"My great aunt is a seer. She predicated Ruby's death-" Brendan broke off with an exaggerated huff when Cole stopped dead. "What?"

"Seers talk in riddles," Cole complained. "This is-"

God, Jake really wished Cole could judge an audience. But, to his surprise, when he looked over, Brendan was already nodding. "Yeah, and usually I'd agree with you." Brendan folded his arms and studied Cole for a moment. "But she lived by Porter's Lodge for years. I'm not so interested in what she can predict; I'm interested in what she lived through."

God only knew why Cole seemed to deliberate it or why he thought they'd be guided by his decision, but he nodded after a moment and, as Brendan turned to lead the way up the stairs, let out a long, annoyed breath.

"Do you actually need us?" Jake asked as they reached the second floor. It was like a really old hotel from the seventies (or what he assumed one of those would be like!), and there was something about it that made him feel deeply uncomfortable about it all.

"Your case," Brendan reminded him. "Besides, she and I don't get on," Brendan said as he continued to stomp up the hallway. "Well…that's…" he turned and scrubbed a hand over his eyes. "I was a little shit to her when I was younger. She winds me up. We… I'm not going to question her. You are. I'm just checking that you don't miss anything."

"No pressure," Jake muttered to Cole as Brendan continued up and knocked on one of the doors. He was let in quite quickly and Jake skulked forward, not convinced that he really wanted to do this.

Inside was heavy. Smoke hung in the air like a cobweb layer and the curtains were cracked so that only the thinnest slice of light cut through the dull dimness of the room. In the huge chair by the fireplace, a woman sat. Her hair was long and tied into a braid that looked more like a curtain tassel than anything else.

When she looked over it was with milky white eyes and Jake swallowed nervously.

"You have the sight."

Brendan who had drifted over to a table, looked up and over at them, apparently knowing already which one of them Iris Campion was talking about. His face registered no surprise, but he seemed to be studying Jake

Typical. Jake looked away, silently hoping that the issue would just die. Unfortunately, the silence continued until he winced and sighed. "Barely," he argued quietly, not looking at her or in fact anyone.

"It'll grow. You'll be the youngest yet." She said it with an easy confidence that made him want to sneer at her and wasn't that reaction one of a million reasons as to why he'd rather not be an acknowledged seer.

"Iris," Brendan said quietly, taking his gaze off of Jake's face. "Porter's Lodge. We need to ask you some questions."

Her head turned a little and she seemed to be looking at Cole with her sightless eyes. Cole said nothing, but was definitely uncomfortable as he stood, pinned by the gaze.

"Iris," Brendan said again, voice tight. "Please."

She hummed and turned to him. Then she smiled oddly.

"Miss…uh…Miss Campion?" Jake asked, unsure. "May I sit?"

Her gaze swung back around again and she nodded imperiously. Not entirely convinced this was the best idea, Jake drew over a chair and sat opposite her. Brendan continued to stand. Thankfully, Cole edged closer and pulled over another one of the chairs which was something, even if the coward stayed a little behind Jake.

"We're investigating the murders at Porter's Lodge," Jake started. "We…we were wondering what you remembered about it?"

"Tom?"

Tom Redgrave? Jake glanced over at Brendan who had wandered over to a bookshelf and was studying it as if he wasn't listening, but there was no way Brendan was ignoring them.

"Yeah," Cole said. "Let's start with that."

"What were they like?" Brendan asked suddenly. "Sebastian and Ruby. They were responsible for the village, right?"

He still hadn't turned.

Cole sat back like he'd swallowed a wasp, but said nothing as Iris hummed a little. "Ruby was…electric. Exciting. A wild girl from the village. Never could get her to change her mind once she'd settled on something. Her mother was the seer I trained with…" she drifted off and seemed to be thinking about something. Then shook her head. "She had long red hair. When she married Sebastian, she used to pin it all up all sleek and impressive. It would be down after an hour or so."

"And him?" Jake asked, because apparently that was the line of questioning they would start with. "Sebastian?"

"Quiet. Kind. When he stopped using heroin for a few weeks he was fine."

"How long did he take it for?" Cole asked calmly.

"He was using when I arrived in the village, about two months before Ruby set her sights on him. Used it until the day he died, as far as I know." Iris tilted her head in a way that reminded Jake oddly of Brendan. "But he was a good man. He'd come into the village in winter and top up all of our meters, slip electric cards through our letter boxes and there would be food packages for Christmas. At an equinox, the family would come down into the village for the celebrations. He never missed it."

Jake glanced over at Brendan who peered up from where he was looking at the books and nodded. "And Tom Redgrave's murder?" he asked, suddenly realising that having some context actually helped. "The report says that Tom was killed by Sebastian."

Iris actually snorted. "Ruby would have done it," she said without hesitation. "That woman. She was a force. Sebastian wouldn't have had the power to kill a fly."

"She was in a coma," Cole pointed out softly. "After the attack."

"She probably put herself into it, always over-reaching that one." Iris sat back and then looked around. "Brendan, would you?"

He obviously knew what she was asking for. He turned and walked into the little kitchenet and put the kettle on. Then there was the sound of cupboards being opened and cups rattling.

"Ruby was… she wasn't powerful but she was tenacious. Rumour was that Tom Redgrave had come to collect Lysander and take him to Ambros. She wouldn't let him go."

"Sounds familiar," Jake muttered, glancing back into the kitchen and oddly hoping that Brendan wouldn't hear.

"Doesn't it? History always comes in circles. Unless we learn from it." Iris drew in breath. "Lysander wasn't seen in the village for a while. Whatever happened, he ended up going to Ambros once a month for a weekend; there didn't seem to be much Sebastian could do about it."

"And when Ruby woke up?" Jake asked.

"It didn't change. She would come to see us…her mother mostly and they'd sit together for hours while Heather would counsel Ruby and scry far too often. She pushed her powers to the limits for that girl. It killed her in the end." Iris's fingers drummed on the arm of the sofa. "None of the children ever showed a skill with seeing. Probably for the best," she added and then her head peeked up as Brendan came out with a cup of tea for her.

It was hard to tell how she did it. Whether she just had lived being blind for so long that she was that confident with reaching out, or whether her power gave her an extra layer of sight. Either way, she reached for the tea and took it with ease, seeming delighted with it.

"You always did do this well," she added and Brendan practically rolled his eyes, but stood closer now, by the table.

"So you think that Tom Redgrave was killed by Ruby to protect her son," Brendan asked. "I guess that Lord…uh…"

"Percival," Iris said, in between sips. "Percival was Sebastian's father."

"Percival," Brendan continued, the name sounding

hesitant on his lips, "blackmailed Sebastian. I'll start a murder case against your wife unless you give me your son." He drew in a long, annoyed breath, "and we all know how easy it is for Coven Lords to demand their future heirs."

Jake winced.

"Percival put those rules in place. You, unfortunately, suffered at those new laws. He strengthened what the Coven had once had."

Brendan nodded, but said nothing.

"So no mystery there," Cole said. "Next one is nineteen eighty-one. Fountain. Ted Johnson."

"I'm certain that you know how to ask better questions than that," Iris said with an odd smile.

"What do you know of Ted Johnson's murder in nineteen eighty-one," Cole asked, shifting like a teacher had just scolded him.

"He'd come to the village, looking for them. The family was out."

"What...did he ask anything about them?" Jake asked.

"Not really," Iris said. "He seemed to know Ruby and Sebastian. They'd had a conversation and made contact a while ago. He went to Sebastian's funeral."

"The theory was that he chased off an intruder," Jake offered. "And uh...his cousin, Jonah Summers? was...he'd been making noises about demanding money from the main line. Someone said he'd probably gone in to get what he thought was owed and they'd fought-"

"No," Iris said easily. "Have you been there? No-one ever wanted to step foot in that place, no matter how grand it was or how desperate they were for funds. They converted the old ballroom because it was never used. People felt uncomfortable in that place. I was invited in once. Heather, Ruby's mother, never went in. It was...difficult."

"How so?" Brendan asked.

"I went through the entrance once and that was as far as I could manage. There was evil in that house."

"Then why send them there?" Cole asked. "Why send the heirs of Ambros to live in a house like that?"

Iris's eyes jumped to Cole's unerringly. It was hugely uncomfortable as she studied him. "Punishment," she said at last. "Look at the people that lived in that house. Look at the village history. The Lord of Ambros punished them by sending them to that house."

"For what?" Cole asked, almost like a statue where he sat.

Iris shook her head.

"Ted Johnson wasn't in the house," Jake said, not too sure what else to say. "He was in the fountain. And we know what's on the grounds. Maybe Summers was looking for the graves-"

"The graves?" Iris seemed genuinely unsure for the first time.

"The-" Jake suddenly found himself unable to speak and coughed, baffled as to what the problem was.

"What were the rumours?" Brendan asked smoothly, and his lack of concern made Jake realise exactly who was stopping him from speaking. "About Johnson and Ruby?"

"She did kill once for her family," Iris said, eyes still on Jake. "The rumour was that Ruby had been spotted around the property too that day, despite rumours that the family was absent. That hair. It's hard to disguise."

"Why?" Cole asked. "I mean…they knew each other. Why invite him to the property and then kill him?"

"Who said she invited him?" Iris asked, finally letting her white eyes leave Jake's face.

It surprised him when Cole just raised his eyebrows and looked at her with some amusement. "Possibly because according to you she was wandering around the village in disguise and waiting for him? Or did she usually do that when the family went away?"

"You are clever," Iris said a smile playing around her face. "No-one was sure. There were mentions of a child, but Ruby never had another after Phineas. Some said that she'd been having an affair with him and had sorted out an accident. She was linked to many men after her husband died."

"Sebastian died in 'seventy-nine," Brendan said, drawing in a deep breath. "Would she have had an affair with the other Redgrave victim?"

Iris actually cackled at that idea. "Ruby Ambros and the Redgrave family never saw eye to eye. The villagers never welcomed them in because of it. But… as Vivienne and Phineas grew older, there were whispers that the children were unhappy with her about something."

"So you believe that she could have killed all three," Brendan sighed. "And Lorcan over there has a theory that the last body found in twenty fifteen was Ruby Ambros herself." He took in a breath. "Mum said that you had given a prophecy about her death."

"I said that she would see the future and would die in a place she hated fifteen years after the millennium," Iris said, sitting back. "I would imagine it was her."

"Suicide?" Brendan asked. "Regret for what she had done there?"

"Young man, believe me, she gave the Ambros family stubbornness and tenaciousness. She wouldn't have given up. Or felt guilt over what she'd done if she felt the reason was justified. She was like your boy."

The tone suddenly shifted, like the floor had just shuddered and threatened to collapse. Jake, still unable to say anything, couldn't look at Brendan.

"How would you know," Brendan asked, voice so grated it sounded like bricks were rubbing together.

Iris said nothing.

"Answer the question," Brendan snarled, standing and storming close to her. Jake glanced over at Cole who sat as if frozen, watching what was happening with the same unsure horror that Jake felt. What if Brendan lost his temper? How the fuck were they meant to restrain Brendan Campion of all people?

"I've seen him," Iris said after a moment.

Brendan's fists clenched tightly and Jake watched them, trying to keep an eye out for any magic that crackled around them. He still couldn't say anything, and Cole seemed almost spelled silent too. "Doing what?"

"Dying for his family."

Brendan stayed still for a moment or two longer and then snorted. "Funny. I saw him dying because of it," he snapped before he turned on his heel and gestured harshly at Jake. "You finish this off," he ordered. "I'll be outside."

And, with that, he walked out and slammed the door behind him so hard that the little apartment that Iris had seemed to quake.

Jake looked over at Cole who was rubbing at his forehead. Thankfully, his friend recovered quicker than Jake did and sighed. "Who might have killed her?" he asked, sounding tired.

"I don't know. I think...it was a spell," Iris said. "I know that. What I don't know is what the spell was. If it was defensive, offensive, who was there."

"But someone was?" Cole asked, leaning forward, eyes narrowed.

Iris nodded slowly. "They're shadowed. Every time I've seen it, the figures in the background are shadowed, the spell is faded and unclear. All I see is Ruby, staring out the window and watching something in the grounds."

"The body was found at the window," Jake murmured to Cole, feeling a momentary flash of surprise that he was able to speak again. Then he turned to her. "Thank you for your help. We may have to get in contact again-"

She waved a hand. "You still have some time to do so."

God, he didn't want to touch that idea, not entirely sure what it was that she had seen. Awkwardly, he stood up and wandered over to her. "It was lovely to-"

"Liar," Iris said, sounding tickled. "But yes. It's been useful."

He took her hand without really thinking about it. Probably, he should have known better, but he was distracted and half thinking about what the hell he was going to say to Brendan so he was completely unprepared when the images slammed into him like a cinema screen collapsing onto him. A disorientating jumble that made him feel like his mind had split into fragments as it tried to make sense of the images and the fact that, all the while, he was still standing in her room, shaking her hand.

An interrogation room covered in blood. A coffin in a crumbling, ancient looking room. A bronze plaque that was so old it had almost lost the engraving where it sat in a cobwebbed crumbling wall. Red hair and blond close as two people bowed their heads together, whispering. Steps leading down into complete darkness. A scrap of paper caught in the wind, the ornate markings on it fading in front of his eyes.

It made him stumble back and Cole caught him, steadying him carefully.

"Give it two more years," Iris said with some amusement. "You'll get there. Most of what you saw is a while away yet."

Jake tried to regain his balance and then felt his stomach roll.

"Bin," Iris said dismissively. Thankfully, Cole seemed to get what she meant and yanked over the little, silver peddle bin so that Jake could vomit into it, embarrassed beyond words at the fact that he was doing this in front of Cole.

Iris held out her hand to Cole who just snorted. "I'll pass," Cole snapped.

"Will you," Iris asked and, for the first time, her tone changed to something deeper, firmer and more formal. Cole stared at her for a moment and then placed a hand on Jake's back, starting to steer him to the door.

"You don't want to have a seer look into your future?"

Cole snorted and put the bin down on the counter as he led them through the door. The hallway blurred and wobbled in Jake's vision as they stepped outside and headed for the stairs again.

"Fuck. My head," Jake gasped, clutching Cole's arm. "I didn't even think-"

"She's a sneaky old bitch," Cole snapped and then nodded at the old man they passed. "She's only in here because none of her family want her."

Jake sniggered as they walked. "Shush," he hissed. "You'll upset the others."

The look on Cole's face suggested he had no idea why that would be the case, but he continued to half pull, half drag Jake through the lounge they'd gone through before. Then they emerged into blessed sunlight and Cole helped him stumble over to the flower bed where Jake could throw-up again.

When he finished, he looked back to see Brendan staring at him from where he was leaning against his car, phone in his hand. As if nothing could make it worse than throwing up in front of his mate, now he was doing it in front of the guy that he kinda wanted to be when he was older.

Fantastic.

"He took her hand," Cole was explaining as Brendan pocketed his phone and came over. "Think she shoved some images or cracked his brain open to release some."

"Cracked it," Jake said. "Had it happen once before only…you know. From a nice person." Then he blanched and looked up at Brendan. "I mean…"

Brendan shook his head dismissively. "Did you touch her?" he asked Cole.

"After seeing that?" Cole asked, eyeing Jake up with a faint amount of disgust. "Nope."

Brendan clicked his tongue and then shook his head. "Go back, see what the others got. Report to me tomorrow."

"What are you-"

But Brendan was already walking away to his car, his

footsteps short and sharp like he was a one-man army marching into battle.

“Where have you been?” Daphne asked as they walked into their little meeting room.

“Old people’s home,” Cole replied shortly, as if he’d been the one that had been forced to puke up his guts and have his mind invaded.

“Seer,” Jake added as he sunk into the nearest chair and buried his head in his arms.

“A woman who lived by Porter’s Lodge,” Cole added. “She knew the gossip about Ruby Ambros. What did you get?”

Daphne glanced between them and then at Rob who was looking between Cole and Jake with something like amusement. “You’re not afraid of a little old lady, are you?”

“You meet her next time,” Jakes suggested as he reached for the jug of water and resisted the urge to just pour the whole jug down his throat. He filled a glass of water instead and downed it quickly, feeling a strange mix of relief and nausea.

“Colin Grant,” Daphne said, apparently accepting that they both weren’t in the mood. “He and his cousin Paul were attacked in twenty-ten.”

“And they are?”

“On the Ambros family tree. Paul was put into a coma, they took him off of the support spells about three years afterwards. Colin was tortured.”

“And what? You just went in and asked him about his happy experience?” Jake asked.

"Jesus, you are in a foul mood," Rob complained. "What did she do, come on to you or something?"

"We went and asked him what he remembered," Daphne cut over them as Cole drew in breath to snap back. "We told him we thought someone was targeting those with Ambros blood. He seemed to think it was likely."

"He was attacked and tortured," Cole said quietly. "Could he give you a description or anything to go on?"

"No," Daphne said, "He-"

"Someone jabbed out his eyes," Rob cut in sounding perversely delighted by the idea. "Seriously, he took his glasses off and it was gross. Like they'd been scooped out with a sharp fork or something."

How the hell had this guy made it through the interview round? There'd been psychological evaluations and everything.

"Male or female attacker?" Cole asked, casting Rob a withering glare.

"Male," Daphne said with certainty, "He was sure of that."

"Iris Campion pretty much just told us that she thinks Ruby Ambros is responsible for most of the deaths at Porter's Lodge. The woman sounded like a right treat," Jake huffed. "So…were there two of them? Working together? Or is this something else?"

"That theory doesn't make any sense. Why would Ruby Ambros try to wipe out those with Ambros blood?" Daphne asked, nose wrinkling up at the idea as Cole stood up and walked towards the door, disappearing for a moment.

"She really hated the Redgraves," Jake offered, digging his fingers into his head and half talking to the table. "They took her son to Ambros when she refused to let him go. Or so the village rumour went."

"Someone castrated Colin Grant," Daphne snapped. "And his cousin. Neither were reproducing again. Whoever attacked them and kept them for those few days was making sure of it."

Fuck. That was... Jake folded his legs, wincing at the idea.

Cole stared at her as he walked back in, apparently having picked up on the end of Daphne's statement as he handed Jake a glass of water and then cast the family tree up on the wall that they'd left blank for that very reason. "Okay, so is this...it seems as if someone is trying to destroy the line?" he asked, rubbing at his hair.

"How can it not be?" Daphne asked. "Three members of the same family dead at Porter's Lodge when there's a history of deaths in that family? Maybe Ruby was trying to protect her family and was always the one who survived."

"Iris was adamant," Jake said. "It was Ruby that killed Tom Redgrave because he came for her son. The rest... maybe, but that one doesn't fit. Maybe...maybe someone who wanted the family dead approached her. Get rid of the other strands of the tree. She already had an issue with the Redgraves..."

"Apart from the fact that the only family that still can reproduce is the Redgrave family," Cole muttered as he continued to stare at the family tree.

"Wait," Jake said, leaning forward. "Iris said that Porter's Lodge was a place to put family members who were being punished. Maybe... do you think that the Ambros family knew there was someone after them and would abandon people to the threat? Maybe Ruby and Ted Johnson were trying to overcome something together?"

Daphne sat back, like a boss in a meeting and shook her head. "We need to go back to the house," she said decisively. "We need to bring up mirror spells."

Oh fuck.

Chapter Ten

His mum probably wouldn't approve of what he was doing. Hell, even Liaden wouldn't, but Brendan needed to calm down somehow before picking up his son and even he could admit that drinking right now was a fucking stupid plan.

So he stood, to the side of the school, practically chain smoking to keep his juddering nerves under control.

Dying for his family, Brendan thought with a sneer and a long drag. God that woman had some nerve. She was a complete bitch when she wanted to be.

He glanced towards the school gates, ignoring the disapproving glance from a mother as she walked towards them to join the assembled nutters that had arrived half an hour early to collect their children. Not that he could really make a comment, but he'd come early to calm down and work his way through the mini pack that he'd picked up, not so that he could gossip and pass comment on school affairs.

Not to mention he was close enough and subtle enough to reach out with his magic to double check his son. Danny had always been easy to find and get a read of and right now he was starting to tire after a full day of schooling and what Brendan suspected was probably most of a lunch time spent barrelling around the playground like a hyper puppy. In other words, the kid was fine.

Still. Brendan found himself unwilling to walk down to the coffee shop five minutes down the road as he usually would. Instead, three cigarettes in, he speed-dialled Nate.

"Yes?" Nate sounded suspicious as he answered. "What have you heard?"

"Why?" Brendan asked, raising the cigarette to his lips and leaning against the wall as he went to light it. "What should I have heard?"

He managed to take another puff as Nate seemed to debate something. Then the background noises started to change as Nate left the room he was in. "They finished sweeping the lake this morning," Nate said softly.

Brendan forced himself not to react. "And?"

"Nothing," Nate said with a long sigh. "No body. For either Nicolas or Damien. Two months of searching and I can confirm that neither are on the property, we have done every check imaginable."

He was meant to feel anger, a bone deep fury that his son's body had been removed, that Nate hadn't mentioned that they were sweeping for the bodies. But it was…it was almost too much for him to manage to feel anything. "Redgrave's alive then, we're certain."

"Can't rule out that someone else might have picked up both bodies, but…We've had some sightings. Some are more likely than others." Nate's tone changed, "I'm sorry," he said, sounding genuine.

Brendan stared ahead, the leaves of the bush opposite seeming to be vivid and stark in his vision. "Wouldn't have changed anything," he said tightly. "Still dead, isn't he?"

"Yeah," Nate said, "he is. We...your memories. We looked through them from the moment you cast the paternity spell to find him-"

He could only vaguely remember giving permission a few months ago.

"-his head was falling backwards, so we don't have the best image, but the sword was definitely..." Nate's voice became ever so gentle, "through the heart. It was accurate," he said, as if forcing the issue. "And the...Nicolas fell from that window."

"I know this," Brendan said, gritting his teeth.

"We'd pieced together witness accounts, memories. Some saw the...him"

"The body," Brendan spat. "You want to say the body."

"He hit the water. And there was an unaccounted-for figure by the lake," Nate said frankly, ignoring Brendan's comment. "Be it Redgrave or someone else, it must have been them that took the body. And without the body of either Nicolas or Redgrave, we have a limit as to what we can match and how much further we can take this investigation."

"You're gonna declare him guilty," Brendan snapped. "Aren't you?"

"Yes."

Brendan flicked the cigarette on the floor and crushed it, extinguishing it on the damp pavement.

"I have to," Nate said. "Stuart...Boss was right to put him with me. I was dragging it out. He...Brendan, Nicolas tortured someone. I can't get motivation without a body or a witness statement. I'll enter it in and any further evidence might open it up but... he is guilty of the deed." Nate sucked in a breath. "Nicolas Ambros and Damien Redgrave tortured Ted Grey to death. Together."

His heart thudded out a strange beat, almost in his throat as if it might burst out.

"Brendan?"

He couldn't speak to him. Didn't want to. There was a wave of deep, painful emotion that he didn't want to touch at the idea that in a hundred-years' time, that was all that might remain of his son. The statement that he had tortured someone to death.

The fact that it might be true. That was what his son had become because he hadn't done enough.

One minute too late was a joke. He'd been years too late. His mind zig-zagged with sickening speed between a spoiled, evil, destroyed teenager taking joy in Grey's death and a terrified, tormented child forced to torture to avoid his own pain. And he was shit because he couldn't work out which was the more painful image, which one would haunt him more.

"Brendan?"

"Go fuck yourself," he said, but despite the harsh words, his tone sounded monotonous even to his own ears. Slowly, he removed the phone from his ear, dimly hearing the rumble of Nate's words and stared at the phone, almost forgetting what he was meant to do with it.

He needed to hang up the phone and pick up Danny.

His thumb ended the call and then he drew in a breath before pushing off the wall. He cast a quick cleaning spell as he walked, removing the majority of the smell of cigarettes.

The kids were out on the playground, or at least the smallest ones were. Tiny little four-year olds being sent to their parents and he stopped dead, oddly fascinated by the sight as if he hadn't seen it a thousand times before.

Take them home, he wanted to scream at the parents. Hide them.

One little girl caught his eye. Dark hair and big dark eyes, she was busily trying to explain something to the man that had come to collect her and was pointing, her expression earnest and serious as if she was explaining the secret for world peace.

His fingers twitched with the urge to cast a protection spell around her.

"Dad?" a familiar, curious voice asked, immediately drawing his attention down and to his own child.

Only living child.

He stared down at his son for a moment, for a second hating Danny because he was... he was singular. It wasn't as if Brendan was picking up the boys or telling off his sons for having a fight as other parents did. Every time he thought of Danny it was singular.

Son. Child. Boy.

The next instant, he was on his knees, pulling Danny close to him, dimly aware that he was probably embarrassing the crap out of the kid, but too scared to care. His hand cupped the boy's head and he buried his face in the soft strands, trying not to cry.

It somehow made it worse when his son whispered that it was okay.

Pulling away, he studied the little face. And yeah, he and Danny looked similar, but Nicolas and Danny had the same mouth and chin and the same worried expression and the same way of tilting their head the way he did.

Smoothing his thumbs over the boy's cheeks, he tried to smile, even as his vision jumped and jarred.

This one, some part of him whispered. This one would be safe. Protected.

This one would be good.

He stood, pulling Danny close again and something made him look over and he watched, somehow unsurprised when he saw Liaden coming over, short jacket still open and scarf flapping in the wind, hastily wrapped around her neck and her gloves not quite matching.

She didn't say anything, just wrapped her arm around his neck, the other hand reaching down to smooth Danny's hair as she let Brendan bury his head in her shoulder and cry.

He hadn't moved since they'd got home. And at some point, he really needed to stop using Danny as some form of security blanket, but he couldn't give a shit right now. Instead, Brendan sat with the kid on the sofa, Danny curled up in his lap.

He couldn't have explained what made him reach out for the photo album. He hadn't looked at it in years, and certainly never with anyone else present. Danny watched it curiously and twisted around to sit so that he was facing forward, just as the album landed in Brendan's palm.

The kid seemed to know what it was for and silently shifted again so that they could both look through it together. The photographs of Nicolas as a new-born were scant; Lindsey's probably justified revenge for his own reluctance when the child was born.

The first one to feature Brendan and Nicolas had been

taken the day after Owen had tricked him. Danny giggled a little and then looked up at Brendan. "You look so young," he said, delighted.

"Mm," Brendan agreed, staring down at his sixteen-year-old self. "Too young," he said, shifting Danny into a slightly more comfortable position on his lap. "I was only about eight years older than you are now."

Danny's eyes widened. "That's..." he turned up his nose.

God, please let that attitude continue. He watched patiently as Danny turned the page, curious, and sniggered at the sight of Nicolas dressed up like a bunny for Easter.

"That's cute," Liaden said gently, coming to sit on the arm of the sofa. "Why didn't you let me do that?"

"Mum," Danny whined. "You didn't let mum do that to me, ever. Right?" he checked with all the earnestness he could muster.

"Your mum never dressed you as a bunny," Brendan replied, looking up at Liaden who smiled into her tea. Danny shot them both a suspicious glare, but said nothing.

The next few were staged photographs taken by his mum and Owen. Brendan couldn't quite remember when he'd started to get involved in snapping the odd picture with his phone-

Oh. Yeah, he could. "Look," he said with a smile. "I...I gave him a pot of peanut butter and then got distracted by a phone call. When I looked back," he smoothed his fingers over the one-year-old gleefully grinning up at the camera, holding up his peanut butter covered hands in triumph, face covered in the stuff as Danny giggled.

"He must have been sick," Liaden chided.

"God, he was." Brendan winced. "I'd forgotten that..."

he frowned at the idea. Thankfully, Danny reached and turned the page, unusually eager.

There were more pictures from Brendan from that point onwards. The pictures not as clear and as high a quality, but certainly more relaxed and caught in the moment. Nicolas' first steps, some signs of Brendan's own cure for boredom by gelling his son's hair into different styles. Christmas with Nicolas being held by Owen and trying to gnaw his way through a brussel sprout because the kid was weird as hell.

"Brussel sprouts," Danny shrieked in disgust. "I hate brussels."

The memory of holding Nicolas on his lap and then being amused when his son started to pick food off his plate came back so vividly he could almost feel it. His son's small body wriggling, the shriek of delighted laughter as the baby had continued the game with a cheeky grin. Every so often, Nicolas had head butted backwards to look up as if to share the joke with Brendan and then reached out his hands again. Every time Brendan had caught one hand, the other had reached out instead. His mum had laughed and bent down, using a napkin to wipe the baby's hands as he'd shrieked out a long string of noises, as if he'd wanted to chat away.

"We used to celebrate Christmas on the twenty-seventh," Brendan heard himself say hoarsely. "Lindsey always had him on the day itself."

"Lindsey?" Danny questioned.

"Your brother's mum," Liaden answered gently. "We talked about her, remember."

Danny nodded slowly. "She was brave," he said, peering back up at Brendan. "Mum said she was really brave."

Brendan nodded. "More than me," he said, the image of her, scared in an ill-fitting school uniform and telling him frantically about the baby was one that would never leave him.

Mostly because he'd laughed in her face if only to combat the utter terror that had risen up within him at the idea.

Danny shot him a doubtful look and continued to turn the pages. To Nicolas' third birthday, to his son's artistic attempts at writing on the walls and looking back over his shoulder at the camera with a grumpy sulk at being interrupted. At his older nineteen-year-old self with a truly shite hair cut lifting Nicolas in the air and his son's rather disgruntled expression, dressed in pyjamas and with epic bedhead.

He'd got the letter, he remembered. To become an intern for the Elites. First and last to ever do so. He'd been their runner, worked to get information for them and had basically been their tea and coffee boy. And he'd been so delighted he'd woken up the toddler who had tolerated the celebrations for about twenty minutes before bursting into tired, frustrated tears and Brendan could remember feeling so awful that he'd read to his son until Nicolas had fallen asleep, still sneaking disbelieving glances at the letter.

Danny was staring at the letter in awe. His mum must have put it in, pieced it back together and he felt an odd lurch in his stomach at seeing it once again. "Why is it ripped up?" Danny asked, fingers already on the edge of the page to turn it.

"Don't," Brendan said softly, covering Danny's small fingers with his own. "Don't turn the page."

"Is that…" Danny broke himself off looking unspeakably worried.

"I went to celebrate that weekend," Brendan whispered. "They…he was taken that night."

Danny leaned in, snuggling into him. "Sorry," he whispered.

"No reason for you to be," Brendan said, closing the book and looking up at Liaden. "Sorry for being…I'll be better," he promised Danny. "I know I said it before, but…I'll get better at this. At talking about him."

Danny pulled back to smile shyly at him. "I'd like that," he whispered.

He placed a kiss on the kid's nose. "You should get ready for bed," he said, trying to step back into the role of being a normal, functioning parent.

Danny nodded and scampered off without protest. Surprised, he turned to look at Liaden who seemed equally taken aback. "Is it wrong that I'm tempted to milk that?" Brendan asked slowly.

She laughed, sounding surprised. "Smart, I'd say," she said. Then she hummed, moving away to sit in the armchair, placing the now empty mug on the side. "Nate called."

"Not tonight," he said. "I…It's not his fault but…"

She nodded. "And someone called Jake seems to be trying to get hold of you."

Shit. "The Porter's Lodge case," he groaned, rubbing at his eyes.

"Do you still want to take it?"

No. But a thump from upstairs reminded him of why he might have to push on through. "Fuck. I'll call Jake in a bit."

"I can call him and tell him to do one," Liaden offered sweetly. "Nate can-"

"No," Brendan said, standing up and feeling suddenly exhausted. "Where is my phone?"

His wife watched him thoughtfully and then dug her hand in her pocket. "Here," she said, handing it over.

"This was in my pocket," he pointed out, taking it from her palm.

"So it was," she agreed, standing up to kiss his lips. "And very easy to pick-pocket." She moved past him as he dug into his jean pocket again.

"And the cigarettes?" he called.

"Binned them," she said. "Your cleaning charms still leave your mouth tasting like an ash tray."

He debated arguing it and then decided he was just doing it to be contrary. Instead, he dialled for Jake, glancing at the calendar and feeling a slight swell of surprise that it was coming close to the end of November.

"Hi," a nervous voice said on the other side of the phone. "Um...yeah."

Um yeah? Not sure if he had the patience tonight, he pinched the bridge of his nose. "What do you want Jake?" he asked.

"We...um... we were gonna go to the house tomorrow," Jake said. "Take another look at the graves and then the house."

Probably wise at this stage. "Right."

"Okay." The kid sounded brighter suddenly. "So we're looking at leaving early-"

No. "We're leaving at one," Brendan ordered. "I'll pick you and the others up and we'll head over."

"Uh…" Jake sounded as if he were checking that with someone which already started to put Brendan's back up. "Maybe a little earlier? I mean-"

"One." He wasn't moving on it, he thought as he watched Liaden busy around the kitchen. She deserved… something. Breakfast or lunch or a lie in. And there was no way he was getting up at the crack of dawn on the orders of some recruits.

"From the Currock building-"

"Yeah. No." Brendan plucked at the back of the sofa. "From the drive," he said slowly because the idea of going into the office at the moment might be a little more than he could cope with. "Jake…"

"Jake?" the kid said sounding suddenly delighted. "I… yeah?"

Oh for…he looked over at Liaden as if she might help him, but she was frowning down at the back of a ready meal and he felt an odd wave of fondness overwhelm him.

"Bre…uh…sir…Campion?"

Fucking hell. "Just… whatever you hear from the office or the papers, I don't want to discuss it. At all. Clear?"

There was a long pause now. "Okay?" Jake asked, sounding confused, and he'd guess that meant that the news hadn't been released yet or making the rounds on the gossip circuit of the Currock building.

"Great. Tomorrow. One." He hung up before Jake could say anything in reply and then stared at the phone, somewhat baffled as to when the kid had become Jake rather than Atkins.

"You have such a way with people," Liaden said, leaning on the counter.

"I'll cook," he said suddenly, holding out a hand to her as he stepped into the kitchen. "You sit."

She watched him, eyebrow raised. "Brendan-"

"Let me do something," he said, lifting her hands and brushing a gentle kiss to them. "Something useful. For you two." He frowned down at her hands and cupped them. "You are the two that I can actually look after."

She smiled at him, though he could tell she wasn't fully convinced. But she hopped onto the counter next to him and he raised an eyebrow when she scooted backwards to bring her knees up to her chin and wrap her arms around her legs. "Go on then, oh master chef," she encouraged. "Show us how it's done."

By the time Danny came back down, he was mid prep and felt like he might almost manage to laugh as the pair of them sat on the counter and got in his way.

Chapter Eleven

BRENDAN LOOKED DISTINCTLY UNAMUSED WHEN he picked Jake and Rob up the next day. To the point that Jake had a sneaking suspicion that he'd deliberately picked them up forty minutes late just to make them stand in the cold, warmed only by their own spells.

It was a bloody good job that Cole had gone ahead with Daphne after she'd started pacing the walls at about eight-o-clock. And Jake wished he'd gone with them when Rob had opened his mouth as they walked over to Brendan who rolled down the window.

"Have they really shut the case and declared-"

The foul look that Brendan had shot him had actually made Rob almost trip over himself to stop talking and Jake glared because that had been Brendan's one request. They'd been standing waiting for the man for forty minutes and not once had Rob mentioned whatever it was that Brendan seemed to be trying to avoid.

"Where are the other two?" Brendan snapped, looking past them.

"They went ahead." Jake winced as the glare was turned on him and he squirmed.

"When?"

God, he didn't even want to speak. "Uh...they went this morning. About four or five hours ago."

Brendan stared at him for a long enough amount of time that it started to get really uncomfortable, then he jabbed a hand at the back of the car. "Get in and do not speak."

He made them sit in the back too. Something about them smelling like wet dogs before he cranked up the music when Jake tried to ask a question.

Okay.

The drive to Porter's Lodge was quicker than it had been when they'd gone with Daphne. Brendan drove like the speed limit was more of a suggestion and there was a distinct possibility that he was casting spells to get cars to move out of his way. Which was cool and everything, but also mildly terrifying. The further away from London they got, the less traffic there was. The sprawling countryside Jake had admired last time became a rushing blur as Brendan drove through Sussex and hurtled down the tiny lanes.

When Brendan stopped the car at the gates it was with a muttered curse. Worse still, as he got out of the car, he clicked the fob and activated the child locks. Wincing, Jake watched as Brendan made his way to the gates and studied the post before kicking at the ground and making his way back into the car. His movements were tight and furious as he got back in.

"Iron?" he demanded, turning to look at them as the blaring music suddenly cut out like a knife had been plunged into the speakers. "The property is completely encircled in fucking iron?"

"The gate-" Rob started to protest.

"Don't be stupid," Brendan cut him off. "The iron runs

underground. Doesn't matter if the gate is shut or not. You said that there were graves here?"

Jake nodded, terrified that if he said anything he'd get his head bitten off.

"Fuck," Brendan muttered again, getting out his phone.

"I…there was iron surrounding the graveyard," Jake pointed out, suddenly feeling so completely moronic. "I thought…it wasn't enclosed above ground…" he trailed off when Brendan turned to stare at him in disbelief. "Yeah," he winced.

"There wasn't iron-" Rob started to say.

"It was in the yew bushes," Jake confessed. "Cole and I saw it."

"Yew bushes too?" Brendan demanded and then made an annoyed noise and ended the call he'd been making. "Fucking voicemail. They've been here for hours, right? Daphne and Hedgehog boy?"

Hedgehog boy? "Uh, Cole? Yeah. Daphne wanted to look around the house and check the graves." He almost added that she'd wanted to go at night, but held onto that information because they seemed to be in enough trouble as it was.

"Did you go in the house before?" Brendan demanded, fingers flying over the screen of his phone, assumedly firing off messages to various people.

Jake shook his head. "Just the grounds."

Brendan tossed the phone down on the seat next to him and turned back to the wheel. He drummed his fingers on the steering wheel for almost a full minute before he properly shut the car door and put the car into gear.

This time, they drove slowly down the driveway, the thick woods seeming denser than before with the information about the iron. Brendan got halfway down and stopped the car again. He flung open the door, got out and started kicking at the mud banks on the side of the driveway.

"What?" Jake asked as Brendan got back in.

"Iron," Brendan said. "Whoever did it first time around wanted people to be safe as they came in, but weren't taking chances."

"Why can't we feel it?" Jake asked. "We've passed over it, it should be-"

"It's coated in spells. Ground around it has been salted," Brendan replied, starting the car again and driving down at the same cautious speed.

"Ghosts then?" Rob piped up from the back. "It's definitely ghosts."

"Seems like," Brendan replied as they pulled up to the front of the house, next to the destroyed fountain in the middle of the drive. Daphne's little blue mini looked just plain weird on the other side of it; too shiny and new and fresh. Brendan leaned on the steering wheel, his expression hard to read as he flicked his fingers. A blue path lit up from the car, meandered around the entrance and then disappeared into the house. "How far away from the house are the graves?"

"About a ten-minute walk," Jake said quietly.

Brendan actually groaned into the steering wheel. Another twist of his fingers lit the fountain up in blotched pink that made Brendan swear viciously.

"Mirror spells?" he demanded, whirling around. "What the fuck is wrong with you?"

"We didn't do it," Rob protested. "Daphne-"

"You tell me these things," Brendan snapped. "You tell me that you're gonna start casting stupid fucking spells that anger the dead. You tell me about iron. You tell me that they've gone ahead if it's that much of a gap. You fucking tell me these things, you bloody idiotic-" he cut himself off and launched out of the car.

"This sucks," Rob muttered, sinking down into the seat and glaring at the roof of the car. "He's treating us like kids. And you said he wouldn't listen last night. He's not-"

The child lock was deactivated on the car and Jake sucked in a breath because Brendan was halfway towards the house and he definitely had not used the car keys to do that. "Jesus, he's strong," Jake whispered. "He's casting spells like they're nothing."

Rob nodded, looking a little spooked himself. "Probably best to stick with him," he suddenly decided. "Gonna guess that he's pissed off as it is-"

"And why-" Some force knocked them against their respective doors in a hint that was kind of impossible to ignore and Jake stifled the rising frustration that it seemed everyone knew something he didn't. Undoing the car door, Jake winced at the force of the November wind that was rustling the trees into something that almost resembled white noise.

They managed to catch up with Brendan at the huge, heavy wooden door that had been flung open by Daphne or Cole and hung precariously between ivy covered walls that bulged dangerously as if the life was being squeezed from them.

"This is older," Brendan muttered, looking down and

toeing his boot at the spider-webbed cracked paving stones at the bottom of the porch like structure.

"It was the original lodge," Jake tried to supply helpfully. "Henry Ambros' father upgraded it in-"

"Literally do not give a shit," Brendan snapped, looking up from the place where Eric Redgrave had presumably had his head caved in. "Where were your little moronic pals going?"

Okay. Ouch.

"Last murder site," Rob said quietly. "Upstairs, first floor, one of the windows facing the drive."

Surprised that Rob had actually remembered that much, Jake sent him an impressed look as Brendan threw open the second set of old, grand double doors and stomped into the main hall. As much as Jake would have loved to just follow him, he found himself grinding to a halt at the sight of what was before him.

The hall was a massive thing with a huge high ceiling and a grand staircase opposite that could probably fit a car up it with some room to spare. The floor was stone and covered with a red carpet in the middle that continued up the stairs but it was faded, patched and stained. There were two shattered chandeliers in the middle of the hall that must have fallen down and had cascaded shards of glass across the floor.

To the side, there were hallways and doors that were shut off and the whole place was quiet enough that it could make you paranoid about what lurked behind those closed doors. Nervous, Jake shook himself and hurried to catch up to Rob and Brendan who had already navigated around the remains of the chandeliers and were about to climb the stairs.

"Should we call for them?" he asked in a low voice.

"Do not disturb anything," Brendan snapped furiously, not even breaking his furious pace, but managing somehow to half hiss and half whisper the instructions to them. "Do not do anything. You are here because you're idiots and I don't trust you not to find more ways to fuck this up if I leave you alone."

Jake pressed his lips together and said nothing as they reached the first landing which circled the hall. The carpet upstairs was even worse and the right-hand side of the landing looked like it had been abandoned for centuries, not decades. There were bricked up parts to the wall, clumsily done with no attempt at making it aesthetically pleasing.

The left-hand side, where they walked, was a little better. The carpet was faded and saturated in dust, but it looked more as if it had been abandoned than had been destroyed like other parts of the house. The door opposite the stairs was open and showed more light which Brendan stormed through while Jake and Rob followed because, really, what else could they do?

"You two," Brendan barked even as Daphne and Cole turned around from where they'd been standing at the window. "We're leaving. Move."

"We have evidence to-" Daphne started and then yelped when Brendan's magic tugged her forward carefully and she ended up being weirdly encouraged over to them. Behind her, Cole sighed and followed, shifting the bag he was carrying on his shoulder before digging his hands deep in his pockets and shooting a baffled look at Jake.

"The iron goes all around the property," Jake said, not too sure if he should feel more panicked or less.

"No, it doesn't," Daphne said at roughly the same time as Cole said "And?"

"Wait you knew?"

"It's underground." Cole shrugged again as he got closer. "Why bother with the rest otherwise?"

That was...huh... that was a good point. Brendan glanced heavenwards and then continued his storming out, magic almost flaring out around him like a bedsheet a kid had turned into a pretend sail, urging them forward if they dallied too long. "Christ, I don't know if that makes him smarter than the rest of you or more moronic," Brendan muttered as he started down the stairs.

Then stopped.

Across from them, downstairs and towards the exit, the door that Brendan had flung open, the one that Jake had been the last to pass through without touching, was shut.

"I assume you left that open?" Cole asked calmly.

"Yup," Jake answered, stepping down a few more stairs just to see better. He didn't dare step past Brendan who was still glaring at the door as if it should be opening. The fact that it wasn't didn't exactly fill Jake with confidence.

"Are you trying to-"

"Yup," Brendan said, tearing his eyes away from the door. "Shit," he murmured then, slowly, he took another step, hand spreading and palm flat as he moved, clearly ready to conjure at a second's notice. His eyes were fixed above him and only then did Jake realise that there was still a third chandelier, closest to the door and hanging in a far too heavy manner, as if ready to fall any second.

"To the side," Cole muttered suddenly, pointing. "Iris said they never used the main entrance. The west wing has to have another entrance."

Brendan nodded once and then stepped down, apparently happy to lead the way. His footsteps suddenly seemed obscenely loud as they walked, first around one chandelier and then to what looked like a corridor that led down the left hand-

An almighty scream rang out. Painful and terrified as a shadowy figure suddenly launched themselves towards the corridor they were heading for and the ancient looking door that had been left open suddenly slammed shut with a heavy groan.

The figure threw itself against it, shaking the door before it…he turned and pressed himself against it. He looked to be in his late twenties, handsome but his face was already bruised and he was flickering, changing between different versions of himself at different ages, the way that ghosts did.

And Jake knew that face, had seen it in the files that had been given to them by the Council. That was Jonah Summers, the man that the Coven had accused of killing Ted Johnson. The figure turned and banged on the door, his palm flat before he almost tried to claw through it, screaming and yelling-

"Move," Brendan hissed at him, grabbing at Jake's elbow and propelling him forward as a second voice, young and female, started to scream upstairs. "In here," Brendan added, opening the door before almost tossing Jake in as the others followed. Within three seconds, they were in the room, the door shut as an almost silken-like-veil of wards

lined the room. Brendan stood, staring at the door before he kicked it furiously.

"They're awake," Cole said.

"Yes, thank you for that," Rob sneered. "We all really needed you to explain that one to us."

"Waking," Brendan corrected, turning to them. "They aren't aware of us yet, just playing out their own scenes. Any ideas why that might be?" he demanded, glaring at Daphne who was suddenly looking pale.

"Mirror spells are the best way to-"

"Wake the dead and trap them in their final moments," Brendan finished, storming past her. As they turned to follow him, Jake glanced around the room that they were in which looked like some massive lounge thing; sofas that were probably once a deep and rich blue sat in the middle around a coffee table. There was a long table behind it, panelled wooden walls with faded cream and blue wallpaper that reminded Jake of some china patterns his dad's mum collected.

There wasn't a single window or other exit in sight.

Cole drifted over to the bookcase because he was him and was probably going to find more things to correct like the arrogant git he could be. Rob swept an imperious hand at the closest sofa, banishing the dust before he bent over it, groaning into the back of it. "What do we do? Just wait for them to get bored?"

"They'll get angry," Brendan sighed as he walked up to one of the mirrors. There were three embedded in the walls and at first sight you could probably mistake them for three grand arching windows. "They'll realise someone was casting the spell and come for us. The dead dislike reliving their final moments."

"It's just one ghost, right?" Rob asked.

"Four murders," Cole corrected absently as he pulled a book out from the shelves. "I have some supplies," he added suddenly. He took off the bag he'd been wearing and tossed it towards the sofa. Before it could hit, the bag was caught by Brendan's magic and swung over in his direction instead.

"Anything interesting?" Daphne asked, still looking a little shaken as she stepped closer to Cole and the bookshelf.

"Someone enjoyed Dickens," Cole said, looking back down at the book. "Some local history books, some text books from the seventies and eighties. Spell craft books."

Jake glanced over at Brendan who was placing salt and some gem stones on the table. Herbs followed and then string, almost as if Cole had raided items from an old hedge-witch's shop. "Will that stuff actually help?" Jake heard himself ask.

To his surprise, Brendan actually nodded. "Old remedies for ghosts often work better than new spells," he said. "You've swung to the clever side," he told Cole seriously.

Cole didn't seem to be paying the slightest bit of attention. He was still flicking through the book he'd picked up and had Daphne half on his shoulder as she tried to see what he was reading.

"So we're calling for back-up?" Rob demanded, lifting his head from where it had been resting against the back of the sofa. "I mean, you're calling someone?"

"The phones aren't working," Brendan said. "I tried calling both of them," he added with a nod to Daphne and Cole, "and texting. Nothing is getting through – no internet, no signal, nothing. Why do you think I physically walked in the house rather than get them to come out?"

"Wait," Rob yelped, standing up quicker than Jake had ever seen him move. "We're trapped here and we can't even tell people that we're trapped?"

Brendan nodded.

"You said it'd get worse!" Rob cried, coming forward. "That the ghosts would get angry with them for casting the mirror spell."

"Welcome to the predicament," Brendan snapped at him. "We either leave now and risk waking up everything because I will have to hammer at that fucking door to get it open or wait it out and risk that it will take too long for them to fade away again." He dragged a hand through his hair, making it stand up in ruffled prickles. "I assume that no-one brought food with them?"

"I have some oranges," Daphne said quietly.

There was, Jake was sure, a moment when Brendan would have laughed at her, but he seemed to just about manage to restrain himself and nod instead. "That's... better than nothing," he said, before he stared down again at Cole's supplies.

"Why did you bring us?" Rob demanded, standing in the way and apparently unwilling to let the issue go.

"Because you need babysitting because you're all fucking idiots." Brendan swung around to Cole as if to say something and seemed to be momentarily derailed by the fact that Cole wasn't paying him an ounce of attention. "What are you looking at?" he demanded wearily.

"History of the village," Cole said, flicking a page and reading, seemingly unaware of the tone.

Brendan stared at him and then tilted his head. "History of the house included in there?"

"On and off," Cole said, turning from the bookcase and sitting down in an absent manner.

"You two," Brendan said, pointing at Jake and Rob, "Start making talismans with this stuff. We might be able to limit the interaction they can have with us. Not you," he added when Daphne stepped forward. "If you cast the mirror spell, they might sense your magic. I'd rather they didn't."

"It's a valid technique," she snapped suddenly. "And they all agreed with it."

To Jake's surprise, Brendan suddenly seemed to soften a little. "I know," he said. "But there are precautions to dark magic – it's complex and unnatural. You need to understand the natural laws that you are breaking and ensure that you weave ways to deal with the consequences into those kinds of spells. And mirror spells? You need to be prepared for what happens when you stir up the past like that. You should have guidance the first few times you do it in the field."

Him being kind seemed to make Daphne crumple a little and she nodded, her shoulders deflating as she looked away.

As if relenting, Brendan drew her over to a mirror and pulled out a pen. "Now," he said as he reached forward. "You can describe to me the layout of the house, from what you've seen so far."

Cole continued to read, only looking faintly surprised when he looked up and saw everyone else getting on with their own task.

Geek.

Jake found himself sat opposite Rob as they rifled through what Cole had brought. Silver to ward off spirits, Black Onyx for the same, Silkstone to help boost it. Strips of Cedar for protection. There was Eyebright which Jake put to one side (boosting the ability to see visions seemed unwise right now). Larch joined Eyebright. Rob took the Myrrh, Sycamore and Vervain and started to mash it together. "Been years since I've seen this done," Rob muttered under his breath. "Is this like our version of every little helps?"

"Something like it." Brendan wandered back over to them, the drawing of the house on the mirror looking a little filled in with rooms, but still mostly blank. "Look at the walls," he added. "This entire room is patterned, but the wall against the hall is solid blue. They were trying to keep the ghosts out when this was last decorated."

Beyond him, Cole twisted the book around, craning his neck and shifting as if trying to find the correct perspective on something.

"We'll save these," Brendan sighed as he looked at the Larch and Eyebright. "Kinda hoping we might find a way to sneak out without needing a confrontation."

"Scared?" Rob mocked.

"You are no-where near ready for this," Brendan sighed. "And I am no-where near the right state of mind to fight them off and protect the four of you. So yeah, if there's a way around this, let's take it. We can bring back actual useful people tomorrow."

Ouch.

It must have shown on their faces, because Brendan

suddenly winced. "I didn't mean…you're all still training. You're meant to be useless."

Not entirely convinced that was any better, Jake started to fill the small silver cages with the stones and the plants, wrapping them up in leaves and then closing the cages. They were slightly precarious, but already he could feel the energy humming from them. Brendan wordlessly held out his hand for them and then started to weave, storing power and spells of protection into the stones.

"Like that," he offered. "See if you can replicate."

Theirs were clumsier attempts, but Jake managed to catch onto the stones energy and start using it as a focal point for the protections spells. He could manage about half a foot of protection around it, which would mean whoever wore them would have to duck to keep their lower legs protected. Rob seemed to manage roughly the same and Brendan nodded, though Jake noticed that he'd kept hold of the one that he'd spelled.

Probably wise.

Cole was standing up when Jake next looked over, examining one of the mirror's edges with careful fingers.

"What's he doing?" Rob complained.

"The house," Cole said as he continued with what he was doing, "had building works to extend it in the eighteenth century. And this is a drawing room," he added, fingers stopping. "Usually, they have windows. This is in the middle of the house. Roughly."

"So?" Rob asked.

Cole pulled and the whole mirror came away from the wall. He simply placed it against the wall and then turned his attention to the revealed brick work. "So," he said as he smoothed his hands over it. "I think this was a window."

Rob rolled his eyes. "And you think he's the smart one," he muttered to Brendan.

"Well," Cole said. "Assuming this hasn't been touched, there's a possibility that they built the west wing of the house next to walls and then just knocked through. Which means there might be a gap. Wall will be weakest here." He turned to them and shrugged. "Might get us through to an exit."

"Might get us stumbling across another ghost in very tight circumstances," Daphne said, almost curling her arms around herself.

"I mean you could hide a body in there," Cole said thoughtfully. "But they wanted to add a ballroom. Seems relatively like a safe choice that this is unlikely to be a haunted part of the house. And the Ambros family lived in the west wing. They must have come up with a few bits of protection for that side of the house. We go through, find their exit and leave. Gonna guess that's what our ghost earlier was trying to do."

"That was Jonah Summers," Jake said quietly. "His body was never found. The Coven thought he'd vanished after killing his cousin."

There was a long silence.

"His body isn't in there," Cole said after a moment, looking slightly annoyed now. "That's been solid since the west wing was built."

"Here it has been," Brendan said quietly. "There could be an access point elsewhere."

"So what? We just stay here and hope for the best?"

Cole demanded. Then his eyes lit upon what they were making and he hummed thoughtfully. "We don't know how bad it'll get when the ghosts start to come out of their mini pantomimes," Cole said, folding his arms. "And that chandelier could go any second if we try to leave the room that way."

"I can keep it off our heads," Brendan said dismissively.

"And open the door, and potentially dissuade a vengeful ghost?"

There was the oddest moment in which Brendan almost looked chagrined. "You don't think anyone else here is capable of helping me?" Brendan demanded.

Cole actually looked around. One by one as if it was a genuine valid question and he had the power to decide. "Not with confidence," he said eventually.

"Um," Daphne broke in. "Actually-"

"And your way works better because?" Brendan cut in, ignoring her.

"Percentage of likelihood?"

It made Brendan bark out an annoyed laugh. Turning away from Cole, he muttered something under his breath and turned away from all of them as if needing a breather.

"Do you need the wall intact to ward the room?" Daphne asked quietly.

"No," Brendan said eventually, turning back. "Go on then," he said, sinking into the sofa that Cole had vacated. "Have at it."

Cole nodded and crouched, his hand placed firmly on the bricks. For a second or two nothing happened, and then slowly, the bricks started to crumble to dust, a gentle fading away that was unlikely to draw the attention that might have happened had Jake just ploughed through it with a blast like he'd thought Cole would.

Beyond, there was darkness and the faintest hint of another wall about a foot away from the drawing room.

"It's wider than I thought," Daphne whispered, as if that would make a difference. Then she looked expectantly at Cole. "Go on."

Evidently, Cole lacked the self-preservation of a gnat because he shoved his head out of the room without a second thought. Then leaned even further forward before stepping fully out into the dark passage. Surrounded by the grand arches that had held the mirrors, Cole became a shadowy figure as he looked left then right. Then, without a word, he turned decisively right and vanished.

"Does he have a talisman?" Rob asked suddenly.

"Nope," Brendan said, eyes on the ceiling even as magic bubbled around him as he cast some sort of spell. "He's swung firmly back into idiot land again."

Chapter Twelve

It had been a while since Brendan had attempted a projection spell. It was draining and there were usually far more effective, non-magical ways of contacting people at a distance, but there weren't many options at the moment and he could probably use the supplies that Lorcan had brought with him to give him a boost later on if he started to run low.

He was tempted to go for Liaden, but Boss could be a complete dick when he wanted to be and he had no way of knowing if she'd be able to get through to him if Nate was caught up in one of his meetings. Still, it meant getting through the Currock buildings wards (which were somewhat time consuming to bend) and persuade them to realise that he was actually keyed into the wards even if not physically there.

When he opened his eyes, he could see Boss at his desk, eating a hot-dog and flicking through his work. He stopped, tilted his head and then snapped his gaze up to Brendan.

"We have a problem," Brendan started.

Boss actually rolled his eyes and then started to wipe his fingers on the napkin that had come with the takeaway. "Of course you do," he sighed. "Couldn't use a fucking phone to complain about the result of Summers' investigation-"

"Not..." Brendan glared at him, "You think I'm astral projecting because I can't be arsed to get my phone or come in to shout in person?"

Boss actually seemed to contemplate that and then put down the napkin, eyes narrowed. "You're at the house," he said after a moment. "Fucking hell, why can't you use your phone?" he asked staring at Brendan with something like parental disappointment.

"There are ghosts and the kids used a mirror spell," Brendan said, years of dealing with the man allowing him to be succinct. Back before Boss had been Boss you had to otherwise you'd have something thrown at you. "It's getting worse and they're not prepared for this."

"Ghosts? Who the fuck decided to do a mirr-" Boss suddenly cut himself off. "I'll send a squad over."

"There's iron surrounding the property and someone was murdered at the entrance to the building. And in the fountain out the front," Brendan pointed out quietly.

"We train morons," Boss actually groaned. "I'll send a squad. They'll be there in an hour," Boss said, checking something online. "Sunset is a couple of hours away. We won't have long to get you out."

"We're in the middle of the house," Brendan added and watched Boss wince. "Lorcan might have found a way to get us to the back of the west wing. But McCafferty has been here before. He might know-"

"McCafferty has been to a haunted house surrounded by iron?" Boss asked, and it probably was petty that Brendan had to resist the urge to smirk at the annoyance in Boss' voice and the unspoken 'fucking idiot' that Boss seemed to be holding back.

"Yep," Brendan said and apparently, he didn't manage to keep the glee out of his voice because Boss fixed him with an unimpressed glare.

"Go," Boss said, standing. "We'll need to make contact soon. Save your strength for then." With that, Boss's magic reached out and gently nudged Brendan back through the wards and seemed to follow him for a few seconds as his spirit found its way back to his body. There was a strange sensation that felt like a grim nod and then Boss was gone. Somewhat disorientated, Brendan opened his eyes to a nervous looking Daphne, shifting from side to side in front of him.

"I thought you'd fallen into a coma," she whispered.

"Don't be daft," Brendan muttered, feeling a little insulted at the idea. "Nowhere near close to that." He sat up from the sofa and looked around. Goodman's kid was still doing sweet fuck all, Jake had his head half into the wall, apparently looking for Lorcan and the wards around the room were still thrumming happily. Nothing had attempted to crash against them for entry which was a relief. "Lorcan found anything yet?"

"The end of the passage," Daphne admitted. "He's trying to find a way through."

Standing up and ignoring the faint wave of nausea as he readjusted to his body, Brendan strode over to the hole that Lorcan had made, then shoved his head in the passage too.

The idiot boy was at the end of the passage. At some point he must have found a candle in the drawing room because it lit up his features in an eerie manner now as he searched the walls.

"Is it worth crumbling it again?" Brendan asked, trying to keep his tone level and somewhat quiet.

Lorcan's head whipped around and he stared back at Brendan with a strange expression on his face. "I can't tell what's on the other side," he confessed slowly.

Fair enough. Climbing into the passage, Brendan slowly made his way down. Lorcan shifted to one side, still holding the candle as Brendan placed his hand on the wall. It wasn't exactly his best skill, but he could feel the emptiness on the other side and that seemed as good as anything they'd get.

Gently, he sped up the effect of time on the wall as Cole had. It took more magic, but it wasn't necessarily something that would draw the attention of the dead. Slowly, the brick work crumbled to dust and faded away until they could see the hall on the other side.

It was fitted with electricity which was the first thing that struck Brendan. They had to be in the updated part of the house, the part that Ruby and Sebastian had lived in. He stepped out, brushing off the brick dust as he went.

To the right, the hall went on to another door and then suddenly stopped. Clearly, it had been bricked off too, though this had been wallpapered with some truly hideous seventies wallpaper. Taking the risk, Brendan walked down and touched his hands to the wall, then pulled away with a hiss at the feeling of iron within the brickwork.

Clever.

Turning back, he watched as Lorcan placed a hand on the door, the candle he'd been holding extinguished now that they had light.

"You hoping that it will suddenly work this time?" Brendan asked.

Lorcan pulled his hand away as if he'd been burned. A weird flush crept over his face as he looked down the hall. "Do we get the others here or not?" he asked, sounding a little sulky.

The kid really was like a hedgehog sometimes. At the moment, he was practically rolling into a ball and thrusting out spikes. Amused, he walked to the door and reached for it, annoyed at himself as he did it and remembered that Lorcan still wasn't wearing a talisman.

It opened to another very seventies style room but this one had windows. Feeling an odd wave of relief, Brendan headed straight for them, and then hissed in annoyance when he spotted the iron settings for the glass panels.

They weren't getting through there.

He turned back to Lorcan who remained in the doorway, staring across the room. It was a cosier, comfier room for all that it was hideously decorated with mustard coloured fixtures, but ultimately there was nothing of interest in it, other than the family portrait above the chimney.

Oh.

He didn't want to be curious. He absolutely did not want to be curious, but he found himself stepping closer to examine the painting. There was a tall, red-headed woman who was standing up, a blond-haired toddler on her hip while a blond man sat on the chair in front of her, with a blond-haired girl on his lap. To his side, a tall young teenager stood, with auburn hair and a serious expression as he leant in slightly to his father.

It must have been taken from an actual picture, but the

artist (whoever they had been) had captured them all well. And the woman…Ruby, he could see something about the jaw line and the shape of the eyes that mimicked what he saw in the mirror and in Danny's face. And Sebastian, the apparently kind man who seemed to have drugged himself to death, looked tired but pleased, arms around his daughter and a loving expression on his face as he watched her. Vivienne (and wasn't it strange to think that the sweet little girl in the picture was now the formidable Lady Ozwald), was grinning as she leaned against her father's chest and stared boldly straight at the camera.

Brendan stared at the toddler, even if he didn't want to. At the big blue eyes that were frustratingly his own shade and the curious expression that Nicolas had inherited.

He hated it. If only because it meant that the child in the picture looked as innocent as his son had once been and Brendan was all too aware of what that toddler had become.

He forced his gaze across to the other boy in the picture. That had to be Lysander Ambros, who his mother thought Phineas had killed, who his great aunt said had been taken from the family by his grandfather. He'd have been going back and forth by the time that the photograph had been taken. Lysander looked far more serious than the others even as he leaned in a little, but neither parent seemed to be reaching for him and it annoyed Brendan more than he could say.

What would he have given to have been able to have had his son even for the weekends?

"Come on," he said, dragging his gaze away. Lorcan was still standing by the doorway and looking deeply uncomfortable. "I imagine that most of the windows are lined with iron too." He strode out into the hallway and walked in the opposite direction.

The hallway narrowed a little and there was a door opposite. He went to open it and then frowned as something behind him caught his eye and caused him to turn.

There were stairs.

They'd clearly been added in; the carpet was different and the new walls were thinner and flimsier. And, as Brendan stared up the stairs, he was suddenly struck with the realisation that he was in Phineas' childhood house and, up the stairs, might be his room.

So he turned away and opened the other door.

It was a conservatory that had been something of a greenhouse and now looked like some strange overgrown Victorian sitting room. There were poppies in the corner and Lorcan wandered over, touching them gently. There was Bloodroot and Boneset for healing and Goldseal to purify.

"They were promoting healing," Brendan murmured as he looked around, fingers tracing over some rather old, but still functional looking tools. Lorcan was still examining the poppies. "What are you doing?"

"They're opium poppies," Lorcan replied, stepping back.

Jesus. "Was she encouraging him?" What kind of a woman had Ruby Ambros been? Had she actually been trying to kill her husband? Send her son away? Uncomfortable with the thought, Brendan turned and made his way through the tangled plants and pushed through until he got to the wall. There was a door that took a few pushes before it gave way to reveal the room beyond.

It was a ballroom.

It made Brendan let out a disbelieving laugh. There was

an actual fucking ballroom? Who the hell would have come here? The thing was though, as he walked in, he could see that it had been slowly converted. It must have been a century since the last ball had been held in the room. There was what seemed like a bar but was actually a kitchen to one side of the room, though it looked ancient, and there was an uncomfortable smell as he stepped close to it. There had been a table, but it was on its side and half hidden by huge motheaten curtains that barricaded the windows.

The lights suddenly switched on and the whole place lit up from being half lit by the windows. The electric lights weren't enough to put everything in stark illumination, but it was enough to make the room look painfully abandoned.

"No ghosts," Lorcan whispered. When Brendan turned to him, he shrugged. "There's nothing. No screams, no signs. They'd be stuck in their own replays still."

True. "Still need to find a way out," Brendan said. "The windows and walls have been lined with iron on this side of the house."

"Keeping the spooks out," Lorcan said. "But the boundary lines keep them in. Why not just ask for help?"

"Coven families are ridiculously proud," Brendan said and fuck, they were gonna have to go upstairs which was pretty much the last thing he ever wanted to do. "They'd never admit to the Council that there was a problem." He glanced over and walked back towards the conservatory, "How much experience have you had with Coven families?"

"Enough," Lorcan replied. He seemed to be quite happy to follow Brendan. "Should we let the others know where we are?"

"The ghosts won't get through my wards. Seems safe

enough to wander here. Why waste the time?" Brendan replied, steeling himself as he went back into the hallway and, without giving himself time to pause, began to head up the stairs, mind racing.

They were going up too far.

"What?" Lorcan demanded as he almost ran into Brendan's back. "Why have we stopped?"

"It's taking us up to the third floor," Brendan said, pressing his hands to the wall and then hissing. "Fucking iron," he muttered as he continued up the stairs.

The top had a door which was locked but that wasn't too much of a problem given that he and Nate had once spent an entire year trying to beat each other picking locks (which was not a skill that Boss had agreed to them learning). Lorcan raised an eyebrow but said nothing as Brendan forced it open.

The door swung onto another landing and this one was airy and bright. There was a wall at the end, but it looked like it had been designed that way and Brendan could imagine that there were probably just layers of brick and iron in between the west wing and the original part of the house.

It surprised him that most of the rooms were pretty much empty, even the bathroom had been stripped back to its fixtures. The kids would have all moved out and taken what they wanted with them, he supposed. It was impossible to tell who had lived in which room, except for the fact that there was a clear master bedroom that was still furnished, covered in layers of dust.

It was old fashioned though, Brendan thought as he edged in. The kind that felt too still and silent, as if you were being watched, though in this house that could absolutely be the case. There were flower patterns on the bedspread and long curtains that framed the huge windows…no, not window. It was a door. The master bedroom had a balcony.

"Finally," Brendan muttered, walking over and forcing that lock as well. Then he stepped out into the fresh air and stared at the darkening skies and across the grounds. It wasn't the best sight; the trees were thick and the house wasn't so high that he was above the trees, but they were higher up and it did give some view of the side of the house.

"That's where the graves are," Lorcan said as he came to stand next to him, quietly nodding ahead and Brendan could fancy that there was a part of the tree line that looked thinner than others. Lorcan gently tapped the balcony railings with his foot watching it suspiciously. "They'd have been able to keep an eye on them."

Maybe. Leaning slightly on the railings, Brendan tried to peer around the side of the house to see if anyone had arrived yet, though it seemed bloody unlikely, and then huffed and pulled his phone out of his pocket. Switching it on, he held it out as far away from the house as he dared and waited.

The mobile buzzed with missed calls and messages and Brendan dialled instantly, going for Boss even as he winced at the idea of ignoring Liaden. He'd send Lorcan for a snoop and then call her later, he figured.

"Where are you?" Boss asked after two rings.

"On a balcony on the west wing, around the side of the house. Top floor."

There was a pause. "And how the fuck does that help us get you out of there?"

"Jump?"

"With all that iron in the brick work? Try again," Boss said, the 'moron' strangely absent from his words if not his tone.

It made him blink and peer down at the grounds, trying to see if he could spot anything. "How the hell did you get here so fast?"

"Stuart," Boss said, the sound of people calling to each other in the background. "Set up a portal spell here years ago and re-awakened it when he was mentoring." He paused and then almost seemed oddly tickled. "He didn't mention that, I take it?"

"No." Brendan glared down at the grounds, half-hoping he might spot Stuart and be able to throw something at him.

"And we've found the graves," Boss added, sounding slightly impressed by that. "Stuart's not taking it well if that helps."

"Probably dickish of me to admit that it does," Brendan sighed. "Any ideas? The west wing of the house seems safe, but it's locked up tight. Nothing in and nothing out." Next to him, Lorcan slipped away and back into the master bedroom and then the hallway. Brendan turned and watched, flicking a spell at the door to keep it open no matter what.

"Boss," he said, as Lorcan disappeared through the door, the tracking spell that Brendan had laced him with on the stairs keeping a close watch on him. "Who submitted this request?"

"What?"

"Whose idea was it to come here?"

There was a pause. "Lorcan's," Boss said after a moment, voice suddenly changed. If they'd been sitting face to face,

Brendan imagined Boss would be watching him with narrowed eyes. "Why?"

"He's quick," Brendan replied. "Clever."

"Too clever?"

That was the question. "Not sure," Brendan admitted. He glanced around the room again, half sure that Lorcan was probably finding a way to listen and-

Wait.

Despite the old-fashioned pattern, the bedding looked so much newer than the rest of the house. The duvet seemed dusty and abandoned, but the style was far more modern and there were a few little pots and bottles out on the top of the chest of drawers and there was a door that likely led to an en-suite...

"I'll uh...I'll give Liaden a call," Brendan said, still staring at the room. He reached in with his magic and, after a moment's examination, poured out the items from the left-hand side bedside table. Two bottles of pills, a dream catcher and some Vaseline fell onto the bed along with a small thin notebook.

"-got six of us on the grounds looking at the walls. We've set up a base, used the iron to draw a safe area-"

Brendan summoned the Vaseline to him and looked at the label. Putting Boss on speaker phone, he looked up the branding of the tub and drew in a long breath when it looked to be a recent design. As in the past ten years recent.

"-we've moved both cars into it. Though watching Summers climb into that mini was worth my time-"

Brendan summoned the pill bottles over too. Pain medication and stuff to help the kidneys. All prescribed to Ruby Ambros in twenty fifteen.

"Shit," he hissed down the phone, cutting over Boss. "Ruby Ambros was living here in twenty fifteen."

There was a brief pause. "You're certain," Boss said without making it sound like a question.

"Yeah. Which means it's highly likely she was in the house during all of the murders. She has to be the body in the second-floor window..." Brendan hissed. "Which means we are currently stuck in the house with her spirit. A house that she lived in for almost half a century."

"What are we dealing with?" Boss demanded.

Brendan scratched his head. "She was growing opium for her husband. Her son was taken from them and given to Ambros. My great-aunt linked her to most of the murders... I'm seeing nothing that detracts from the theory that she might well have killed all three..." he hesitated, "four. We saw another ghost. Jonah Summers."

"And you're standing in her room," Boss double checked.

"Iron laces everything in the west wing. She can't get in here. She..." he froze at a strange sound. "Lorcan," he called louder.

A hissed shush floated through the doorway.

"Boss, I'll call you back. I can hear...creaking."

"If she put the iron in, she knows the weak areas," Boss warned. "Every single person you have named had Ambros blood."

"I was never claimed-"

"You better hope that she gives a shit about that," Boss replied sounding really pissed off. "Go. Call when you can."

Hanging up, Brendan walked cautiously back in, tossing the pills and the Vaseline onto the bed as he headed for the doorway. Lorcan was at the door to the room that had been shut, except now it was open and now there was a figure in there. Staring down at something that no longer existed.

Brendan came to a stop, a little behind Cole and watched as their breaths faintly fogged the air as the figure tilted his head, still intently gazing down. Dimly, Brendan supposed he should feel some small relief that it was a male figure in front of them and he appeared more as if he was in deep mourning than anything else.

Then, slowly, the ghost turned his face to them.

"Shit," Lorcan whispered.

Yeah, Brendan could echo that. The man in front of them was dressed splendidly, but he was dressed in older clothes, more Georgian than anything else. He had the sharp cheekbones that seemed to have been carried through the family but darker hair, pulled back into a long tail behind him.

And then, as he watched, the ghost lowered his hand, the palm cupping in a move that was unmistakably the sign of someone smothering another.

Then the man turned back to his work, looking down again at whoever he was killing. And, as he turned his head, Brendan spotted the lines along his neck, the line of blue bruises and there was a flicker as his face suddenly turned pale with blotched red, as if he'd been choked to death.

"Get to the stairs," Brendan whispered. Lorcan remained frozen, so he shoved at him. "Go," he snapped, a little louder.

It was too loud. The man's head snapped to them again, more focused as if acknowledging them this time. Lorcan stumbled back and then obeyed, moving towards the stairs because the idiot still wasn't wearing a talisman.

"You are," the ghost whispered. "Are, but aren't." The head tilted curiously to the side, fingers reaching down to stroke over whoever it was that he had killed.

It was a small room, next to the main room.

And the runner under the door was a dull grey...

Brendan reached for the door handle and yanked the door shut. He could hear an almighty wail that suddenly vanished when he slammed the door shut and the iron was fully connected.

He crouched and locked it by twisting at the tumblers. One step back and he could see the organisation of the rooms and winced.

Christ, that had to have been a nursery.

The urge to be sick threatened and, for a second, Brendan was sure that he'd give into it. But he turned on his heel and headed back towards the staircase where Lorcan lurked looking unsure.

"You banished him?" Lorcan asked as Brendan swung him around and directed him down the stairs.

"Locked the door. There was iron in it. They must have trapped the ghost inside." And Jesus, maybe the insanity of Phineas Ambros and the terrifying strength of Vivienne Ozwald were making more sense because living next to that for their childhood would surely mess anyone up.

Christ, Lysander might have even been eager to leave.

"All the way down?"

"Where else can we go?" Brendan snapped at the idiot in front of him. "You need a talisman."

“They’re becoming aware,” Lorcan hissed, stopping and turning. “We waited too long.”

Yeah. Brendan gave him a gentle shove again. “It is what it is,” Brendan huffed, half tempted to throw something at the kid. “Down.”

Chapter Thirteen

"I SWEAR," STUART SAID, ALMOST TROTTING to keep up with Boss, "if the graves had been visible-"

Nate resisted the urge to smirk in pleasure when Boss whirled, becoming a silhouette against the headlights of the cars that were giving them their light as they set up operations. Folding his arms as he sat on the bonnet of the little blue mini, Nate waited for the show to begin.

Annoyingly though, it seemed that whatever expression was on Boss' face was enough to make Stuart back away, hands raised in the air as if in supplication.

"Daylight's fading," Omar pointed out quietly as he double checked the circle they'd created with crystals. "Do we have any ideas about getting into the house?"

"Campion's made contact-"

"Astral projection again?" Faye asked, tugging her jacket around herself a little tighter.

"No. Via a phone call," Boss muttered, somewhat scathingly, which seemed unfair given that Brendan had done it earlier. "They're locked in the middle of the house, but he can get up to the top balcony."

"The recruits?" Omar asked.

"They're fine." Boss scrubbed a hand over his face and then stared over the door that they'd had zero luck trying to force. "The minute we start trying to get into that house with magic, we're going to stir the ghosts back up again. Johnson at the fountain and Eric Redgrave at the door."

Nate nodded at the reminder as did the others. Johnson had been screaming at whoever had dunked his head into the fountain and then crashed into the brick work when they'd turned up while Eric Redgrave had been stuck in a strange loop of suddenly crashing to the floor, head seized and slammed in a clear ambush.

A vicious ambush, he remedied, staring at the crack in the stone of the porch.

"And let's try not to piss them off. If the pair out here are linked to the ones inside, we could make things a lot worse for them inside if we get them going again."

They all looked at each other and then Nate grinned over at Omar. "I'm pretty sure you're the person least likely to piss anyone off," he said hopefully.

With a long stare, Omar sighed and walked out of the protection circle and towards the front door.

"How is he?" Nate asked, sobering quickly as Boss stepped close to him and checked over the talisman that Nate had created while the others had been listening to Stuart whinging about the graves.

Boss hummed. "Unsurprisingly, give Campion a problem and he'll take it as a personal insult. He seems fine. The most on it that he's been in ages." He lifted the talisman over his head and turned towards the door. "Do you have some of Campion's storage crystals?"

Nate nodded and dug into his pocket, handing one

to Boss. "On a scale of one to ten," Nate said, glancing up at the fading light, "How likely is it that Brendan has finally learned not to fling his magic around like he's got endless reserves?"

Snorting, Boss shoved his hands in his pockets and followed Omar to the door.

Great.

Inside, Jake watched as Cole had returned looking pale, being almost propelled into the room by Brendan. "Talisman," Brendan snapped at Jake, holding out a hand.

Almost stumbling over at the order, Jake summoned the spare talisman from the table and gave it to Brendan who roughly shoved it over Cole's head and then stomped to the chairs. "We have a problem," Brendan sighed.

"There's a fucking ghost upstairs," Cole jumped in. "He..." he shook his head and looked away, sinking down into the nearest chair.

"Not our biggest problem," Brendan said shaking his head. "You were right: that body on the first floor was Ruby Ambros. She was living here until twenty fifteen which also means, at the moment, she is our best bet to be the killer."

Oh.

"Wait," Rob said, standing up. "Seriously? We're trapped in her house, she's a ghost, and she's a fucking killer?"

Cole was staring at Brendan in horror and then at the walls where Brendan's wards still shimmered. With a nervous look, he walked close to the door and placed his hand on it over the wards.

"Could you do this if the walls were lined with iron?"

"No." Brendan was staring at the door. "Open it."

Jake stood, heart in his throat as he watched Cole blink at Brendan and then look around at the others. An odd expression crossed his face as he glanced back at Brendan and then he turned, hand reaching slowly for the handle and opening it.

The hall beyond was tinted, as if they were peering through a sheer scarf, and seemed to be empty.

"Are you blocking sound?" Daphne asked, stepping a little closer to Cole. Brendan nodded, fingers drumming slightly on the table before something passed through the veil-like wards.

A scream tore through into the room, female and terrified. The sound seemed to shudder down Jake's spine and made him suck in a gasp. Cole didn't appear to react to it, but instead stepped to one side and seemed to be peering up the stairs. After a moment, Daphne made a strange sound and joined him.

"What?" Brendan asked, standing.

"There's…" Daphne turned, eyes wide. "There's a girl on the stairs."

"Ruby?"

"Way too young," Cole murmured, eyes fixed on whatever was happening.

"Way too old," Daphne argued. "She's dressed like…" Daphne suddenly swallowed. "Oh god, I think it's one of the original occupants."

It was a perverse horrified fascination that drew Jake closer. Standing with the other two, he craned his neck to see. There, on top of the stairs was a girl, young, too young, little more than a child, dressed in a long dress that seemed to swamp her. Her blond hair was loose, and she was on her knees, begging someone and shaking, terrified-

And then her chin was lifted as if being moved by another and she trembled worse than before.

Abruptly, she fell backwards and the horrific scream that accompanied her was painful to hear. The sounds of bones breaking made Jake wince as she crashed to the floor of the hall, broken body staring up as she lay in the middle of the collapsed chandelier as if it wasn't even there. Then she whimpered and tried to move, painfully dragging herself as if frantic to escape something that they couldn't see.

Then something opposite, over the girl's body, caught Jake's eye. A woman watched them. Pale and old with gleaming blue grey eyes and the smallest smile on her face. She stood by the bricked up east wing, seeming completely aware and unnervingly intent. For all that she looked old, she didn't appear frail or worried.

Nor did she seem to be lost in her own death.

Cole slammed the door shut and pressed back against it. The noise, the screams, the sharp blue eyes, all vanished like fingers had been snapped.

"Fuck," Brendan hissed. "She's aware of us. She isn't reliving anything…" he shook his head.

"Was that Ruby Ambros? Has she tried to attack us?" Daphne demanded.

Brendan shook his head. "The others are out on the grounds," he hissed suddenly.

"She's trapped in the house," Cole said. "Surely."

Brendan let out an annoyed breath. "I'm going to call the others," he muttered. "Stay here."

How…

Brendan disappeared behind the wall again leaving them behind.

"Great," Rob called. "Thanks for that," he added sarcastically and then looked back at them all. "He's treating us like we're useless," he complained.

"We're trapped," Jake argued. "It's not exactly fun for anyone." He turned to Cole. "You said you saw a ghost upstairs?"

Cole nodded slowly. "A man. He was...he suffocated someone..."

Daphne winced and looked away and then tilted her head. Bizarrely, she then knelt down and started to cast magic down at the carpet, ripping up the motheaten pattern to reveal the stones underneath.

"Why?" Rob asked, seeming past the point of being too surprised by anything that she did.

Daphne didn't reply, instead continuing to create a free square of space before she flicked her hand at the floor. Upon it slowly started to appear the names from the Ambros family tree.

"Here," Daphne said, pointing at the names towards the top. "I think that girl was Avis Ambros, the daughter of Henry Ambros. She would have been fourteen when she died according to the dates on the grave."

"And your ghost?" Jake asked, glancing over at Cole who had stepped closer. "Any possibilities?"

Cole's hazel eyes scanned over the names, just as the wards suddenly rippled.

"An attack?" Rob asked, unfolding his arms.

"Could just be Brendan reworking and strengthening

the wards," Daphne pointed out, but her voice wobbled with nerves.

"There," Cole said suddenly, pointing at a name in the middle of the tree. "William Ambros."

"You're sure?"

Cole nodded. "He... I think..." he looked away. "His eldest son died the same year he was born according to that. I think that was who he was killing."

Jake sat down, not really caring that there wasn't a sofa where he'd been standing. "They really are mad," he whispered. "The Ambros family. All this..." he looked around and then up at the others. "Is this just like their version of a mental institution? Let the mad deal with the mad?"

"Imagine living here," Daphne whispered and she looked ill as she leaned against the wall. "Night after night knowing that these...how could you raise your children in the same building as a ghost who killed his own child?"

"She stayed," Rob said with a harsh swallow. "She stayed beyond needing to." He eyed them all up. "So how far do we think that Ruby Ambros had gone?"

The wards fluttered again.

"So," Cole said looking up at the ceiling, "here's a question. Potentially, the people living in this house did so as a punishment. Haunted until they obeyed or went mad." He tilted his head as his eyes dropped to theirs. "So what was here that drove William Ambros to kill his son and Ruby Ambros to kill anyone that ventured onto the property?"

Oh fuck.

"The east wing," Daphne whispered, eyes round with

terror. "Every family member sentenced here seemed to have tried to lock it away, protect themselves somehow. They boarded everything up."

Jake batted his hand as if scrolling through the family tree until the original family members that had lived at the lodge were shown. "Cecelia, Henry's mother, Constance, Henry's wife. His children: Emma, Avis, Susanna, Agnes and Henry. His other two sons never stepped foot in here. Richard was executed with him and Robert Ambros was taken by the Council and never reunited with his family."

"Henry Ambros Junior died shortly after birth," Rob butted in. "Then the deaths are as follows: Avis, Cecelia, Susanna, Emma, Agnes then Constance. By the time Robert Ambros came to the property in 1507 the house was abandoned."

"Someone was in the house," Jake pointed out. "She was begging someone, then thrown down the stairs. That's thirteen years before the last death."

There was an awkward exchange of glances and Daphne pursed her lips, apparently annoyed that she couldn't think of an answer. He suspected that she was exhausted and probably beating herself up about the mirror spell…

"I'll go and talk to Brendan," Jake offered, heading towards the gap in the wall even as he felt a flicker of nerves at the idea of doing so. "See if he knows what's happening with the protection spell too. Be back as soon as I can."

He didn't bother to look back; the only indication he had that the others weren't following him was that he couldn't hear them squeeze through the gap in-between the wall.

By the time he found Brendan, the man was out on the balcony speaking into his phone, arms resting on the precarious looking railings. Jake stood, suddenly unsure as he glanced back down the hallway that he came from; at the empty rooms behind and the closed door next to the only furnished room.

He wandered through an open door and into the smallest room. Peering around, he wasn't exactly sure what he was looking for, only that he wanted to wait for Brendan's tone to soften a little.

Outside, the light was turning into the dim blue of approaching sunset and the grounds were becoming silhouetted shadows. But he could see a sweeping clearness that probably had been the gardens at one point, surrounded by walls and thick shrubbery to create hidden, tucked away clearings by the house. Dimly, over the tops of these, he could almost see the path that they had followed, the one that snaked around the house, yet seemed to keep them at some distance from it.

It should have been an amazing place to grow-up, he thought as he stared across the grounds. Although at least some had been given the chance to grow up, he realised as he turned slowly back to the door and walked into the hallway once more. It was curiosity that had him pause outside the door by the master bedroom, the one that was locked and looked unnervingly normal for what had happened inside. Faintly, he could hear creaking, as if something was pacing.

"It's locked," Brendan said quietly.

The unexpected sound of his voice made Jake jump

and snap his head towards the man. Brendan was leaning against the door frame, arms folded and watching him with narrowed blue eyes.

With a last, unsure look at the door, Jake stepped away from it and nodded. "Uh... we...what do you think is in the east wing? Because we thought that maybe-"

He broke himself off when Brendan raised an unimpressed eyebrow and stomped past him.

Right. Yeah. If they'd figured that out then maybe Brendan had too. Not sure what to do, Jake watched as Brendan headed for the wall at the edge of the west wing. Then inclined his head towards the stairs where the spiral staircase became straight.

They made it down about halfway before Jake became aware of Brendan stopping and lighting up the area with a spell and making it so bright that Jake almost winced. He turned and stared awkwardly as the man traced his hands over the walls of the stairwell.

"What are you doing?" he asked, curious.

"There should be another level," Brendan said, moving down a step. His face suddenly smoothed and he reached into his jacket pocket, bringing out a biro. He started to trace the wall, coming down a few more steps which forced Jake to take a few more steps down, until there was a fully shaped door in front of them.

"But the walls are lined with iron, right?" Jake asked. "We can't get through with magic."

"Mm. Unless it's not a wall," Brendan said vaguely and then seemed to refocus on Jake. "There's a pretty big hammer in the conservatory. Would you mind?"

By the time Jake made it back upstairs, the others were awkwardly gathered on the staircase and Jake found himself clambering over them to give the hammer to Brendan.

"You really think-" Rob begun for what didn't sound like the first time, "that you'll get through the iron with a hammer?"

"I'd imagine it's an iron cage for the bricks," Brendan replied. "If it's only on one side of this wall then we should be fine. And there was a door here."

"Would she know that?" Daphne asked quietly. "It's Ruby's house after all."

"We'll soon find out," Brendan replied, hefting the hammer as magic flashed up it briefly to reinforce it, though how well it would work when the hammer was smashing into iron was anyone's guess. Then Brendan swung.

Plaster rained down on them, and Rob put up a hasty shielding spell when it looked for a second as if Daphne had forgotten why she shouldn't. It only took a few swings to reveal that, behind the plaster, there was in fact a door, covered with thin iron mesh that almost seemed like netting.

Ignoring the iron and kneeling, Brendan studied the lock and then started to pick at it which was...Jake looked away, not really sure if he was allowed to see that skill. There was a click and then a few more swings with the hammer. Then the door was freed and opened.

Beyond it lay darkness, only slightly illuminated by the light from Brendan's spell. With a quick gesture, Brendan seemed to redistribute the light, casting across the tiny space and showing that it'd opened into a short hallway that seemed to lead to a dead-end.

"There's a door on each side," Cole murmured as Brendan clambered through.

"And it's silent," Daphne whispered. "Maybe we're still in the safe part of the house."

"Maybe," Brendan replied, but he sounded doubtful. "We'll stick to the west side first."

"You can tell after all those stairs?" Jake asked, surprised.

A flick on his hands again had the wall on their right shimmering for a second and Brendan nodded towards the other side. "That has iron in it," he said. "So does the wall ahead." With a determined stride, the man headed towards the door and went for the handle.

It opened.

Beyond, dimly lit through weak light streaming through heavy curtains and the spell Brendan was using, there was what looked like a desk and bookshelves. A yank at the curtains pulled in more light as the spell ended and it was indeed a study or library of sorts.

"God, you're gonna get too excited by this, aren't you?" Rob muttered to Cole who was looking around with interest.

"How long do you think this has been closed off?" Daphne asked curiously as she went to the desk and flicked through the papers upon it.

"Not long," Brendan said as he stood in front of a shelf, looking at a small framed picture. He lifted it to study and Jake got an all too brief impression of a coloured photograph.

"S.A." Daphne said as she picked up a pen. "Sebastian Ambros?"

Glancing over, Jake paused as he saw Cole suddenly pale. "What?"

"Why would it be closed off with iron?" Cole asked, his breath fogged...

Shit.

Brendan whirled, a sharp movement of his fingers bringing them all closer to him as he looked around.

"We need to get out of here," Daphne breathed. "Before-"

"We need answers," Brendan corrected. "One ghost is better than the six on the other side."

"I can't see anything," Rob snapped. "Cole's just being a paranoid-"

The figure of a man stood in the doorway suddenly, flickering unsteadily in the jumping light. His expression was cruelly amused as he stepped forward, brown eyes sweeping over them and dismissing all until his gaze rested on Brendan. "You're all grown up," he said, stepping forward a little bit.

"Who are you?" Brendan demanded.

"I used to watch you," the man continued, stepping even closer. "Oh, but you were so well protected. Still have no idea how she did it." He thickened a little, that was the only word that Jake had for it. Became something like a normal man, non-descript with brown hair and eyes and a tanned complexion. There wasn't a single file that resonated with his appearance and yet Brendan stiffened suddenly.

"Mr Pembroke?" he asked in some disbelief. "You...you moved abroad," he said, sounding baffled.

"You know him?" Cole asked, swinging his head around in a disturbingly owl-like fashion.

"He...was my next-door neighbour," Brendan said

with some disbelief and then something crossed his face. "You were-"

"Spying on you? The child never claimed by Phineas Ambros? Of course." The man...Mr Pembroke smiled. "I did always wonder if your mother would grow suspicious of me. She never did. I found her...much changed from the girl I remembered."

Dimly, Jake could hear Daphne whispering to herself.

"Did they end up taking the boy?" Mr Pembroke asked, getting close, smiling. "So many fascinating things to pass-"

Brendan raised his hand a fraction of a second after Daphne raised hers and it was her spell that hit first, cascading around the room as Pembroke wailed suddenly and then misted forms rose up, engulfing Pembroke until the ghost stood at the door as if still alive, tilting his head in mild mannered curiosity as the mirror spell took full effect.

At the desk sat an elderly woman. Made of the same fogged substance as he, Ruby Ambros was sat back in her husband's chair, one delicate eyebrow raised and wow, how many times had Jake seen that exact expression on Brendan's face?

Pembroke snorted. "I thought Maeve would see through me first. I spent far more time with her than with you."

Ruby continued to watch him. Brendan was staring down at Daphne with something like reluctant admiration before he strode across the room towards the door. "This side," Brendan said, walking through the image of Pembroke who was still smiling at Ruby.

"You do know that you are far too late?" Pembroke said, his bravado fading a little as he seemed to become unnerved by her calm silence and wow was it awkward to walk through him when it seemed as if he was staring at them with that expression. "Everything is already in motion. It was too late as soon as I had the letter."

"We have our own plans," Ruby said after a moment. "We always adjust."

"We?" Pembroke asked sharply. "And who exactly is 'we'?"

Ruby simply smiled. "But you have proven to be useful. In so many ways. The information-"

"I have given you nothing," Pembroke snapped. Cole, who had been the furthest away suddenly hesitated, looking back over his shoulder.

"Cole," Jake hissed.

"I have lost track as to how many potions I've given you," Ruby said frankly, reaching for a glass to sip, watching him with cool blue eyes.

Pembroke faltered, looking worried suddenly. "You wouldn't kill me here. You wouldn't dare."

"Needs must," she said, finishing her drink and standing. She brushed some stray hairs off of her skirt and then sighed. "It is unfortunately rather slow."

Pembroke was breathing quicker now and hurled a spell at her, or at least tried if the hand gesture was anything to go by. But nothing happened and his horror made it apparent that he had intended for there to be an obvious effect.

She sighed and moved past him, seemingly unconcerned. Pembroke reached for her, but he couldn't seem to grip properly or have strength to do anything as she opened up one of the bookshelves-

Cole reached through Ruby gently. Part of Jake knew what would happen as Cole's hand reached for the same hidden hook that Ruby had used six years ago. Next to him, Jake heard Daphne draw in a breath as the wooden bookshelf was opened to reveal a contorted corpse. Despite Pembroke's attitude, Jake felt a flicker of pity because the fingers were clawed, the mouth hanging open in an endless scream and the smell suddenly horrific.

"We should go," Cole said, his voice hard as Ruby reached calmly for the dying, flailing man and started to guide him in.

"She doesn't look remotely bothered," Daphne whispered. "She-"

As Cole stepped into the hall, Brendan slammed the door shut behind him and then reached into the bag, salting the door strip and taking out small lines of iron to lay underneath.

"Pembroke is not on the family tree," Rob said as Brendan stood. "Right?"

"Gonna guess it wasn't his name," Cole muttered as he headed towards the stairs.

"There's no-one he could be on the tree," Daphne argued. "Wrong age or wrong gender. That was…he didn't sound as if he were willingly spying for her," she added looking at Jake. "She was-"

They all stopped at the sound of something going through a wall. Brendan stood there, fist half in the opposite side and staring at the wall, panting.

The four of them stood in awkward silence as he shook his head. "Go back to the stairs," Brendan ordered.

"Are you-"

"Go." The snapped command left almost no room for arguing. Unsure, they all scrambled back, back into the stairs where Cole closed the door over so that a sliver of the room beyond remained.

"Should we-"

"No," Cole said, staring at the door as if confused by its existence.

They all jumped at the sound of a dulled explosion. "Think that's Campion?" Rob asked nervously.

"He's gonna burn through his magic," Daphne worried, shaking her head. "Why is Brendan so angry about-"

Jake sat down on one of the steps. "Well…it was his old next door neighbour….Pembroke? in the study and…I mean he asked if the boy was taken so seems like maybe…maybe he had a hand in Nicolas Ambros' uh… kidnapping?…if that's the right word?"

The others suddenly looked as uncomfortable as Jake felt. Cole's fingers drummed on the door knob for a second as if he were having a silent debate with himself.

"We should go downstairs," Rob said, sounding awkward. "Leave him to it. I mean, shit, imagine not realising your next-door neighbour was a spy plotting to nab your kid?"

Cole blinked and stared at him. "Why would anyone suspect that?" and then sucked in a surprised breath when the door was yanked open by a pissed off looking Brendan. Rob yelped and stumbled back, just about catching himself from tripping the rest of the way down the stairs.

"I suggest *you* go downstairs," Brendan snapped.

"I-"

"Fuck off," Brendan hissed and Rob suddenly was moving down the stairs. "One of you go with him," he ordered, turning back to the hall. "Genuinely don't give a fuck who it is, as long as you keep him out of trouble."

Cole turned.

"Not you."

Huh? Puzzled, Jake turned to see if there was some obvious reason, but Brendan wasn't looking at them.

"I'll go," Daphne said quietly. "If you're going back to the entrance hall, I'll be more trouble than anything else."

Jake nodded. "You might need to do it again."

She smiled. "I'll stick my head out of the drawing room. It might draw their attention," she offered and then with a last unsure look between Cole and Brendan, turned and vanished down the stairs.

"And why not me?" Cole asked once she'd gone.

"I have my reasons," Brendan muttered. "We're going to have a chat with Ruby Ambros."

Chapter Fourteen

CLEVER OR TOO CLEVER?

Boss's voice kept ringing in Brendan's ears as he watched the two lads in front of him as they explored the room that would open back onto the landing where he'd first caught up with Lorcan and Daphne.

Either way, he was keeping the lad with him.

The room they were in was moth eaten and probably hadn't been touched in a century. There was a family painting on the wall again, but this time there were different faces, an older style of dress that seemed roughly to be in a Victorian style and only a man, a woman and a young boy. A child's tin soldier was on the floor just peeking out from under the collapsing sofa.

There were more books again, but age and neglect had mostly gotten to them and they were almost crumbling, too fragile to handle without equipment and impossible to tell if they were family secrets written down or just penny books picked up from wherever the family had shopped.

"Were any doors open when you and Daphne first arrived?" he heard Jake ask Lorcan quietly.

"No," Lorcan replied. "But then we went to the windows straight away. The east wing was all boarded up and we only walked by three doors. All shut. Same as you did."

"Are we really doing this?" Jake asked, turning to Brendan as he sat at the table with the three talismans. "Walking over to her murder site?"

"You can swap with Daphne if you want," Brendan said clicking his jaw as he continued with the spell. Linking them all together should manage to create a bubble of protection, as long as they remained within a certain distance.

For a moment, it seemed as if Jake might actually argue, but then the boy slumped and leaned his chin on the back of one of the precarious wooden chairs that Brendan had taken. He looked like he wanted to say more. A lot more.

Mercifully, he remained quiet, instead watching Brendan closely as if to get his head around the spell he was using.

"How many graves were outside?" Brendan asked as he weaved threads of magic together, the light a soft blue that he always thought looked ironically ghostly in a spell that was meant to repel the damned things.

Lorcan gestured for the bag and pulled out a rather dog-eared, stained notebook and laid it on the table. Brendan let his eyes flick between the spell he was weaving and the hastily scribbled diagram.

"Henry Ambros," Lorcan said, pointing a finger at the largest square that had tiny neat script like writing next to it, and why did it not surprise him that Lorcan had insanely neat handwriting, even in a rush? "His sister was with him. Then his daughters, wife and still born son. Next three graves are more recent-"

"Relatively," Jake butted in, starting to rock the chair that creaked in warning against the harsh treatment.

"William Ambros, our study ghost with his infant son.

Wife too. Then a hundred years or so later are Jeremy and Roberta..." Lorcan paused and glanced up at the portrait on the wall, "Who...might be those two?"

"Sebastian?"

Lorcan shook his head. "If he's on the grounds, he wasn't buried there."

Right. Brendan studied the diagram, not really sure what was bothering him about it. "We step out of this door and we're in the oldest part of the house and Ruby's murder site."

"But...we're heading for the door, right?" Jake double checked.

Lorcan let out a breath. "Previous generations closed up the east wing and you want to-"

"They won't let us out until sunrise," Brendan argued. "I'm not sitting and waiting-"

"But you could, right?" Lorcan challenged. "Rather than casting on everything and anything and forgetting that we have no food to help you keep up your strength."

It made Brendan's jaw ache to keep it clenched shut as he glared at the boy. Thankfully, it seemed the foul look he was shooting Lorcan was enough to make the boy throw up his hands and turn away, shaking his head.

Wait. The boy.

"Where's Richard Ambros?" Brendan asked, mind already racing to answer the question as he asked it.

"Buried at Ambros, I'd imagine," Lorcan said after a slight pause as Jake tilted his head and leaned in to look at the diagram.

"No, he...the son, right?" Jake asked, peering down.

"You're asking about Henry Ambros' oldest son. The controversial execution?"

Lorcan turned around, eyes narrowed. "Controversial is a bit of a-?"

Jake looked genuinely pleased to know something Lorcan didn't. "The...it's the execution that caused a shadow over the Council's beginnings, right?" he double checked with Brendan.

Kid needed to get some confidence. Silently, Brendan nodded.

"The Council decided he was too old to risk leaving alive. He'd just turned thirteen. Contemporary accounts make hints towards him being starved and beaten while kept in prison for over a year. Kid was eleven when he went in." Jake traced his finger over the graves, meandering between the squares that Lorcan had drawn to represent each. "We studied it in history, about the ethics of the Council and how much they alienated the remaining Coven families in those early days." He frowned as he looked up at them both, brown eyes narrowed in confusion. "Surely they sent him back to his family? His body I mean."

Lorcan stared at him and then suddenly pulled the notebook forward, flicking to a new page as he started to roughly sketch out something that looked like half the outline of the house. Then he tore the page off and did it again, the shape changing slightly.

"Trying to work out where the chapel would be?" Brendan asked quietly.

The kid paused and then glanced up, an odd expression on his face for a second. He nodded. "Obviously the east wing," he muttered, "But we need to narrow that down; we can't just wander aimlessly."

"Chapel?" Jake asked.

"Family Chapels. Families have them inside so that they can pray or cast with ease. Most old families have a family chapel. And sometimes," Brendan added, looking over at the door, "the dead are buried in the Chapel, not the garden."

"Wait, you think…you think that this is all because of Richard Ambros?" Jake asked, sounding stunned.

Lorcan opened his mouth and then shut it again, slumping against the wall in an oddly defeated manner. Probably because he was an arrogant toe-rag and hadn't seen it first.

"Abused children," Brendan said, trying to ignore the sudden twist in his stomach at the idea, "when killed can often become vicious. A child's fury without an adult's logic. From his point of view, his parents let him be taken, let him be killed. He was executed before his father; a fact that has added to the weight that many in the original Council were looking for vengeance rather than justice."

"Probably justified," Jake murmured.

"Either way. If the mother buried him in the house then it would explain a lot. Those sorts of strong emotions carry their own power to influence a place. And then with Ruby's killing spree-"

"She killed the first time to protect her child. Maybe that…that grew? Maybe she became obsessed with the idea that she was protecting them?" Jake looked over at Lorcan. "It would explain why Lady Vivienne finds the topic… awkward."

Lorcan chewed at his lip, eyes on the page. "That has merit," he said slowly. "But his mother…Lady Constance and her daughters also died in this house. So either you have a family protecting him or…or potentially a lot of abused, upset children wandering around the east wing."

"He might have turned on his sisters," Jake pointed out, wincing a little as he said it. "They were safe and protected, he wasn't. My mum…there was a story where my grandma lived. Said a family bought their freedom, but didn't quite have enough for their eldest son; the slave master put up the price suddenly, some sort of twisted payback or something." Jake shook his head in disgust at the idea. "The boy died, but he'd been told all sorts of things. He came for his family in the night. No-one went by the property; my grandma banned my mum from going anywhere near it whenever they went to visit. She said it felt like…hurt. Raw hurt. As you say, a child's fury without an adult's logic."

"And five hundred plus years of it?" Lorcan pointed out. "That's not going away in one night, Campion, no matter what you do."

"We can burn the body." Brendan finished with the spells and lay the talisman down on the table, glancing between the two lads that stood almost frozen in front of him. "But first, we are going to have a chat with Ruby."

"Burn the body?" Jake replied looking stunned. "They'll…Jesus…" he looked away. "I feel like there's gonna be an army on the other side of that door just because you said it."

"Don't be dramatic," Brendan sighed as he tossed them back the talismans. "And don't stray further than three feet away from me, otherwise you'll be outside of the protection."

Jake let out a wobbling breath but nodded and slipped the talisman over his neck. Lorcan stared down at his, thumb rubbing over the silver cage holding the stones and plants he'd provided. Then, as if suddenly aware he was being watched, he straightened and slipped the talisman on too.

"Good spell work," he muttered.

Maybe the kid was just a bit weird, Brendan thought as he nodded and strode to the door, hefting the back-pack once more. Then, letting out a breath, he opened the door, almost prepared for anything except the sight of Ruby Ambros opposite him, waiting.

She flickered. Mostly appearing as the elderly woman he'd seen in the study, but sometimes there was a jolt and she was younger, hair red and pinned up, slipping out of its braids. She said nothing, instead tracking him with all too familiar blue eyes.

He refused to be cowed. Especially by anyone with the surname of Ambros. Instead, he took a step forward, pleased when her eyes flickered down as if estimating the reach of his protection spell. Behind him, one of the boys was breathing loudly and he could see his own breath fog the air in front of him.

A scream echoed out in the distance, beyond the messy bricked up hallway and there was the sound of something scratching.

He took another step. And another.

And then nearly swore when the door behind him slammed shut, closing the boys within.

"You'll thank me for it," she said slowly, turning to survey the hall below, her back to him and her arms stretched out along the railings looking like a queen showing off her land.

"Why?" He glanced back at the door. His magic wasn't flaring up, so the pair weren't being attacked and, in fairness, they hadn't been attacked by anything in that room.

She didn't reply, but inclined her head and he eyed her up cautiously before tightening the spells around him, lessening the range but thickening the protection. It allowed him to stand by her side as she suddenly became younger, eyes sharp and focused on the stairs.

The girl upon it was young and blond and he sighed at the sight of her again as she fell to her knees, eyes red as she begged something that he couldn't see, scrambled at what must have been a hand at her throat and screamed with such terror that Brendan found he had to look away. Towards the door below, Jonah Summers still clawed at the door and then stumbled back, turning to flee down the gallery, stumbling with frantic footsteps as he went.

"They're harmless," she said, fingers smoothing over the rotting wood as if it were still luxuriously polished.

"You killed him," Brendan said, nodding towards Jonah as he appeared again, stuck in his loop.

She smiled. "We have a motto," she said, watching the man flee from her. "We keep our secrets." She nodded down at the man. "He did not understand that." She shrugged. "He was weak."

"And Tom Redgrave?"

"My children were little when he died. Do you think I would allow his ghost to wander?" She flickered and vanished, reappearing suddenly, further away and walking away from the hall. "My first foray into dark magic. Necromancy. Soul destruction."

"People rarely come back from that," Brendan pointed out, still watching down below. Now that he was looking for it, he could see the way that the door rattled sometimes as if someone was battering at the door, even as Jonah tried to open it.

Ted Johnson had been found in the fountain. Had he still been alive when Jonah had been running for his life? Had one tried to help the other?

"I was lost years before that day." She inclined her head towards the middle of the stairs. "For years I was convinced you could still see the blood engrained in the stone steps." She turned to look up at him. "Can you see it?"

He forced himself to look away from the girl begging on her knees and instead swept his eyes down the stairs, yet there was nothing that he could obviously see that would hint towards the atrocities that had occurred on the staircase.

Then Ruby was no longer beside him. When he looked down the hall, she was stood by the archways that led to the windows where she had died. With a last glance down at the hall, he pushed off the banister and followed her, sparing a glance at where Jake and Lorcan were. "Why do you say you were lost?"

She merely smiled at him as he watched her, unwilling to lose track of her or have her behind him, yet all too aware of how hard that could be with a ghost.

"They like you," she said nodding down at the drive as he stood next to her and finally (*finally!*) got a glimpse of Boss below. The cars that had driven them in were within a circle and there were tunnels dug along the drive to reveal the iron. The sun was almost down, setting behind the trees and making the branches look like blackening claws in the burning pink of the sky.

"Still, there is over twelve hours to go," she mused as she watched below, "Before the sun rises again."

"Is that a threat?" he asked.

"If I wanted you dead," she said softly, "you would not have been born."

It shocked him enough that he turned his head to stare at her, but all he saw was the archway and the shadows that played along the ripped wallpaper as the sun fell beyond the tree line.

Chapter Fifteen

THE DOOR WOULDN'T OPEN. No matter how much he shoved and pressed and rattled it, nothing fucking happened. Frustrated, Jake pounded his hand flat on the door before leaning against it, half convinced he might be able to hear what was happening.

It took a few seconds to realise he was alone at the door. Baffled, he turned and swept his gaze across the room. "Cole?" he asked quietly, peering around.

He wasn't in the room. Instead, Jake's eyes lit upon the still ajar door at the edge of the room and he felt a sudden moment of prophecy that something awful was about to happen.

"Cole?" Jake yelled as he stormed through the door and into the darkened hallway. "What-"

His friend was sat on the floor before the study door with it open because he was a fucking moron. Opposite, the study they'd been in earlier was darkened and Jake froze, hating that he couldn't fully see within anymore. "Is…is the ghost-"

He jumped when the figure appeared close to the door frame. The cobweb of broken capillaries suddenly much clearer and one eye too bloodshot to be dismissed as normal. He was so close that if Cole had been standing his breath would have hit the figure. But Cole didn't even flinch, tapping pointedly on the salt and iron that Brendan had placed across the doorway making the ghost hiss with frustration

"Why are you talking to him?" Jake asked, voice dropping to an almost whisper, as if that would make the ghost not hear him.

His friend turned to look at Jake as if he were stupid. "Because we're trying to solve a case?"

Seriously?

"What was your real name?" Cole asked, shifting to tuck one of his legs in a little closer to his body. It should have looked silly; him sitting crossed legged on the floor like the ghost was going to tell him a bedtime story, but Cole looked worryingly at ease with the situation.

The ghost sneered at him.

"She blocked off the stairs," Jake reminded Cole cautiously. "Even Ruby Ambros didn't want to deal with-"

"She blocked it off because she couldn't use the study anymore. What else was the point of being on this level?" Cole asked, rolling his eyes. "Or maybe it was added protection when her kids were upstairs. Who the fuck knows or cares?" Cole turned his attention back to the ghost. "Your real name?"

The man smiled. "Do you honestly believe that it would help you?"

Jesus. Jake scrubbed a hand over his face and found himself leaning back against the wall. "We can't even corroborate that he's telling the truth. He could lie over and over and we'd have no way of telling. He'll just lead us down a dead end." He winced. "Pun not intended."

But Cole was still watching the ghost. "How many people did Ruby Ambros kill in this house?"

For fuck sakes, sometimes it was like talking to a brick wall with Cole. The ghost suddenly tilted his head in a motion too quick to be possible if he were alive. "Far more than you know," he whispered, sounding delighted. "Too many for her to leave."

Huh?

"And you weren't spying for her?" Cole pressed. "Willingly, I mean?"

"You saw," the ghost said, his image jolting a little. For a second, he was younger, but it was almost too much of a flash, hardly long enough to even process it had happened, let alone see what the image had been.

"But you came here," Jake said, curious despite himself. "Why would you come here if you didn't know you were spying…had she spelled you to come here?"

The ghost said nothing. Instead, he reached out, the air in front of him rippling as he dragged his fingers along the boundaries created by the iron. "She's a bitch," the ghost said eventually. His eyes fell to the iron bar at the bottom of the door.

"She's dead," Cole said quietly, not moving even as Jake straightened, slightly unnerved by the ghost's focus on the iron bar.

The ghost's head snapped to theirs slightly, suddenly intent. "Did Brendan Campion have more children?"

"When did you die?" Cole countered.

The ghost seemed to weigh it up, glancing between them. "Two thousand and eight," he announced.

"No," Cole lied smoothly. "No more children."

The ghost's head tilted, slowly, until it was at an angle that made it almost look as if his neck had snapped. The air grew colder, their breath becoming more and more obvious and Jake tried desperately to steady his breathing because it seemed as if the ghost…Pembroke – whoever he was, was listening to something.

"Liar," the ghost breathed, eyes staring at Cole.

The temperature was dropping rapidly now and there was the strangest sensation of something vibrating in the air, the taste of it almost metallic. "Cole," Jake said, staring at his friend's shoulder. "Close the door. We should go downstairs," Jake hissed.

"Yes," the ghost practically purred. "Run."

"Ambros is dead," Cole said suddenly, fixing his gaze upon the ghost. "Phineas is dead, his heir is dead. The line is done."

The ghost stared at him and then smiled. Then laughed. Deep, amused peels that echoed off the walls. "Are you certain?" he asked.

"Cole," Jake yelled, grabbing his friend's shoulder. "Come on. We need to-"

The lights, both from spells and candles, went out and left them completely blind.

Brendan ran his hands over the rough brick work. Apparently, no-one had ever tried to hide the haste and panic with which the wall had been created. Even the cement had finger marks in it in places. There was no iron work, but he could feel the hum of century old spells within.

Another scream had him glance back along the hall.

From this angle, he could see the young girl's face and felt a flicker of regret that he hadn't actually paid attention as to which of Henry Ambros' daughters they had thought it was.

She was long dead. There wasn't much that could be done for now except push on and end whatever the fuck it was that had killed her. Still, it was hard to turn away from her and move his hands over the brick work, tracing the weaving within the bricks to the seed point. He ended up crouched down, fingers resting over where the focus stone had to be.

It was an old method, one that he had sort of replicated with the talismans. A popular spell formation from the Georgian times when flowers and the natural world had been at the height of fashion. They'd thought them impervious and able to hold spells, giving root and focus so that the caster could easily keep a spell going. That was until some bright witch had figured out that you could overload the stones and shatter them, collapsing the spells stored within.

He pushed his magic, holding out another hand to scoop up the recoil that would come because like hell was he letting that go to waste if he was expending magic. Then smiled when he felt the little stone within the wall start to tremble and crack from his magic.

The temperature lowered as he did it, but Brendan ignored the signs, focusing instead on that tiny window of opportunity...

The stone split and the magic crashed out. He barely caught it and swore as his hand went numb, skin smoking and a feeling not unlike sunburn scoured across his skin. But he could feel the foreign magic settling within, topping up his reserves. Eyes flicking back to the scene that played out on the stairs again, he lifted his hand to the brickwork and collapsed it as he and Lorcan had done what must have been an hour ago.

Only something must have rebounded because suddenly, the scene caused by Daphne's mirror spell flickered and came to a stop. And he knew it without fully paying attention to it. Slowly, Brendan paused in what he was doing and turned to look over. The girl, blond hair streaming as if she was caught in a breeze, stared up at him, eyes intently fixed upon his, no longer tormented by her attacker or her violent death.

Then she vanished.

Shit.

He glanced at the wall as it collapsed to dust and winced at the smell that rolled over him, one of damp and mustiness. Tossing a spell with a flick of his fingers into the passage, he lit it up and peered down at the empty, abandoned passage with a frown.

Slowly, he stood and stepped in then paused, sudden tension creeping over him.

He knew what he'd find, even as he turned.

The blond girl stood before him, bruised and bloody, her head sometimes not quite staying on straight on her neck, jerking as if it was balancing rather than staying because it was firmly attached. Her big brown eyes were fixed on him and she jolted and jarred, though unlike Ruby her appearance never changed.

"You should be resting," he said gently.

He wasn't prepared for her to scream, doubling over as if suddenly struck by a spell. Nor was he prepared for the wave that hit him and sent him skidding back as whatever it was she screamed out hit the protection spell. He ended up on his knees, scrapping along the wooden floors and pulling a mostly rotten rug with him then yelled as the bricks suddenly reassembled in front of him.

By the time he made it to the wall, it was just that again.

A wall.

Jake and Cole collapsed out of the hallway wall in a flurry of dirt and dust, stumbling gracelessly along the new hallway. Jake could have sworn for a moment he heard something click, but then Cole was opening a door that seemed to be miraculously unlocked and gave them a barrier between them and Mr Pembroke, flimsy thought it probably was, Jake thought, panicked as they slammed the door behind them.

"Campion has my fucking bag," Cole hissed as he scrambled to his feet, rubbing a hand over his cheek and then wincing when he saw that their breath was still visible.

"Protection spell worked," Jake spluttered as he reached out for...huh... a table to help him stand. He gasped for clean air as he stared down at the scarred desk and then peered up at the shelves beyond that were filled with dead plants and ancient looking bottles. A glance to the left showed a row of windows, bare from curtains that displayed the dark sky beyond, everything below it lit with moonlight.

When he looked over at Cole, his friend was glancing around as if stunned before he moved quickly over to the shelving unit.

They were in a potions room. Which meant there were supplies.

They fumbled through the drawers without speaking, rifling through and disposing what they didn't need. Above them, the old potion bottles wobbled threateningly from their violent desperation and Jake kept glancing up, half terrified one would fall.

They both knew what the Lady of the House had probably used the room for.

Salt.

Turning, Jake grabbed the small glass container and started to pour it over edge of the wall they'd crashed through.

"Don't," Cole yelled. "There's no fucking way of knowing how they're moving around."

"Fuck it," Jake yelled and turned to the door.

Locked.

Annoyed, he placed his hand over it to cast and then yelped as his hand went numb. "It's locked with iron," he called.

Cole froze and then looked up. "We haven't been followed," he said as he slowly rose from the drawer he'd half tossed out onto the floor.

"Think it's a safe room?" Jake asked. "Seriously? She probably created half of their deaths in here."

Cole stepped into the middle of the room, eyes darting over the two tables and then turned to the huge windows rattling the locks.

It was hard not to hope too much…but to Jake's shock, Cole twisted the handle and then they were staring out at the empty sky and the overgrown garden below.

"We can get out," Jake whispered, feeling dumb. "We…" he backed up when Cole gestured and then felt like offering some protest when Cole actually climbed up onto the window frame and stuck most of his body out looking for all the world like he was about to jump to his death in the freezing November wind. "That's still a way to jump," he murmured, staring down at the ground. "They liked their high ceilings."

Cole twisted and crouched to peer down at him and grin before he flashed a cheeky wink at Jake and suddenly reached up. His body almost looked like it was lifting and swinging to the side. For a second, Jake thought he was being grabbed, but Cole swung again and found footing in the brick work to the side.

"You climb?" Cole asked sounding like they were in the middle of a conversation.

"I…not haunted houses," Jake snapped, peering out. Cole had to be hanging onto something, but from his angle it looked mostly impossible.

"Might have to jump then," Cole grinned, lowering already. "You know spells to float, right?"

"You are such a dick," Jake hissed. And then, with a steeling breath, climbed onto the window frame as Cole had. At this vantage point, there didn't seem to be an obvious useful place to aim a landing on the garden down below. "Did we see this part before?" he called, glancing around.

"Pretty sure we got distracted by the graves," Cole called, already closer to the ground than to the window. He jumped and Jake sucked in a breath.

Bastard landed on his feet like he was part cat and grinned back up at Jake. "Want me to cushion your landing?"

"Shut up," Jake muttered as he turned his back to the grounds and stared at the brick work above the window, fingers still gripping the edge. Above, was a row of decorative bricks that stood out a little and he sucked in a breath before he let go over the window with one hand and reached for them. His hands were slipperier than he would have liked, but the brick was fucking cold and rough as sandpaper so it didn't matter too much. It was harder than he liked to admit to let go and reach with both hands, but he just about managed it. From there, it was easier. Patterns in the brick work made it surprisingly easy to climb down and Jake doubted that they were the first ones to realise that.

It was only when he landed on solid ground that he felt a wave of relief and guilt swamp him. "We're out," he gasped, still unable to believe it. "We should have grabbed the others."

"We're not out yet," Cole pointed out, nodding across the garden. The bushes around the edges surrounded them like a wall. "Come on. Campion wanted to see the east wing, right?"

Right. "Daphne and Rob?" Jake asked.

Cole hunched his shoulders and blew into his hands. "I…I dunno. One thing at a time. They're in Campion's protection room, right?"

"He must be out of magic by now," Jake muttered as they got close to a window that was useless because it was covered on the other side. The plants were so overgrown that they were having to climb over them.

"So he's probably in more trouble than they are," Cole pointed out as they neared the next set of windows that was equally as useless. He pressed his hand against them and then hissed. "Iron," he murmured. "They must have taken out shares in the stuff."

"Windows are newer than the building," Jake murmured.

"Huh?"

"The windows. They've been replaced. Relatively recently." Jake gasped as a particularly icy blast of wind wafted over them. "Look for older windows if you're trying to get back in."

Cole glanced back at him and then nodded, shoving his hands into his pockets as if to try and warm them. "Fine," he said, oddly petulant.

They walked along the wall of the house, around walls that stuck out further into the grounds to accommodate a different part of the building which also had protected windows. Beyond it, was a garden wall, about half a person taller than they were, covered in crawling vines and enclosing the area that they were in.

"I fucking hate climbing," Jake muttered as Cole started forward.

If Brendan were honest with himself, there was a tiny part of him that was almost delighted with the idea of finding a secret passage. But there was far more of him that was gleeful at the idea he got to kick in the doors and no-one, not even Boss, would be able to condemn him for it.

The first door that he came to splintered apart easily. No iron in these parts to cause difficulties.

He cast again, aiming for more light and coaxing fluttering, fragile flames onto the stubby candles that still, somehow, remained. Stern, humourless faces stared down at him and he sucked in a breath before the realisation hit that he was standing in a portrait gallery.

He increased the lights, stepping in and kicking at the threadbare rug in the middle of the room as his eyes fell upon a portrait of a man towards the end of the room.

The man in the painting was in profile. He had a thick, dark auburn beard and was almost frowning at him. His clothes were dark and his chin was lifted in scorn, while his narrowed eyes appeared as if they were following his every move.

On the long walls, close by, was a larger portrait, a family portrait. It was basic: a man standing in the middle with dark hair, his much blonder son by his side and a blond woman. There were two little girls and a little boy with them. It looked like they were in some sort of church or a prayer room.

It'd be too much to hope that there'd be a label on the paintings, or some kind of date. But, while there was a signature at the bottom of the portraits, and not all the same signature, it was hard to get any other kind of information from it. Sighing, he looked around further. There were various children and young girls on the wall, assumedly Henry Ambros' daughters. There was one of another woman, but her hair was hidden and it was hard to tell if she was the same woman in the family portrait or not. There was a painting of a place that looked slightly familiar…

It made him pause to study it reluctantly and step closer. Scan his eyes over the grand looking castle that overlooked a great lake, high up on a steep hill.

Ambros Castle.

It was impressive. He could remember being a kid, and having some vague incomplete understanding that somehow, he was linked to the place and being fascinated. For years it had been like a fairy-tale place…he wasn't even sure when it had changed. He remembered being six and feeling enchanted, and then being twelve and treating the place like it has been designed to torment him.

He wasn't sure when he'd ever studied the castle in a way that was…not without emotion because, realistically, that probably wasn't possible, but he had to wonder if there had been a time when he hadn't been crippled by the onslaught of agonising questions. He could admit to being surprised at how little Ambros Castle must have changed for there to be such an accurate picture of it in this family gallery. There were three towers around the outskirts, all of various heights and yet his eye was drawn to the one closest to the lake, slightly away from the main keep and the family quarters. It rose above everything else and there was no way he could be objective about it. He found his hand reaching out for it as his eyes automatically tried to measure the difference between the tower and the lake below.

How far had his son fallen? His finger dragged down, tracing the path. He'd been stabbed, dying. Had he gone before he hit the surface of the lake? Part of Brendan hoped so; the force with which the body would have hit the water…

His hands clenched uselessly on the oil-soaked canvas, nails almost tearing into the image and he leant into the image for a moment as a wave of grief hit. Different from usual, but still able to steal his breath and make him not give a shit about where he was or the danger he was in. He was barely surprised when he felt the tears on his cheek and he pushed away from the painting, feeling half blind from it all.

This was useless.

Shaking his head, he stormed towards the door he'd come through, back into the hallway and striding along until he found the next door. He was almost uninterested in his safety as he opened the door.

In front of him, a ghostly body hung from the ceiling beam. Slowly creaking and swaying as the unseeing eyes looked past him, backwards and forwards, backwards and forwards. He stopped, staring, and kept his breathing quiet as he stared at the girl's bloated and burst-veined face.

How many people had died in this fucking house?

He needed the kids. They'd been able to give a better guess as to who was swinging in front of him. Annoyed, he stepped out of the room, closing the door once more and looking up the hall-

He stopped when, out of the corner of his eye, gone before he could focus on any detail, he could swear he saw a boy watching him. But, when he focused on the hallway, it remained empty and eerily silent apart from the creaking noise of the still swinging body and his own breath.

It made Brendan pause and try to quieten everything, as if by staying completely silent and still, he might catch whatever it was that was stalking him. But the only thing he could hear was his own thudding heart and the only thing he could see was the hallway ahead with its peeling walls and thick layers of dust.

The next room was empty and sparse compared to the one previous, but he couldn't quite work out how to explain that. And, even as he walked down the hall, something prickled along his spine.

There was something at the end of the hallway.

Still, he'd been trained well enough that he ignored the gut-reaction to just walk down to the end of the hall and face it or dare the fucking thing out. Too many lectures from Boss, Brendan thought grimly as he opened the next door.

He winced as he opened it and immediately heard the sound of someone pulling themselves along the floorboards. At first sight, there was nothing that could be seen, but he could damn well hear it as he peered cautiously around the room. In the centre, was a mostly collapsed bed and there were wardrobes with the doors half hanging off, the curtains had collapsed years ago and lay in a crumpled pile on the floor.

As he stepped in and carefully walked across the room, he spotted her and drew himself to a horrified stop. The girl on the floor was barely older than the girl on the staircase and was making choking noises as she grabbed at her throat and tried to crawl away from something, then screamed when something hit her leg, the phantom limb shuddering with whatever spell was being used on her.

From the direction, it seemed as if someone was sitting on the bed, firing spells at her and slowly killing her.

He spun, just about catching sight of the boy this time. Dark haired and terribly thin. Older than he'd first thought.

When he glanced back at the girl on the floor, she was still crawling, desperately aiming for the door and then gasping in agony and curling around her arm protectively, even as the other desperately scratched at the floor, almost clawing her way forward.

Outside, he came to the end of the hallway and frowned. It was like a rotated L shape, the hall leading off to the right and yet…

He stepped to the left side, hands smoothing over the walls, not really sure what he was looking at and there was something not quite right. He tapped his hand on the wall as he turned to look down the side of the corridor that he hadn't examined yet.

Then back at the wall.

Then back at the way he'd just come.

There was something…

Chapter Sixteen

"ARE YOU GOING TO DO something?" Daphne heard herself snap at Rob.

Funny. She almost bit her tongue afterwards, hating how it had sounded. If there was one thing she truly despised, it was sounding like she was a nagging housewife, but Rob was being such a pain. And so lazy. It was as if he genuinely thought he was helping out as much as the rest of them were.

"What like?" Rob asked, head phones on as he listened to music. "Can't call, can't text, can't leave. Can't do anything," he added petulantly, scrolling through his playlist.

When she said nothing, he smirked as if he'd won and went back to his music. He was sprawled across the sofa and she stared at him a minute longer, torn between seeing his logic and still refusing to be anything like as lazy as he was, even if being active did seem pointless right at that second.

A little bored, she wandered over to the bookshelf that Cole had examined earlier. She'd narrowed her selection down to two books when there was a sudden jolt to the room and the protection wards flickered.

Rob, when she looked over, was frowning but seemed determined to studiously ignore what was happening. Heart in her mouth, Daphne took one step towards the hole that had been created in the wall. Then another. And another.

It was only when she was about an arm's length away from the hole that she noticed her own breath again.

"Rob," she whispered, freezing where she stood.

He must have been watching her, because he came over, headphones still on, though she suspected that nothing was playing. His gaze jumped to her breath and then he froze as well, looking towards the hole.

"Shit," he whispered. "But...the only two ghosts in this wing of the house were surrounded by iron so..."

A loud crash upstairs echoed and it was too far away to work out what it was, but loud enough that it was clear something was going wrong.

"He better not drop this spell," Rob breathed, stepping back suddenly. "Fuck."

"Maybe it's another one," Daphne whispered. "One that was hiding or-"

She screamed suddenly as a figure appeared in the hole, recognising it immediately as the ghost from the study.

No.

"You can't," Daphne heard herself mutter frantically. "You can't...the iron-"

"The focus is shifting," the ghost said, tilting his head as if to listen to something. "They're distracted." He smiled and his fingers walked across the air pointedly. "You're not their concern right now."

It should have been a good thing, but the way the ghost said it was almost as if...almost as if they would suffer because of it.

"You can't get through this," Rob sneered suddenly.

"These are Brendan Campion's wards. No way you're getting through that."

"You've seen how he casts," the ghost smirked. "This? This is going to start to weaken. And I don't need it to weaken much," he said, gently moving his hand across the boundary line. "Now. I want you to tell me a few things."

"No," Daphne hissed at the same time as Rob asked, "What sort of things?" Horrified, she glared at him, but Rob shrugged, hand white around his phone as if it would turn out to hold the answers to their predicament or become an effective weapon.

"How many children does Brendan Campion have?"

What?

"Two. One living and one dead," Rob answered instantly, nose wrinkling at the question. "What?" he complained when Daphne glared at him. "How's that going to help him?"

"Nicolas is dead?" the ghost hummed for a moment. "Is he buried?"

Rob shook his head and then huffed at Daphne when she grabbed at him. "It's common knowledge," he snapped. "We don't know," he said, turning back to the ghost slowly. "His body wasn't found."

The ghost seemed to be deeply considering the answer and then smiled. "He had a wedding ring on. Campion," he seemed to consider it. "How old is the other child."

Something in her screamed in protest even as Rob answered. "I dunno. Like nine, I think? Still in primary school."

There was a cruel smile. "Let's see if we can start to drain Daddy a little quicker, shall we?" he asked and then stepped back into the shadows. "Make her watch someone she cares for die. Ambrosius vivet."

"What the fuck does that mean?" Rob asked and the question hadn't even made it from his lips before the wards started to shudder.

"Brendan's filtering a supply of magic into this," Daphne whispered, stepping back. "I don't know if he's stopped to examine how much magic he's using at the moment."

"Fuck," Rob muttered, looking up. "But...I mean... he's meant to have almost endless reserves. Right?"

Daphne swallowed. "God, I hope so," she said before she turned to look at him. "We need to strengthen these though," she said as she clutched the protection charms they'd made. "Now."

Outside the east wing, Jake thought it was pretty fair to say that they had encountered a problem.

There was a fucking massive boulder in front of the door.

Wiping at his mouth, Jake gasped and doubled over, trying to remember how he'd found it cold outside. "How far has it moved this time?"

"Not far enough," Cole complained as he leaned back against the wall, hair sweat slicked and panting. He ducked down and pushed against the door again and then shook his head as he stood back up. "Fuck," he breathed. "We need to do it again."

"Nah," Jake said, shaking his hand up at Cole. "You do it. Your fucking idea."

"I dealt with the brambles," Cole complained, nodding at the wall they'd vaulted over half an hour ago. They'd found themselves, somehow, in what had to be the old servants' courtyard for the east wing which seemed so fucking weird that Jake couldn't quite get his head around it. Of course, a Coven family would have had servants. Kitchens. Washing facilities. And of course, the entrance to the servants' side of things would be blocked. By a rock. That had runes carved into it to make sure it was unaffected by magic.

Cole seemed obsessed by the idea that a lever, their brute strength and a lot of desperation would budge the damned thing. He glared down at the huge stone and then looked suddenly inspired. "I got it," he announced gleefully. "Explosion."

Jake stared at him, hand cupping his mouth for a moment, trying not to yell. "It's impervious to magic," he said, feeling like he was talking to a three-year-old. "We would have done that half an hour-"

"Explode something next to it. The force of it could help us move the rock."

"Explode something," Jake said, doubtfully.

"You exploded stuff as a kid, right?"

"You haven't met my mum," Jake pointed out, trying not to imagine what her reaction would have been to him doing something so stupid when he'd been a teenager.

"So?"

Not worth the discussion. Shaking his head and refocusing on the point, Jake sucked in a breath. "There will need to be force on it when your explosion happens."

Cole nodded as if that was a perfectly fine thing to be happening. Muttering to himself, Jake picked up the broom handle they'd found and reinforced and started to push against it again, having to run his magic up and down it to keep the wood intact.

A blast of heat made him wince and flinch and then nearly cheer when the boulder finally shifted in a great lumbering flop, not unlike what a whale might be like if asked to roll over on dry land. It didn't exactly go far, but finally, Jake could see the door.

Cole stumbled a little, looking pale as he reached for the door.

"You all right?"

"Overestimated myself," he replied honestly and then looked annoyed at having done so. With a wary glare in Jake's direction, he pulled at the doors, splintering wood and half pulling it apart with his bare hands until they could climb inside.

Unlike the grand halls and galleries in the main part of the house, this was small and narrow, forcing them to walk one behind the other. Within three steps it was pitch black and Jake reached blindly for Cole's shoulder. "I'll go up-front," he said. "I can light the way."

Even without light, Jake could see how much Cole hated the idea. But, thankfully, he conceded the point and stepped to the side. Holding out his left hand, Jake lit up a glow within his palm, like a magical torch, and squinted at what he could see.

There was something eerier about this part of the house, and it wasn't just the knowledge that it was boarded up. It was that there were still plates in a huge old tub, trays still laid out, some heavily stained from the centuries. The kitchen, when they stepped in, had things scattered all over the place and it looked like some earthquake had hit it. To the point where Jake half expected there would be a body.

But there was nothing.

"What do you think happened to them?" Jake asked as he stepped through gingerly. "The servants, I mean."

"Ran," Cole suggested as he silently followed. "They didn't live onsite. I'd bet that they stopped coming or ran home one day and never came back."

"Not even for a wage?" Jake asked doubtfully. "Desperately hungry people can overlook a lot of things."

"They didn't take anything," Cole said quietly. "Look around. How much would half this stuff have fetched five hundred years ago? Yet it's all on the floor, there for the taking-" he broke off and glanced down in disgust. "Desperate people would have come back to steal."

"Dead people don't steal," Jake pointed out.

"Think the mass murder of villagers, even in a Coven owned property, would have attracted some attention," Cole argued. "Or do you think they killed the whole village and some wanderers just moved in at a later date?"

"We are talking about the Ambros family, right?" Jake checked. "Who knows with them."

Cole said nothing, but nodded after a moment or two. "Fine. Your theory sounds more plausible. Don't rule mine out though."

They meandered through the huge kitchen which was bigger than most of the other rooms they'd been in and then back down the little corridor again. The pantry cupboard they avoided like the plague, but there was a little polishing room that still had metal candlesticks standing expectantly and a few tiny pieces of jewellery still neatly placed upon the table that seemed to be struggling to hold itself up, despite the spells that must have been layered through it.

That was scary. Even the jewellery had remained.

At the end of the wall was another door that was locked when they tried it. Jake shoved a spell at it, splitting the lock and letting the door creak open.

Up the tiny, narrow staircase, was a body.

For a moment, at instant glance, he thought it was a ghost. But it was bone and hair and the ragged remains of a dress that he could see and Jake glanced back at Cole, shaking his head. "Two bodies," he breathed. "Two bloody bodies that Stuart missed."

"In fairness," Cole said as he knelt down to study the remains, "he didn't come here and cast mirror spells all over the place."

"In fairness?" Jake queried. "When did we decide to be fair to him?"

It made Cole look up with a smile before he glanced back down.

"Will we have a ghostly visitor?"

Cole shrugged and seemed to peer past Jake, up the stairs as if he might be able to see an answer in the shadows. "Guess we'll find out," he said as he stood and carefully stepped over what was probably a woman.

It was safe to make that assumption about an old skeleton in a dress, right?

They climbed silently, Jake sure that Cole was paying attention to what was behind while he kept focused on the ascent.

The top of the stairs looked to have been bricked up as well and Jake found himself having to do that same time spell on the wall as Cole and Brendan had previously, hating how much effort it took, but out of options when it came to quietly creating a passage through the walls.

He stepped out into the hall beyond to be met by Brendan Campion's raised hand. They stared at each other for a moment or two, baffled.

"How?" Brendan asked, sounding doubtful.

"Ghost in the study threw us into another room. Climbed out one window, broke into the servants' entrance for the east wing," Cole said, sliding past Jake. "You?" he asked, peering around in undisguised interest.

"Came through a wall," Brendan said slowly, glancing between the two of them as he stepped back. "Be careful," he seemed to settle on saying, "there are ghosts and no iron in this part."

"In a loop?" Cole asked, already halfway down the hall.

"For now," Brendan allowed, still seeming distracted. He touched the talisman around his neck. "You were attacked?"

"Pushed," Jake said, a little embarrassed by how relieved he was to have the man with them again. "Why?"

"I didn't feel it," Brendan muttered, spreading his hands and pulling up some magic between them; the misted shape too faded for Jake to make out what it was, "the others…they're still in the room?" he asked, studying the mist carefully, before making a sharp gesture that sent his magic into Jake's talisman, briefly illuminating it as Brendan magically fiddled with something.

"Yeah…" Jake glanced over at Cole who remained expressionless. "We haven't seen them since you last saw them. I don't know…that ghost, the one that you sort of…" he trailed off, a little awkward about how to phrase it, "he…I think he managed to get through the iron."

Brendan's brow furrowed. "Get through the iron?" he repeated doubtfully as he looked up. "Did you do anything?" he asked suspiciously.

Ah. Jake shifted awkwardly and tried to catch Cole's eye. But for some reason the idiot tilted his chin as if about to do battle. "We had a case to solve," he said.

Brendan stared at him and then banished the mist. "A case?" he replied angrily. "A case? Do you see where we fucking are?"

"Take opportunity when it knocks," Cole snapped back. "We may never get a chance to question him again."

Jesus Christ, Cole. Tact!

Jake barely had time to process any other reaction before Brendan stepped forward, almost squaring up to Cole. "I told you to leave it alone," Brendan almost shouted and Jake stared, shocked when Cole didn't so much as flinch at having someone bellow so close to him. Instead, Cole watched Brendan with an inscrutable expression which Jake was sure was irritating Brendan even more.

"He talked to him," Jake said. "He didn't-" He broke off when Brendan held up a hand to shush him, wary of having his voice cut off again.

"You," Brendan sneered at Cole, "do not leave my side."

Cole tilted his head, eyes narrowing. Then he let out a disgusted noise and turned away, muttering under his breath.

"What was that?" Brendan said, like a dog catching a scent, clearly reluctant to let it go. He reached out to pull Cole back and shoved him against the wall. "I swear to god, Lorcan. If you are deliberately-"

"Hey," Jake said, reaching forward to do who knew what but somehow ending up with his hand on Brendan's elbow, trying to pull him back. "He...he's socially shit, but he isn't deliberately trying to wind you up."

Cole jerked his head to Jake, as much as he could. "Socially shit?" he gaped. He seemed to be oddly accepting the way he was pinned against the wall, not yet fighting back, but Jake could see him flexing as if he were tempted.

Brendan on the other hand, turned to Jake slowly, expression baffled as he looked between Jake and Cole. "You don't think he's..." Brendan looked at Cole again, as if struggling to find the right word. "Suspicious?"

"Cole?" Jake asked, floored.

Brendan looked away and then with a large huffy breath let Cole go. "I am watching you," he warned, pointing at Cole in a vaguely threatening manner.

"And how fucking glad I am," Cole snapped sarcastically, pushing off the wall where he'd been shoved.

"Socially shite," Jake hissed at him in disbelief which actually made Cole look away, his fists opening and closing every three seconds, but Jake thought that under all the bluster he could detect that Cole was a little more shaken than he wanted to let on. "Shut up," he hissed at Cole as his friend opened his mouth.

His friend got a pinched look but wisely (for once) held his tongue. Then his eyes seemed to fall on something and he went very still. Freezing, Jake turned very slowly, noticing that Brendan seemed to sense that something wasn't right and was starting to turn too.

Down the furthest end of the corridor, a hand was sticking out of one of the doors, the fingers curled into a claw that dug into the floorboards as, slowly, a matted tangled head of hair came into view. The motion so heaved and desperate that Jake felt shivers flood down his spine as his breath started to thicken in front of his eyes.

He was the closest, Jake realised dimly, frozen in a sort of horrified fascination as the body clawed its way out of the room, jerking and jolting like static. The tangled mess of hair dipped closer to the threadbare remains of the carpet, the back bowing up like a rising hill.

"Jake," Brendan said quietly. "Step backwards. Very carefully."

The movement was almost hypnotising and Jake turned his head without fully turning away from the sight, unable to tear his eyes away. The woman's back continued to rise, the knobbly, thin spine lifting up and then, suddenly he was faced with a pair of blue eyes, red rimmed and fixed unnervingly upon him.

He stared back at her, taking a few steps forward despite distantly hearing his name be called. And as he stared at the figure in front of him, the world around them shifted. The rotting rugs became thicker, stitched beautifully and gleaming with colours, and the heavy rich curtains were drawn to let through the flooding daylight. In the midst, the woman in front of him was neat, her hair drawn back sleekly with a head-dress resting towards the back of her head, still staring at him with unblinking blue eyes.

He turned and, instead of seeing Cole and Brendan and the breaking walls and collapsing plaster, he saw another woman in the new hallway. Older, paler and less well put together. She was greying, her hair drawn into a long plait and her dress looked like it had once been beautiful and sewn to fit a healthier woman.

When he looked back again, an even older woman was standing next to the young woman, hand on her shoulder.

Striking, and with her chin tilted in a royal manner, she was dressed in full mourning black, hair dragged back into a head-dress and eyes a misty, clouded grey.

"See," she hissed.

He turned back again to the ill-kept woman, but there was nothing there; the hallway was empty.

"See," the two women hissed.

There was nothing to see. Except when he looked back, they were both dead, standing still but wounded, horrifically wounded as if they had been tortured. The young woman's face was scratched and blood stained her night clothes, one arm twisted, bloody and useless. The old woman had her hair around her throat and eyes scooped out. And, when she opened her mouth, her tongue was missing. Instead of words only a terrible, anguished scream could be heard-

It hit him like a blast of power, crashing him back into the wall, almost crushing him against it until his vision started to blur and, for a second, he thought he saw a shadowed figure, the impression of an image, a smile and he thought, in the space of a blink, he saw a room…

But then he felt something give way against his back. He was half convinced that it was his body that had crumpled under the power. But instead, he was crashing across carpet and down the stairs, his body battered as he tumbled down part of the way and then lay, stunned as he blinked up at the high ceilings of the hall.

The hall…

Stunned and aching, he sat up and winced because his arm and back protested in such a way that he wasn't sure something hadn't been torn or broken. But he managed to roll over and clamber gracelessly to his feet, hand on the wall to help him balance as he stared back at the way he must have come.

The wall looked the same as it had when he'd given it less than half a glance walking up and down the stairs hours earlier. Frantic, he twisted around, eyes scanning the hall.

He was alone.

For now, he thought, as his gaze rested on the window where Ruby Ambros had died, half hidden by the archways where the shadows lurked.

If there was one thing this bloody house was teaching him, it was that anything could come for him.

His heart lurched when he realised that he was standing in the exact place where he had seen the young girl begging, only she wasn't looping there anymore. Christ only knew where she was, he thought as he took a hesitant step down the staircase.

A lack of ideas led him back to the door to the blue drawing room where Daphne and Rob had to be. He knocked on the door, softly then growing in volume when nothing happened, almost convinced if he did it long enough that Brendan's silencing wards might fall and allow him to be heard by those inside.

Frustration had him slam a hand against the door, forgetting himself for a moment. Then he froze, suddenly aware of how stupid he was being.

Turning, he stared at the grand double doors that were no longer rattling as if someone was banging and desperately trying to get in, and there was no longer the phantom of Jonah Summers running and trying to claw his way out through them.

Jake stared at the doors and then up at the first-floor landing and at the chandelier that still hung, twisting threateningly in the air above.

What now?

Chapter Seventeen

Brendan watched as Lorcan continued to pound at the wall where Jake had gone through, roughly the same time as their crawling ghost had vanished. The boy was tenacious (or committed to his role), Brendan had to give him that.

"It won't crumble," Lorcan said with a last slam of his hands.

"I'm aware," Brendan said, folding his arms.

"You just don't care?" Lorcan challenged.

God, he really was getting under Brendan's skin. "He's fine," he said, as his mind started to race with options. "The protection talisman has calmed down and is still working which means he's still alive and nothing's attacking. He's just been thrown onto the other side of the wall."

"And you're sure of that?" Lorcan challenged, "Because from what I understand, you can't tell if Robert and Daphne are all right-"

"Because they're in the room I've warded," Brendan snapped. "And I had jack shit to do with their talismans. Thought you were meant to be clever," he goaded. Turning, he stared back up the hallway and then, after a private war with himself, turned to Lorcan and pushed him against the wall again, this time in a firm manner than with anger.

"What are you doing?" Lorcan asked, looking confused, but not fighting back.

"I am not spending the next few hours watching out for vengeful ghosts, trying to keep the others safe and all the while keeping one eye on you," Brendan said, shifting his grip so that he held Lorcan by one wrist. His other hand came up to angle Lorcan's head so that their eyes met. When he reached for his magic, he frowned, a little surprised by how much he seemed to have overestimated himself tonight.

He was out of practise. Still, he wasn't about to let Lorcan run around as he had been.

"Are you plotting to hurt me?" Brendan asked, pushing with his magic. It wasn't neat or elegant and most telepaths would have hissed at the bastardisation of their magic, but he didn't particularly care. As a truth spell, he'd found it worked perfectly fine, if a little unconventionally.

"No," Lorcan hissed. "I just don't like you at the moment." He drew in an annoyed breath at the last part of his comment and wriggled.

"Are you trying to hurt or otherwise harm anyone that we walked in with?"

"No," Lorcan said, clearly trying to break both eye contact and the force of the spell ploughing through his mind.

It wasn't hard to keep him still. "Did you know about this place? Did you know what we were walking into?"

"Yes," Lorcan answered. He winced and then tried to look away again before letting out a groan of fury. "You don't interfere with people's theories," he said tightly, cheeks flushing a little. "I didn't want to skew them."

Brendan tilted his head. "What?" he asked, because of all the answers he'd expected-

"I knew the rumours," Lorcan explained. "I told you, my family comes from here. You and I are related. But I don't know the full story. No-one does. I wanted the others to be...unbiased."

Dear god.

Slowly, he let Lorcan go, pulling back his magic and watching with... he didn't know what emotion he was feeling as he let Lorcan go. Oddly numb? he wondered as the fight he'd been preparing for slipped away like water between his fingers. Baffled.

A bit... amused?

"You acted like this because you wanted your fellow recruits to be unbiased?" he checked, then covered his mouth when Lorcan nodded. Strangely, despite everything, he could feel amusement starting to win.

"What?" the boy asked, bristling again.

"And so far," Brendan said, dropping his hand and trying to keep his voice level, "Would you say that the rumours seem to be founded in fact?" he asked, brushing his magic through the boy again, but softer this time, enough that it might indicate a lie rather than force an answer out of him.

It worried him a little that Lorcan couldn't seem to feel the spell upon him. "Locals say it's haunted," he offered after a moment.

It was hard to tell who was more surprised by Brendan's bark of laughter, himself or Lorcan. "Well they aren't fucking wrong," he murmured, looking down the hall and then back at the – Jesus, Jake had been right – the socially dense boy in front of him. "Any other rumours?" he asked and then pressed his lips together when Lorcan stared at him warily. "Think we might have blown past your worry about bias. Besides, I'm an experienced Elite. Think I can use my own common sense to weed through the stories."

Unsurprisingly, Lorcan remained a little uncertain and Brendan was almost certain he was now weighing up the validity of that claim and then shrugged. "Can we do it while we head in a direction?" he asked, a little snippy.

Brendan nodded and started to walk back along the hallway where their crawling ghost had been earlier.

"Local rumour," Lorcan said after a second or two, "says that the Ambros family started adding to this place years in advance. The mother of Henry Ambros was a seer," he said ducking under some heavy cobwebs. "She created this place, created the rooms in the belief that she would save the next generation. When the Coven fell, she promised Constance Ambros, Henry's wife, that her children would be safe."

So far, not surprising, Brendan thought as he headed back to the misshapen looking wall close to where he had first come in and ran his hands over it, feeling for the magic within. "Go on," he said when he realised that Lorcan had fallen silent. "What other rumours are in the village?"

"But the boys never came to the house," Lorcan said, sounding annoyed. "Richard Ambros was executed, Robert Ambros taken by the Council to be 're-educated' and Henry Ambros Junior was stillborn. They say it pushed the family over the edge. Slowly, the servants stopped coming to the house. The family were becoming more unstable and the pay wasn't worth what they had to put up with. They were scared. Until, one day, roughly ten years later, the house was locked to visitors."

"What?" Brendan asked, turning his attention to Lorcan again because he'd started to ignore him given there was nothing shocking being said. "They locked the house after ten years? Most of them were still alive then, right?"

Lorcan nodded. "There were the daughters, a nursemaid that remained with them, Constance and Cecelia. They say that the nurse fled one night and found refuge in the village and told them of terrible things, reasons to stay away. And it was she that, when Robert Ambros returned to the house years later, told him to burn it to the ground."

"Burn it?" Brendan asked. "Why did she say it should be burned?"

Lorcan opened his mouth a few times. "Necromancy," he said eventually.

Brendan froze, hand on the wall as he turned to Lorcan and then looked around the walls as if seeing them anew. "Ruby," he breathed, "she said that she dabbled in it to eradicate Tom Redgrave from the building. It never occurred…every person that dies here is trapped," he said, turning to Cole, "the original occupants…they were attempting necromancy here?"

Lorcan shrugged. "That's the rumour," he said, staring at the wall.

Brendan lifted his head to look up at the ceiling. "Richard Ambros is buried inside," he mused, "sacrificial magic is needed…" part of his mind raced and then he turned to Lorcan. "How long was it after his visit here that Robert Ambros died?"

"A year," Lorcan said slowly.

"Headaches and voices," Brendan said, remembering his own searches into the Ambros curse. "Some said it was Constance, yeah?"

"You know more than you let on," Lorcan said in a mulish tone.

"You really want to go there?" Brendan questioned, with a glare. "You say necromancy? I think they tried to resurrect Richard Ambros using the girls. Years later, Robert walks in and his whole family have torn themselves apart while he'd lived in the lap of comparative luxury and, on top of it, was by all accounts loyal to the Council. The Council that had ruined them." He cut himself off, unwilling to debate the curse with Lorcan as it was.

But it would make sense, he thought reluctantly. Whatever was in this house might be the root cause of the curse. Which meant that if there was a curse threatening…

Not now, he almost hissed at himself.

"So how did you fall into this?" Brendan asked as he studied the wall. When Lorcan shot him a confused look, Brendan sighed. "Elites. Training. What made you apply?"

Lorcan shrugged. "Seemed like a logical option."

And that was it, apparently! None of the enthusiasm that Jake showed or the tentative hopefulness of Daphne. "Because?"

The boy breathed in an annoyed sigh. "You interviewing me for a promotion?"

"Curious," Brendan said honestly. "Can't really get a read on you."

That made the boy look over. Hazel eyes narrowed a little and then Lorcan looked away. "You did a good thing," Lorcan said awkwardly. "Killing Lord Ambros."

Ah. "So that made the Elites a logical option? Help us do more of the same?"

Lorcan almost seemed to be squirming, which was amusing enough to keep the usual terrors threatening from the mention of what happened in Ambros Castle at bay. "And I like being clever," Lorcan added, not looking at him still. "Knowing more than others."

That almost made him smile. Pulling the spell off the boy, he shook his head.

"Except," Lorcan said slowly, "I have no idea what we're doing. With the wall," he added when Brendan stared at him blankly.

"Oh," Brendan shook himself and tried to refocus. "Well…there's a third floor, right? The west wing is separated from the main house by layers of brick and iron, so we're not getting through there, but maybe…" he stepped back, "maybe we can get through here."

Lorcan glanced between Brendan and the wall a few times. "You think there are stairs here?" he demanded.

"I know there are stairs here," Brendan said, grinning. "I'm just debating how much noise to make." He stepped back. "I have a feeling all hell is about to break loose."

"And this is…something to smile about?" Lorcan double checked nervously.

"Live on the wild side," Brendan suggested before flinging his magic at the wall, this time without caution or care, and it was like being able to fucking breathe again after all that sneaking around.

As far as he was concerned, the ghosts could fucking go do one.

Downstairs, Jake neared the huge double doors cautiously, half his attention focused on the chandelier above as he tried to calculate the odds of it falling just as he reached the door. The nearer he got, the faster and harsher his heartbeat became until he was certain that Daphne and Rob could hear it, despite the silencing spells that Brendan must have used.

As his angle of perspective changed, he froze, able to see down the corridor and glimpse the man who knelt in front of the door. He looked perfectly alive except for the way that he flickered, sometimes younger – almost a young teenager and then older as he had been approaching thirty when he died.

The door that Jonah Summers' ghost leaned against remained closed, a large arched wooden door that almost looked like a front door itself, and he guessed, had probably led to where Ruby and Sebastian Ambros had lived with their children. He could tell that Jonah Summers' ghost knew he was there, the man's head turned, just a little, as if listening to something that he wasn't yet convinced deserved his full attention.

Jonah Summers must have felt Jake's gaze practically boring a hole in the back of his head. Turning, he revealed a swollen cheekbone and an ugly series of bruises across his neck, a bloody nose, ears and even bloody eyes.

"You'll be joining us soon," Summers said, staring dully at him. "In this prison," he spat.

Jake shook his head slowly. "You don't want that," he said gently, stepping forward even as his magic brushed against the talisman again, as if checking the magic was there, small help that it might be. "We're investigating your death," he added, Cole's mutterings about opportunity whispering in his ear as he carefully placed one foot in front of the other. "Records state that you fled after killing your cousin, Ted Johnson."

Wailing, Summers disappeared causing Jake to wince as he felt more than heard the scream. There was a rumble, not unlike the sensation of an underground train passing underneath and Jake's attention swung back up to the chandelier, his mind distantly noting that his breath was once again visible.

The boy that appeared again was certainly Summers. He looked to be about thirteen, hair gelled up and dressed smartly but with wide brown eyes that stared at Jake. "We used to climb trees together," the boy whispered. "Play tricks on little Rupe Hawkins down the road."

"Did you come here together?" Jake asked, trying to focus fully on the boy and not make it so obvious as to what his concern was by continuing to look up. *Self-fulfilling prophecy,* his mum's voice warned.

"They owed us," the boy said and then flickered, becoming the man without his death wounds. "We were family too and what did we get? My mum died because we couldn't afford the medical care. Other kids would laugh, say we lived in a shed." For a second, he became younger, so much younger, a scared tiny kid and then he was back, an adult, his face covered in blood. "Ruby tricked us. Told us we could come in. Help ourselves if we helped her."

Jake looked down the hallway where he had seen Summers begging and clawing and the door and realised that he had absolutely no idea how the man had died or even where the body might be. "You got separated," he said quietly.

"It was fine," Summers sneered. "We did her dirty work. Buried bodies, ran around after her. Yes ma'am, no ma'am, three fucking bags full ma'am," he added with a sneer, sticking close to the walls, eyes suddenly narrowing on Jake. "We did nothing to deserve it." He was coming closer, face alternating between shadow and light from the windows as he walked. "But that brat…that creepy little shit…always made you wary that one."

Child? A quick flash of dates flicked through Jake's mind and he forced himself to keep his position. "Phineas."

Summers nodded. "He was watching Ted. All day, watching him. Never got why she let the kids stay with us when we made deals, but they did. Ruby and Ted were outside and she…apologised to him…" he shook his head, as the room started to tremble. "Could see it happening. Like a bad film. And that kid he…" Summers trailed off and held a shaking hand to his head. "In here," he hissed. "I could feel him. Rooting around. And her. The pair of them. Telling me to be quiet, to hush up, to forget."

"But you couldn't," Jake said, starting to eye up the distance that was between them.

"I wanted," Summers said, his voice growing louder, "what I was owed. They weren't silencing me. I knew too much. I could cause so much trouble. I could-"

He broke off suddenly, eyes fixed on something and Jake almost wanted to back against the wall, hating the fact that the ghost was now distracted by something behind Jake. It sounded like…like a repetitive thud. Like in films when someone heaved a huge piece of stone against the gates to a castle or something.

"No," Summers snarled, vanishing suddenly and, as he did, the wind suddenly seemed to pick up and Jake could hear the clinking of the glass and crystal shards from the chandeliers as they hit each other, both on the floor and up above. Backing against the wall, he winced at the feeling which was not unlike small whips lashing past and, as the debris in the hallway was picked up and swirled around, he thought for a second that he could see a line of flickering figures at the middle of the stairs, facing the doors. It seemed as if he could only catch a glimpse of them when the light hit them in the right away…

A blood curdling scream rang out and Jake turned, stunned as Jonah Summers threw himself at the door again and then turned, staring at something that was no longer there. He clutched at his hair, almost seeming to rip some of it out before stumbling forwards then away, crashing down the hallway to hit the door and try to crawl his way through it, all the while clutching at his head as if it were being split open.

He was looping.

Jake didn't know if it was relief or pity that flooded him, but either way, whatever emotion it was nearly stole his breath away.

But it was nothing compared to the feeling that hit him when the doors suddenly gave way, lurching forward and open. He could see figures flying backwards onto the driveway beyond, but one snuck forward, ducking under the fierce winds to get closer to Jake.

"Atkins?" the man asked, needing to raise his voice to

shout. "Where are the others? Where's..." he paused as he presumably spotted the ghost of Jonah Summers, back in his loop and running at the doors as if they were still locked. "Holy, fucking hell," the man shouted, gaping at the sight.

Another figure came through and Jake was certain that as long as he lived, he wouldn't shake the image of Boss glancing at the begging ghost and then just walking through it as if he genuinely couldn't find a shit to give. It didn't interrupt Jonah's pleadings one bit, but Boss headed for them and his wards seemed to make things bounce off him. "Where the fuck is Campion?" Boss demanded. "Why are you here alone?"

Unable to tell if that was an attempt to insult him or Brendan, Jake gaped and then turned to the drawing room. "I...he's warded that room. I can't get back in but Daphne and Rob are in there." He watched as the other man continued to look around and seemed to freeze as he caught a glimpse of what was on the staircase.

"And where is the fucking moron himself?" Boss demanded.

"Upstairs. The three of us were there together...I got thrown through a wall," Jake said, squinting up. "I couldn't get back-"

"They can change the structure of the house," the other man sighed and shook his head. "I swear, Brendan's like a fucking bloodhound for this stuff."

"Are they safe?" Boss yelled over the winds. "The two in there?" he asked, nodding at the door.

"I don't know," Jake replied, raising his voice to be heard, "I think there might be a ghost attacking from the other side."

"Do you know which ghost?" the other man asked.

"I don't...Brendan said it was his next-door neighbour? From when he was a kid?"

The two Elites exchanged a look.

"The ghost...I think it might have broken through iron bindings. And there's nothing in the drawing room...just Brendan's wards."

Boss said something, but his words were lost to the wind. Dimly, Jake thought he could see the figures of what he guessed were the rescue team in the entrance way, but the wind had picked up so much that no-one seemed to want to break through and into the chaos.

He watched, perplexed, as Boss reached into his pocket and dug out a shining roll of...was that iron? It looked like thread it was so thin but as he started to uncoil it, Jake could see the way that it held its shape and realised exactly why Boss was wearing such thick gloves. He marched over to the door to the drawing room and started to shape the iron around the door, pressing it against the wards so that they started to flicker. Then he flicked bursts of magic at the wards in a strange beat.

The other man, when Jake looked back was eyeing up the stairs.

"What about the others?" Jake called, glancing at the doors.

"They're holding the doors open," the man said, glancing back. "We should be fine for a while." He fixed his dark gaze on Jake. "Boss?" he called. "You good here?"

"Wait," Boss snapped and Jake watched as the wards started to collapse.

"You broke through?" the man asked.

"No, Nate," Boss shouted in derision. "I asked Brendan to put it down," he said as he reached for the door and flung it open. As the wards fully shattered, a scream, a very human, panicked scream reached their ears. "Keep him back," Boss ordered before he stepped in.

Jake moved forward before he was conscious of it but the man…Nathan Summers maybe? grabbed him and pinned him to the wall. "Stay," he said and flung a quick warding spell around him before heading through the door as well.

Fuck. Jake thumped his head on the wall and stared ahead and then up, his breathing harsh and hard in his chest and then let out a strangled whine as the image in front of him started to shift.

No. He didn't want this. He hated this. It was like holding up an umbrella to stop a flood and he panted, gasping to take in a few last breaths before-

A coffin in an ancient room, some antique marks peeping out from underneath the ragged, half rotted rug, and Jake stared at it, at the shapes, not sure what rune had been drawn because he couldn't see the rest of it. There was a foot over one edge, but Jake's perspective wasn't quite right to see who the foot belonged to, only that the person, whoever it was – a man perhaps? – was turning.

Then he was outside, staring up at thin clawing branches that seemed to threaten the grey sky above, creating an almost perfect frame for his vision and then he was looking down. He was in a patch of woodland, with what looked like an almost shallow crater underneath thick visible tree roots. In the shallow below the tree, through the woven branches, Jake could see Cole crouching down, one hand clearing away some of the earth as crystals formed a circle around him and an image of a dead woman flickered. Across from him, someone stood with their arms folded and head down, but Jake couldn't quite work out who it was, more concerned with the worried expression on Cole's face.

A gaping opening surrounded by stairs on either side and a balcony above, blood on the carved podium piece that looked like a winged creature. And suddenly, he was there. Standing in front of the gaping darkness and able to turn around and look at the hall around him. It was all cold stone and far grander than anything at Porter's Lodge. Dust sheets and fading wards layered everything and he could feel traces of Council magic being erased by the ancient building.

When he looked back, the darkness was gone and all that remained was a wall with a painting upon it, but it was too dark to make out the shapes. It didn't matter that he walked close to the wall, that he placed his hand on the painting, that he knew there was darkness behind it.

The image slipped away and became a window and he stared out at the driveway of Porter's Lodge.

"I said that she would see the future and would die in a place she hated fifteen years after the millennium."

A woman's voice and it took him a moment or two to place it as Iris Campion's from…god, had it only been the day before? He stared at the window, trying to work out what it was that Ruby Ambros might have seen.

He turned slowly and walked to the balcony edge, having the strangest sensation of seeing himself against the wall and seeing Daphne running to the exit of the drawing room door, her arm at a funny angle and shaking.

All emotion was distant. Uninterested, he turned his gaze

to the stairs at the point where the split began and where the women stood.

The women. Something about that tickled at his memory, at his thought process, but it was beyond his grasp, like chasing the seed of a dandelion when it was caught by the wind. All of them suddenly looked up and he raised his gaze too, and his vision flickered-

"Jake?" a woman's voice was screaming and he thought he could feel hands on his shoulders. "Jake-"

And he could see magic suddenly, see the veins of it running through the house and there was something lining parts of it, like plastic wires keeping the magic in and, tangled around the very walls was a dripping cruelty, like a cancer, spreading and coming from above him in the east wing.

But that wasn't the only sickness that the house suffered from. There was a twisted ball of something similar in the west wing. When he turned, he could see it almost growing in power, had the vague idea that some outside force was helping it in some way.

He didn't know if it was panic or protectiveness that drove him, but he pushed with his mind and with his will. He pushed through the magic outlines of rooms and even through what should have been the imperviousness of iron, until he could see the study and the man who snapped his gaze to Jake.

There, something in him spat.

So he pushed. Focused this time.

"There's a seer," the ghost of Brendan's neighbour sneered, though at what Jake didn't know. Yet, something in the house stirred.

"Not yet," voices whispered, sounding like there were a dozen of them speaking as one, even as he pushed again. "Not-"

This time the push made him almost forget his body. Like being swept away in a torrent of water all of his making, he was static and lost. Distantly, there was a scream and then his awareness of his body came rushing back as he stumbled against hands, his fingers tingled as if they'd been singed-

"Jake!" voices were shouting his name and he slumped suddenly, sucking up breath like a drowning man spat from the sea. He fell on whoever was in front of him and shook, unable to keep himself up as his mind struggled to understand what he'd just seen. He could feel the knowledge from the vision racing away from him, as if sucked back by the outgoing tide of magic and leaving only a few of the images imprinted.

Somewhere, Mr Saunders, his old teacher was grumbling about him wasting his seer ability.

A rough hand grabbed his chin and Nate studied him carefully. "Fuck me, this place fucking sucks," he said, grinning as if delighted in it. "A vision?"

Gasping, Jake nodded and looked around. Then his eyes found Daphne who was still shaking with nerves but staring at him, brown eyes warmed in concern. "Your arm," he said. "Are you okay?"

She nodded and he could see the faintest tear streaks on her face, slightly tinged with mascara. "Rob's…he's not breathing," she cried, shaking. "Boss is with him."

"He's retreated," Jake whispered, pulling back and slumping against the wall. The wind and oppressive feeling still whipped around them, but it didn't feel quite so much like a thousand and one things were clashing all at once anymore. "The ghost…Pembroke?"

"Yeah…well…some sort of ghost," Nate said. "Think that was you, kid. Seers and ghosts. Always eventful," he added. "Either way, dick face disappeared. Just got them to deal with," he said, nodding up at the stairs and the occasionally flickering figures, still only visible when the light hit right.

"I saw them," Jake whispered, staring at them. "I…I don't think they're trying to hurt us," he said, standing.

"I don't," Daphne agreed, her voice cracking and breaking. "I've seen a ghost trying to hurt us. They aren't."

Nate glanced between them both and then up. "Fuck," he muttered after a moment and Jake had a second to wonder if Summers was aware that other words existed. "Daphne… how d'you feel about going back in. Helping Boss?"

It terrified her, Jake could see, but she squared her shoulders and raised her chin with a nod. "I could come up there with you."

"No," Nate said. "I can't keep you both safe and, at the moment, our seer here is our best protection and weapon. Boss'll keep you safe, promise."

Jake wasn't sure if it was patronising to say that he felt a sudden wave of pride for Daphne as she went back in that room without too much protest. He spared a glance back at the door and could suddenly feel the spells keeping the door open. It wasn't stunningly powerful, but it was continuous.

"Come on," Nate said, pulling Jake forward. "We'll get those two morons and then get out. We'll deal with this properly once the house has settled."

Jake took a huge breath as he approached the stairs and the figures above. "I'm not sure how I'm going to react to walking through them," he said honestly.

"Me neither," Nate admitted. "Kinda curious though."

It shocked Jake into a disbelieving laugh and to put one foot on the steps.

Chapter Eighteen

IT WAS LIKE SOMEONE HAD set off a bomb in the centre of the earth and a sucking well of gravity was trying to drag them back down. Thankfully though, Brendan thought, his spells must have been holding because while magically he could feel the forces around them battering against his wards, physically the stairs were pretty easy to climb. Lorcan seemed to find it even easier and Brendan almost fondly wondered if the kid was even aware of the magic around him keeping him from tumbling down the stairs and breaking his bloody neck.

"These were the main stairs," Lorcan said quietly. "Better than the servants' stairs." He seemed to debate it for a moment. "There was a dead body on those."

"And you didn't think to mention it?"

"In this place?" Lorcan asked doubtfully. "What's one more dead body?"

"We've found one dead body that was attached to a pissed off ghost," Brendan pointed out, wincing at a particularly strong blast of a magically reinforced wind and, for the first time, feeling a little wary of his own magical reserves. "Was there another one?"

"No." Lorcan seemed content to mull over that as they

climbed. "Do you think that every person who died here became a ghost? Because of…" he pointed upstairs.

"Yes." Brendan winced as they got to the top of the stairs only to find another wall, made of flinted stone this time rather than brick. "So perhaps we need to keep an eye out for your staircase ghost. Would you?" he asked, indicating at the wall.

Lorcan blinked at him in surprise, but acquiesced though with noticeably less flare and more care to not just fling magic around.

Could learn something from him, a very Boss-like voice echoed in his head and Brendan pushed it away to watch curiously at the sight that was revealed as the bricks crumbled away in front of him.

Disappointingly, it looked like the other hallways in the house though maybe more dilapidated and more furnished. He could see wax candles all over the floor as if they'd been dropped and scattered around.

When he moved to start forward, Lorcan held out a hand in warning.

"What?" Brendan demanded.

"Look," Lorcan said quietly, his other hand reaching towards the wall where faded marks were scratched into the stone there. He stepped closer using magic to create light in the palm of his hand to make it easier to study the inscriptions.

"What are they?" Brendan asked. He could see, at a glance, some containment runes and something that looked a little like the symbol for the dead.

Shit. It wasn't a surprise, but it was unnerving to have such a thing confirmed. "Guess that confirms the necromancy theory," Brendan said. "Are the runes there to boost it?"

"No," Lorcan said. "It's to contain it. To foil the spell. Someone stopped it."

Brendan glanced at him and then nodded to continue forward. They both walked onto the top level that was thick with dust and cobwebs, the stale air almost suffocating as Brendan breathed in.

"Remind me," Brendan said as he spotted a door ahead. "The graves."

"Mm," Lorcan said, turning to look at him. "What about them?"

"Who buried them?"

Lorcan stiffened and then let out a shuddering breath. "I don't know," he admitted. "I never thought about it." He folded his arms, the gesture surprisingly young, and eyed up the next door. "You're getting low on magic reserves, right?"

"I'm fine," Brendan snapped a little, forcing the door and then stumbling through it. He blinked at the sight of the books, the vessels in there…

A workroom. Nothing that he was interested in. Shutting the door, Brendan ignored the longing look that Cole shot it.

"You don't think that-"

"I think that we know what we're looking for," Brendan said, continuing down the corridor. "And it ain't that. We're looking for the chapel."

He could tell that Lorcan was annoyed by something. "If you know something-"

Lorcan opened his mouth and then looked away with a shrug. "Nothing relevant," he said. "But you never know."

Jesus, the kid was a cryptic little shit, but as they rounded the corner, Brendan nearly gasped at the feeling that radiated from the door opposite. Twisting, furious pain tore at his wards and he nearly stumbled with the agony of it.

Lorcan grabbed at him, looking warily worried. "Gonna guess this is what we need," Lorcan said quietly, continuing to eye Brendan up with concern. "You sure?"

With an annoyed glare, Brendan shook the kid off and strode forward. The door was wooden and cracked, the stone around it blackened as if scorched by something. Within three paces of the door, he felt his wards hit something.

Then he was crashing backwards, the air knocked from him before he skidded along the floor and his fingers tangled in the rotting carpet. When he looked up, Lorcan had tucked himself into a nook in the hall and was peering at him before looking back at the door.

In the way stood a woman. Dressed only in a nightgown, hair long and loose and wavering between being a younger, blond haired woman and an older grey haired haunted one. Her eyes looked almost too big for her gaunt face and she shook as she stared down at him, the result not helped by the flickering quality of a ghost anyway.

"What are you doing?" she whispered, eyes fixated on him. "You know what I do. You know."

Brendan placed a splayed hand on the carpet as he knelt up and stared at her, a quick glance at Lorcan seemed to show that the lad wasn't even on her radar and he was... Brendan blinked as he thought he saw the boy scribbling on a well-used piece of paper. "You cannot bring him back," Brendan said, standing and hissing inwardly at how difficult it was to simply remain upright against the power battering against him. "You didn't."

She shook her head, not moving, and the movement was uncomfortably jolting and jarring. He stared at her, not entirely sure he could work out how she had died from what he was seeing but she was so uncomfortably thin and frail that he was almost expecting her to collapse which was a stupid fear to have given that the woman was already dead.

"He's my son," she whispered and the words hit him. Robbed him of breath and he opened his mouth, then shut it, unable to really think or even process because he'd ruthlessly shoved away everything in this god forsaken place that reminded him of Nicolas.

He swallowed, trying to find words.

"He's gone," Lorcan said with his usual lack of tact and then he gasped when he was shoved against the wall, pushed as if being pressed to death and he let out a strangled, shocked gasp.

Brendan threw up a ward, breaking the ghost's hold and then yanked the lad behind him with magic. "Shut up," he hissed as Lorcan skidded behind him.

"You," she said, stepping closer, her eyes furious, yet still looking so thin. "You failed your son. I will not fail mine."

Not screaming at her felt like some impossible task, but he managed it, keeping his hand behind him and spreading his fingers to remind himself that he needed to keep the idiot lad safe.

"Our children always return to us. As you are now," she murmured to him, almost like an incantation that grabbed his attention.

The implication made him press his lips together in

frustration and impotence because he'd rather have slit his own throat than have had his son walk into this nightmare place. "Hardly the same-"

"We both had our sons, our eldest stolen from us," she said, coming closer and Brendan took a step back, hand making contact with Lorcan for a moment before the lad took the hint and stepped back too. "Both fought to get them back."

"Both failed," he said, the words as cutting for him to say as they probably were for her to hear.

"But I was his mother," she said, eyes narrowing. "And he was my boy."

The implication made him snarl at her. "I'm not getting into this," he hissed. "And don't you dare imply he meant less to me than yours did to you."

"You accepted the replacement child," she said, dismissively.

He nearly flung something at her, but his vision was wavering just a little and he had a moment of sudden horror that Lorcan's warnings had been absolutely right. The magic gathered to his command, but he was almost out. Even what he'd borrowed earlier was fading and all he had for back-up was a recruit who had so little magic, it was almost a joke.

He let it go. Reluctantly.

"Unlike you did with your daughters?" he asked, narrowing his gaze and pushing Lorcan back again without looking as the idiot attempted to stand at his side to face this...woman. "What did you do to them? Your other children?"

The floor started to rattle and shake and he reached back, gripping Lorcan's thin jacket without looking.

“You,” she screamed at him as the wind picked up. “Have no concept of this place. Despite your heritage-”

“This ain’t my heritage,” Brendan snapped back. “I am not an Ambros.”

“Phineas Ambros,” she said, as if starting a chant, “Nicolas Ambros. Daniel-”

This time nothing could have stopped him from flinging a wave of magic at her as she nearly said the words because he’d lost one child to the fucking Ambros family and there was nothing in this world that he would allow to claim his youngest son as an Ambros too. And he didn’t care that he could feel the warning signs of magical exhaustion creeping up on him as his muscles started to ache as if he’d run a race and his teeth almost begun to hum.

The blast that he hit her with, the sweeping push to get her away from them and to wound what was left of her awareness was like a sonic explosion and he could hear her screams of agony.

He staggered to his knees once more and Lorcan grabbed at his shoulders. “You’re so fucking stupid,” the boy was snarling at him. “This is so fucking stupid,” he added and then looked up at the door before glancing back at the way they’d come.

“Go downstairs,” Brendan gritted out. And then froze when Lorcan reached behind him and pulled out a small pocket knife.

“What?” he managed to gasp before Lorcan made a tiny incision in Brendan’s fingers and then pulled out a tissue to dab the blood. Then Lorcan dropped his hand and Brendan blinked at the tiny wound. A wave of pain flooded through his mind like a migraine, like wires were twisting behind his eyes and he gasped, head falling to the floor.

When enough of the pain had passed, he blinked up and watched as Lorcan placed the smeared blood upon the door.

"I mean, I guess?" Lorcan said. "Right blood line, similar circumstances."

Fucking hell. "I can't protect you," he ground out.

Lorcan glanced back over at him. "You don't say," he murmured almost absently, even as the wind started to pick up again. He seemed to hesitate suddenly. "Will you be all right?"

Did he look like he was going to be all right? But in the grand scale of things, Lorcan didn't have the strength, magical or physical, to pick him up and Brendan still couldn't even lift his head fully without feeling like he was being repetitively shot in the head. "Wait," he said as he felt something… something was different suddenly. There was a pattern…

Boss was at his wards downstairs. Relieved, he re-called his magic and nearly cried with relief when it staved off the worst of the effects.

"The Elites are in the building," he said, clambering laboriously to his feet. Lorcan peered at him suspiciously and then seemed to decide he had little reason to lie.

"The wall?" Lorcan asked. "They won't be able to get through?"

"They're fresh," Brendan said. "And I'd bet a lot more prepared." He stumbled to his feet and to the door where Lorcan was holding the tissue to the wood. "Don't be an idiot," he huffed and held out his hand for the knife.

"Sure," Lorcan said, handing the pen-knife over after a moment. "Why not. Let's do a toss-up between magical exhaustion and blood loss."

"You're being dramatic," Brendan dismissed as he drew the knife down the inside of his arm and created a shallow cut, then smeared it against the door and pushed with the other hand.

The door swung open with an ominous creek and the gathering wind suddenly died.

"That can't be good," Lorcan whispered as he stepped into the dark room. His hand lifted and he flicked his fingers in a sharp staccato movement and some candles lit up revealing the contents of the room.

Originally, it had probably been a chapel. Towards the front of the house there were two huge windows that had been boarded up and even part filled in with different stone. In between the windows, there was the alter and a runed table on it where someone might cast spells or kneel in prayer.

The pews were rotting and collapsing and looked like they'd seen a fight of some kind. Some were shattered and smashed. But there was also the collapsed remains of a bed and, in the centre of the room, the stone work was different, carved with deep runes in a huge circle.

Warily, they stepped forward and Brendan stared down at the grave, a strange feeling shaking lose within him and...jealousy?

She'd gotten a grave.

He knelt, hands pressed to the runes and stroked his fingers into the grooves. Strangely, the image of the tree at his mother's house hit him and he couldn't help but think the tree was better. This was...in so many ways cruel. The poor boy that had been locked away by the Council had been buried and locked into stone again by his own mother.

His blunt nails scraped the stone. His own son was probably suffering something like this, but not even surrounded by people with misguided good intentions. Who the hell knew what Damien was doing to his child's body.

Lorcan drew in a shocked gasp and Brendan looked up and back-

Behind the door, as Lorcan closed it over, was a skeleton and, on the heavy wooden panels of the door were scratch marks. Some of the whiter lines were random, but within the hatchet mess was the start of a word.

HE

The door was yanked out of Lorcan's grasp to slam shut with a thunderous roar of power.

Shit.

Brendan raced forward stumbling around the lad, and both of them scrabbled to find purchase on the door, digging in their feet. And both of them were skidding, forwards, unable to find a way to keep the fucking thing from closing.

"Go," Lorcan hissed at him.

"I am not-"

"You can open it," Lorcan shouted. "I can't and we can't both get through and hold it open. You go first."

No. That was his gut reaction, but he hated that Lorcan's words made sense. Frustrated, Brendan twisted, half in and half out as he pulled at the protection amulet around his neck and hung it around Lorcan's instead, even as the boy scrabbled at Brendan's jacket for a moment with one hand as if unsure to hold on or push him away.

"Five minutes," Brendan promised. "I'll be back with them in five minutes."

And then he was outside and Lorcan twisted as if to follow, but, as he'd predicted, the door slammed shut and Brendan stood alone in the hallway, feeling like a complete shit.

Or at least he did until he spotted the piece of paper that Lorcan had shoved into his pocket.

On the floor below, the sound of something slamming shut made them both freeze and Jake and Nate stared at the wall ahead. They were towards the front of the house, far too close to where Ruby Ambros' body had been found and Nate was holding his hand to the wall in confusion.

"That didn't sound good," Jake murmured, looking up.

"No," a female voice behind them agreed easily. "It didn't."

Jake looked over at Nate who scowled at the wall and glanced up at him before turning from where he was knelt to peer at Ruby's ghost. The woman stood flickering in what could almost be called a calm way between a young girl, a red headed beautiful woman and the elderly woman who'd died at the window.

She had Brendan's eyes, Jake realised nervously. That was a freaky reminder.

As she stepped forward, Nate sighed and turned to the wall, his palm reaching out towards her, parallel to his body. The smooth circle of a protection ward blasted out, almost visible like air when it's hot.

Ruby paused, frowned and then raised an eyebrow in

annoyance. "I do not intend harm," she said, as if peeved by Nate's actions.

"No," Nate said in a sarcastically understanding tone. "Wouldn't harm a fly, right? Just terribly misunderstood." He rose, brushing the dust from his hands and when Jake glanced over, he could see marks along Nate's forearms as if someone had gone at them with a marker pen.

"No. I am responsible for every modern ghost in this house," Ruby said looking remarkably unrepentant. "But you know," she said, reaching out and becoming almost worriedly solid as her fingers traced the outline of the boundary spell that Nate must have put up, "that actions are one thing, motives are another."

Nate's mood seemed to dip further. "You and your great-grandson are just peas in a pod, right?" he asked and his left hand went back to the wall, palm flat upon it.

"It has been said," she murmured, eyes lifting to the wall. She still looked annoyed by them.

"You stayed," Jake said, watching her, his eyes sliding to the window and then to the wall, the proximity occurring to him for the first time. "And…you came out of your loop quickly…you weren't murdered."

Her blue eyes swept over him and it was impossible to work out what she was thinking.

"And this didn't happen last time…" Jake turned to Nate and then to her. "You…" he looked back at the staircase where the figures had been. Then he looked at the wall.

"She's keeping it up," Jake said, spinning to Nate. "It's her spell. It's why Brendan got through but had it close up again. Family can get through."

Nate's eyes closed briefly before he turned. "He's in there," he said to Ruby. "I don't know your motives and I'm not sure I care. But if you put this wall up, you were trying to contain what was upstairs."

She hummed as if unconvinced by his words. "It's inconsequential now," she said as the wall suddenly begun to shake. "Like a bull in a china shop," she said, shaking her head before vanishing even as a very pale Brendan appeared on the other side.

"You genuinely look like death," Nate greeted.

Brendan shook his head and then held out a demanding hand to Nate who stared at him for a long moment and then huffed. "Thank you, Nate," Nate said, voice heavily sarcastic, "for coming and rescuing me even though I've been a dick to you this week-"

"We do not have time," Brendan snapped.

"You are pushing it," Nate hissed as they stepped into the hidden corridor and Jake stared at the huge stairway that looked like it too had only recently been revealed. "I should be dragging you back down to Boss-"

"Lorcan is up there," Brendan said and, to Jake's surprise, he avoided the stairs. "Here," he added, shoving the piece of paper he was carrying at Nate. "Do you have supplies for this?"

Jake watched as Nate blinked and took the piece of paper to study briefly then looked up at Brendan in surprise. "This looks like…well…necromancy," he said.

"Fight fire with fire," Brendan said and opened up the door to one of the rooms on that floor, past the room where Jake winced to see the girl from earlier desperately crawling away from something on the bed and into the next room down where a girl stood on the bed, looping a rope around her neck.

"Uh..." Nate turned to Jake. "I am really sorry about this," he said.

"Why-" Jake yelped as he was flung forward and in the path of the girl as she was about to hang herself and rock off the bed and into the air.

His mind already had the tell-tale signs of a building headache and being flung into the path of the ghost was like opening up his already exhausted mind again, a door flung wide to the world of the dead and he was there suddenly watching as the girl, a beautiful, thin, terrified girl with tears in her eyes slid her head into the noose and-

She saw him. And they were there standing in the room as it had once been. A large, depressing stone room, the hangings looking plain and unloved and the candles flickering as the sun set casting blued half shadows across the empty room. She had long brown hair and frightened, red-rimmed hazel eyes that filled with tears as she trembled.

"Who are you?" she whispered to him.

"Who are *you*?" Jake asked, and then stepped closer, hand almost passing through her as he looked up to keep eye contact. Above them both, the rope around her throat coiled all the way up to the sturdy chandelier above that rocked ominously making Jake think nervously once more of the chandelier in the main hall.

"Susanna," she whispered and then looked above him to the edge of the room, a tear slipping down her cheek.

"Why?" he asked. "Why are you doing this?"

"My brother," she replied, still shaking. "It is the only way..." she trailed off and then let out a sob.

He reached for her hand, dimly surprised when he could make contact. "You've already done it," he told her gently and she looked down at him in shock. "I'm a seer," he said carefully. "You're dead."

She blinked at him a few times and then trembled even harder. "I don't..."

"You don't need to," Jake said, squeezing her hand. "Just...rest. You can rest."

It took a moment or two, but Susanna looked down at him and then nodded. "I want to," she sobbed, the tears falling quicker now and he winced, sure that Susanna hadn't been any older than sixteen if that, the same age as his youngest sister. And then the present sunk in, the room fading to the dark, magically lit room and the ghost standing in front of him, bruising around her neck and she was flickering.

"Rest," he said, feeling something damp under his nose.

He was aware of something behind him and she looked up as well. When he turned, it was the old woman with the long braid from earlier who was watching the girl... her granddaughter with sorrow.

She met his gaze and then faded and, when Jake looked back, Susanna was gone too, the bed empty. Coughing, Jake stumbled back, touching his hand to his nose and staring in shock at the blood that dripped between his fingers from where he'd swiped them.

"Shit," Nate said, sweeping forward and guiding him to the floor as Brendan, with a hesitant look at the bed, climbed upon it with what looked like spray paint. "Okay so...kid's got some juice," he said to Brendan with a grin then looked back at Jake. "We need to get you some storage crystals. Like that idiot over there."

Brendan ignored the two of them and Jake had never seen paint bend the way it was with Brendan so he guessed that Brendan was using magic to paint the ceiling. Nate flung a hand towards the bed in an attempt to reinforce the rotting thing.

"You sure you're drawing that in the right place?" Nate asked, hands returning to Jake's face to support him. "Because you can't do the entire ceiling and fuel it-"

Jake blinked up at Nate and then turned to look at the ceiling, feeling a flicker of surprise at what was there.

Oh.

Cole was a fucking genius.

Chapter Nineteen

DAPHNE HOVERED NERVOUSLY AS BOSS continued to cast resuscitation spells, almost feeling as if it was her that was struggling to breath.

"You need to tell me what happened," Boss snapped.

"But you're-"

"Jesus woman. I can multi-task," he snapped. "You want to be an Elite then do the same. Panic and talk."

Something in her objected to his tone, but she was more relieved by the sight of this gruff man who seemed unfazed by what had happened and that made her feel almost as if she was over-reacting to the ghost. "The...he broke through iron upstairs. He was draining Brendan...I mean Mr Campion by pressing on the wards."

Boss actually rolled his eyes. "That fucking moron," he muttered. "You think he'd monitor his spells. Arrogant twat."

Opening her mouth, Daphne almost swallowed her tongue when Boss gave her a furious glare. "Then?"

"The wards started to collapse and..." she gestured to the room that looked like a tornado had gone through it. "He went for Rob and..." she gestured helpless at him. "Is he breathing yet?" she asked, horrified by the way her tears shook her voice, the numbing spell on her arm not helping to steady her emotions.

"He will," Boss said, a little gentler than she expected. "The spook got through fucking iron," Boss muttered to himself, even as he adjusted something with the spells trying to get Rob's body to start functioning again. "Ghosts can't do that," he said, shaking his head before he looked over at her. "He say anything?"

Daphne pressed her lips together. "He…asked how many children Brendan had and…he said Ambrosius vivet" She shook her head. "Ambros lives."

Boss pressed his hand against Rob's chest and his fingers spasmed as a roll of light crashed through Rob, shocking his body in a quick bust. "You got out the door," Boss said, looking over at her. "Before I got in, you came out."

"I…I think someone…something else was here," Daphne whispered. "He was distracted."

Boss winced and then his magic crashed light into Rob again, making his limbs jolt and jerk. This time, Rob suddenly gave a gasp and started to cough, eyes wide as Boss sat back. He glanced at her as he did it and she could feel an odd sudden pounding in her head.

"Come here," Boss said, as Rob hacked up a dry scream. With a casual and competent air, Boss examined Rob, looking into his pupils and checking over him with his hand aglow, a scan to check for damage that Daphne was impressed to see because it usually took an awful lot of concentration to do. Boss paused around Rob's ribs longer than anywhere else but didn't seem surprised by what he was finding.

"You too," Boss said as he continued the scan. "You'll need to be closer."

"Why?" Daphne asked.

She needn't have asked. Even as the words left her mouth there was an almighty lurch followed by every door suddenly slamming shut.

"Another one?" she asked, glancing around the room, warily and trying desperately to not show her fear in front of Boss as he finished the scan.

"Nope." Boss started to wrap up Rob's chest with the gauze he'd produced from a back pocket. "Shut up, Goodman," he huffed. "It's bruised ribs. Not years of torture." He turned his attention back to Daphne. "I imagine they're facing the original pissed off occupants. Stay close because I'm not that idiot Campion and I'm not warding a whole pigging room for three people."

She opened her mouth to defend Brendan and then slammed it shut when the house started to rock like an earthquake was trying to shake it apart.

Oh god.

"Why was it so important?" she asked. "All of that, just to find out if Brendan Campion had more children? And then before he…" she struggled with the right terminology for what Jake had done, "He wasn't talking to us. Whatever distracted him…he wasn't even speaking English-" Rob sobbed and curled up next to him and Boss looked down and tapped a finger to his head. The next second Rob was out cold.

"It was the old tongue," Boss said. "I get some of it, but his accent was…" Boss shrugged and then sighed. "As for the rest…" Boss trailed off and seemed to be debating something before he looked at her, face expressionless. "Pretty sure it means that he thinks whatever remains of Ambros is going to go after Daniel Campion."

Cole stood alone in the room. The candles flickered precariously and he swept a glare at them before he stepped away from the door and stared at the word scraped into it, fingers tracing it even as his breath started to become visible.

"You should not be here," Constance's ghost whispered to him and Cole spared a glance at the skeleton that looked like she had died clawing at the door.

So much for reliable graves, he thought, oddly amused.

"No," he agreed, sighing before turning around. "I probably shouldn't."

"There's something..." she continued, stepping close and he had been trained well enough that, as much as he wanted to flinch away and hide, he refused to move. Her transparent hand reached for his chest, pressing into it, which was a fucking weird sensation, and then moved down to his wrists and the hidden bindings there.

"Council bindings," she spat, blazing eyes rising to his. "They should be ended."

He said nothing as she moved away, softening in her appearance as she moved closer to Richard Ambros' grave.

"The door will not open for either of us," she said sadly as she knelt close to the grave. "I can make death come quickly for you."

He snorted and stepped away from the door, leaving her alone with the grave and stepping closer to the alter, studying the destroyed pews. "You didn't do this alone," he said, crouching to study the splintered wood and then stared at the chunks missing from the wall.

"They turned," she whispered. "They came for me. They didn't understand."

He was certain it was her that hadn't understood. She'd lost her mind by the time she'd died, that much was clear and he pressed his lips together because he doubted there was any point arguing the point with her.

"The three of us, trapped here forever," Constance almost sung as she pressed her hands to the grave, and he was half convinced that she would try to pull Richard's body up through the stone.

He looked down and pressed his own hand to the floor, trying to keep the movement casual as he subtly cast out and down with his magic.

The floor beneath wasn't terribly thick. Thicker than modern houses and probably the depth that would usually be between a window and the floor. He debated it carefully because if he blew out the floor he had no idea what could be below and he had no idea what her reaction would be to him disturbing Richard's body. Still, it wasn't hard to push down and create a circle below.

He stood, still turning the idea over in his mind and half wondering if it would be easier the further away from the grave that he was. But the alter, when he stepped up, was even thicker and harder to break through.

Shit, he thought as he stared up at the windows, at the runes and carvings that would have prevented her from leaving. The magic here was more stifling than even the iron had been in the west wing.

"He failed us," she whispered sadly. "It's the next generation that should be protected, not ourselves. Henry…" she sobbed and it was the sound of a long-harboured anguish that he couldn't quite understand. Still keeping quiet, he strode to the wall and placed a finger upon it, walking around and stretching out gently. The noise of his short nails scraping across the stone rang out louder than he believed possible in the heavy silence.

"Why did you come?" she asked, sounding lost.

"We keep our secrets," Cole replied automatically, stopping to look at her mournful expression.

Constance snarled like a wounded animal. "You're one of Ruby's. That bitch," Constance said, suddenly on her feet. "She locked everyone in here. Like they did. Forced us to relive the past. Prevented us from living-"

"You're fucking dead," Cole snapped. "And they were in their loops anyway. It was you she was trying to stop."

"But I won't be stopped," she said with manic, delighted laughter. "It can be finished-"

"There's nothing to resurrect," Cole sneered at her, taking a violent pleasure in telling her the truth. "You know there's nothing there. You just can't bear the idea of it. You failed. You failed every single one of your children."

She screamed at him and he was knocked backwards by the vicious blast, crashing into the boarded-up window and hissing in pain as the protection spell Brendan had placed on the amulet flared up in response to her magic. His breath caught at being stuck between the two, his chest feeling as if it was being squeezed.

"You failed the next generation," he laughed, trying to keep her attention. "Every single one of them condemned for what you did. Even Robert."

"He was theirs," she sneered. "He came and saw what they did and still stayed loyal. Richard was mine. Is mine. He will rise and bring with him glory-"

She stopped, turning her head suddenly and looking

down at her feet in shock. He felt her magic start to flicker and fade.

Finally.

He slid down to the floor and coughed, relieved beyond words. An almighty wail erupted from her and the floor around the circle he had cast lit up.

Jesus, Brendan really was strong, Cole thought as he scrambled to a kneeling position, panting. Any loose stonework was rumbling like sand on top of an engine and the floor was slowly become brighter where the circled runes must have been drawn on the ceiling of the room below.

Thank god. Cole hadn't been completely certain that Brendan would understand his idea let alone carry it out given his earlier suspicions. A wave of...relief (he was determined to call it relief) flooded through him as he watched the light get almost unbearably bright, Constance trapped within the binding circle, screaming.

He edged around the room, getting closer to the door and towards her body, reaching into his pocket for the lighter he'd stolen from Daphne earlier. As he reached for her, he froze, spotting something on the wall behind the body.

The incantation was clear and the runes to hold the spell had been scraped into the wall with what he'd guess to be the broken chips of stone, left over from whatever fight had taken place in the room centuries ago. He fiddled with the lighter for a moment as he debated options, the object dancing in-between his fingers absently, twisting and spinning before he reached into his pocket again and pulled out a crystal, holding it tightly as he stared at the wall, pushing the memory into the gem to contain it with absolute clarity so it could be studied later.

Then he wiped his hand over the wall and dropped the lit lighter to the body, using the little magic he had left over from the Council bindings that were warm in warning against the skin of his wrists to make the flame hotter; hot enough to burn through bone. Behind him, Constance's screams turned from frustrated anger into terror as her body started to burn.

The door burst open, Brendan at the opening, panting and with sweat dripping down his face from exertion. Barrelling in behind him was Jake, his lower face covered in drying blood along with another man that Cole suspected was Nate Summers.

Trapped, Constance howled as her ghostly figure collapsed and shuddered, rippling through various ages of her soul as she flung herself at the boundaries created by the circle of runes. Her fury was such that she couldn't even form words as overwhelming vitriol seemed to crash through the room, her last attempts at vengeance.

Summers glanced at Cole, tugged him back a little and then flung his arm at the burning body, turning the flames blue and speeding up the process.

"You all right?" Brendan asked, eventually tearing his gaze away from Constance to glance at Cole.

He nodded. "She barely had time to get started."

A slightly disbelieving look was swept over him, but Brendan eventually accepted the comment and then leaned against the wall, arms folded as he slid down it and sat to watch Constance's soul be burned away. "Not entirely sure you should have known how to do that," Brendan said after a moment. "Trapping the souls of the dead in a rune-"

"I read," Cole replied, bracing himself for an argument.

"I for one am pleased that you do," Summers said as he too sat by Brendan as if the pair were settling down to a bonfire. "I reckon that you might have read it in one of those dark books lurking around the house."

The intention was appreciated, but in the end, would be pointless. There was no way that the Council would believe that he of all people had just happened to come across the right answer.

The house rumbled and shook, as if shaking off something foul and finding it agonising to do so. Cole winced and glanced over at Jake who looked equally pale and Cole felt the smallest twinge of guilt because perhaps bringing a fledgling seer to this place hadn't been the wisest idea. But then Jake glanced over and grinned, an expression born of relief and giddy triumph. The body within the fire was almost gone now, nothing but ashes. Opposite them, the ghost of Constance Ambros was fading with mourning wails as she still frantically reached towards the body of her dead son, buried beneath the stone.

"Poor woman," Jake murmured.

"Poor kids," Nate said, a slight edge to his voice.

Brendan, Cole noticed, said nothing, but watched Constance's last flailing attempts to get to the body of her son. And it was hard to make out his expression in the firelight as it cast shadows upon the man's face. Maybe pity. Or fear. Grief? Whatever it was, he looked like something carved in marble, pale but with his eyes oddly bright.

You failed your son, Constance had said.

For a stupid, really stupid moment, he nearly opened his mouth, but Nate nudged Brendan and the friends turned towards each other, quietly murmuring and the moment passed like water slipping from cupped hands.

Chapter Twenty

December

THE LAST FEW PIECES WERE being dismantled and removed from the house and Brendan stood in the hallway, staring up at the staircase, his mind a million miles away.

"You gonna do anything?" Nate asked as he put down the pile of books he'd been carrying.

"I've been warding most of this place for the past month," Brendan pointed out, swiping a hand across his face. "Thought you said that all that was done?"

"Council decided that they wanted a few more books," Nate said with a shrug. "Though I argue that whatever geeks wanted to trawl through these should have come here themselves."

"Maybe let's not have more untrained people in this mad house," Brendan suggested. "That the last of it then?"

"Fucking hope so," Nate said and then took a last few looks around. "Should burn it down."

It had been suggested. In fact, he gathered it was being hotly debated. But, for now, Porter's Lodge was locked down with spells, wards and runes. It would be locked up and routinely patrolled while the Council ensured it had found all that it needed from the building. He reached for the pile of books, frowning at the cover that replicated the runes Cole had spotted upstairs.

"Tempted?" Nate asked quietly.

It made Brendan smile as he glanced up and over from the book he'd been warding closed. "To control the dead?" he asked, looking back to finish the spell before he placed it on the table they'd brought in and started on the next.

"Resurrection."

"I've had conversations about this with far more qualified people than you," Brendan said smoothing his hand over the next text and sighing because it was spells to break prison wards, and he could imagine why that one had been pawed through to the point it looked far more tattered than the others. "It's a warning," he said quietly. "Parents who won't let their children go or who protect no matter the cost." He stared up at Nate. "Imagine if Constance had accepted Richard's death. If Ruby had avoided necromancy. If they'd turned Phineas in after his first murder or not surrounded those kids with death for whatever plots they were constructing."

"According to my uncle, Jonah Summers' death wasn't a great loss," Nate started and then relented, his tone becoming more serious, "But if all that had happened… You wouldn't have been born," Nate said gently. "Danny, Nicolas. Obviously, I'd have bagged Liaden and we'd have a flock of better looking kids-"

Brendan half-heartedly threw some quartz at Nate who caught it easily and grinned at him. But the smile fell off his face quickly and he shook his head, looking around.

"How did the Council not check up on this? I mean… bad enough when it was just Richard Ambros they failed. Those girls…" Brendan shook his head. "How could you do that? How could any parent-"

"Choose?" Nate asked coming over. Brendan let out a breath as Nate slid down to sit shoulder to shoulder with him. "Yeah. I dunno, mate. Different times, I guess. Sacrifice the girls for the son and heir."

Yeah, maybe, but he still felt…as if he were missing something. Maybe. "Imagine growing up here," he murmured, looking around, "be enough to drive you mad."

"It is enough to drive anyone mad," Nate said, picking up the books, now warded, and headed towards the entrance. "Come on," he said. "You'll miss the main event."

Yeah. Watching his friend leave the hall through the front doors, Brendan started to follow, but something crept up his spine and he looked up at the balcony above. Not sure why, he continued to stare when he saw nothing because, somehow, he still felt the uncomfortable certainty that someone or something was watching them, despite the numerous, endless spells they'd placed on the house.

Should be burned, he thought and frowned as he headed for the doors and out into the fresh air.

The Council themselves were coming after the ceremony to ward the house completely shut and to cast the same upon the grounds to avoid anyone setting foot upon it unless they were from the Council.

They headed to the side of the west wing, past the huge amount of cars in the drive (and wasn't that a strange sight?) and down the winding paths that were lined with thick yew trees. It was a short walk to the graves and Brendan smiled as he spotted Jake and Cole standing awkwardly at the entrance to it.

"Lads," Nate said, nodding to them. "All set for Christmas?"

Cole actually looked rather baffled by the question while Jake immediately groaned. "I have family," he complained. "So much family. I swear, I couldn't do a head count."

Nate laughed and looped an arm around Jake, taking him forward as Cole continued to look deeply uncomfortable.

"Hedgehog boy," Brendan greeted, shoving his hands in his pockets.

He gained a filthy look for it, but, in the past month had come to almost enjoy making the kid glare like that. "This seems pointless," Cole muttered as they headed towards the graves.

It did. But the bodies should be put to rest rather than being left in that house, especially as two of the three hadn't manifested that night. A new headstone stood for Richard Ambros, the boy's body removed from the chapel indoors, and the body on the staircase had been, strangely, the wife of William Ambros who already had a grave out here. There'd been nothing left of Constance so her grave was more ceremonial than anything, but Mr Pembroke's body had been taken to the Currock building and was still raising more questions than it answered.

Around the graves, various important people were gathered, including a number of Coven family members that made Brendan shift with wariness, and the only member of the Council to turn up to conduct the re-burial. Very aware of the people gathered and the volatile possibilities, he turned to watch his former mentor as she started to begin the ceremony.

"We are here," Eun begun, dressed in her formal robes marking her as the Dark Lady of the Council, "to lay to rest the body of Richard Ambros, a child that our founders killed to solidify our new order."

She looked around at those assembled and Brendan caught the eye of Liaden's cousin Patience, the Lady of the Buan family, as Eun swept her gaze around, lingering on the Coven families that had chosen to turn up today.

"And perhaps," she said, "it is a reminder of lines we should never cross, even for the sake of winning. The protection that should be afforded to every magical child, Council born or Coven claimed. That families should never be ignored or forsaken, and that the vulnerable deserve help." She looked up and Brendan didn't need to follow her gaze to know she was looking towards the house, towards the murder site where those poor young girls had suffered so much.

Eun's gaze swept back over to the crowd. "And above all, we must use this moment to realise the danger of secrets. I am proud that, this year, we have seen communication between Council and Coven become more open, more honest. That together, we worked to end a threat to us all with the defeat of Phineas Ambros-"

There was the smallest ripple from the crowd which surprised Brendan for a moment because pretty much everyone in attendance had been given the speech to debate and argue over for the past week.

That was, until he spotted who had walked onto the grounds.

To the edge, Vivienne Ozwald stood, fully dressed in mourning black, the dress and coat rich and dark and perfectly tailored to her body. Her still blond hair was piled on her head in an elegant twist and her chin was held high as she seemed to choose not to acknowledge the stirrings of the crowd.

One look at Boss' face told Brendan that she had not confirmed her attendance.

"-it is important that we take steps forward to ensure that such a threat never rises again. That no-one is trapped or forced into desperate measures. That we do not create our greatest threat again."

Vivienne's mouth tightened in a way that could have been her suppressing a frown or a smile. The woman could have been his aunt and yet it was probably the second or third time that he had ever seen her in passing.

"So we lay Richard Ambros to rest and we lay Mary Ambros to rest. We lay Constance Ambros to rest," Eun said, casting her hand over the three stones. "And we do not forget."

"So mote it be," the crowd murmured and Brendan let the words cross his lips in a vague murmur, his attention stolen by Vivienne as she stepped forward and, with gloved hands, gathered soil to throw it upon the coffin being lowered for Richard Ambros.

Eun waited patiently. If she was nervous, she didn't show it. "My Lady," she said when Vivienne continued to stare down for a moment, and Brendan wondered what she was thinking, what she was seeing.

How much she had known.

"Your words," Lady Vivienne said turning with a grace

that only the truly, deeply confident could manage, “are so very apt.” She nodded once, and then moved away, heading towards the ignored stone with Constance’s name on it. For all that her name had been included in the ceremony, no-one seemed to feel the need to place well wishes on the empty grave.

“Why is it,” Nate said, leaning in slightly, “That her words say the right thing, yet sound strangely like a threat.”

Brendan watched the woman and felt a shiver of unease as he watched the last living acknowledged Ambros child and realised that it wasn’t Constance’s grave her eyes were fixed upon, but Henry Ambros’. “I think she meant it to,” he said with a sinking feeling in his chest.

Epilogue

Cole sat on a rickety old bench at the peak of the hill, elbows on his knees as he stared at the building in the distance. It was a familiar view: sweeping fields faded into the vast lake beyond that reflected the setting sun and spilt vivid colours across the sky. It could have been a beautiful view.

He'd never once seen it as anything other than prison walls.

"This seems unwise," Vivienne said as she sat next to him. "If we are seen-"

He shrugged and settled back into the bench, his eyes drawn as they always were to the tower that stood out starkly against the burning sun like a torchbearer, the distance to the lake terrifying.

"Did you really think it would work?" Vivienne asked with a sigh as she stepped close to him and lowered the hood revealing her fine boned face. She eyed up the bench with distaste before sitting down, shifting with clear disgust. "Trying to reveal the secrets of Porter's Lodge?"

"No. Those who do not know cannot be told, right?" Cole leaned back and drew in a long, deep breath. "Thought it wouldn't hurt though. They're a little closer to the truth."

Too far though. Still far too far from the truth.

"Mm," was all Vivienne said, turning her attention to Ambros in the distance and he wondered what she thought about the ancestral home. He watched her, shoving his hands in his pockets. When she turned to look up at Cole, he was struck by how tired she looked. Vivienne had always looked elegant and in control.

She must have felt his eyes on her and she smiled, as if amused. "You are young," she soothed. "And you are clever, Cole, but you have no idea how long I've been playing this game. Sometimes it exhausts you."

He nodded, not really sure what else he could say. It was worse when she stood and cupped his cheek, making him look at her. Then she frowned and picked up his hand, studying the ring on his smallest finger. "I will admit to being impressed," she said slowly. "It's a sophisticated piece of spell craft. The illusion holds well."

He shrugged, not really knowing what to say to it. The reminder of the glamour that was placed over him was hardly a comfortable topic.

Annoyingly, her grip moved down and her thumb ended up tracing over his wrist and the hidden bindings there. "How much did they bind?"

"Eighty percent," Cole said, hating that his voice wavered.

Her lips firmed, but she said nothing.

"Here," he said, handing over the stone where he had stored his memory of whatever had been on the wall. "I suspect it might be useful."

She accepted the stone without comment, without looking at it, though she did place it in her coat pocket. "It's hardly the most difficult spell to find," she said dismissively before glancing over at him pointedly. "We took what we needed from the house years ago."

He had little to say to that. Certainly nothing that he wanted to say. "It might help you find another way," he said tightly. "I'm not…that cost is too high."

They'd had the argument before where she'd called him selfish. An idiotic child. He had a feeling that neither of them were keen to repeat it.

"You really lived there? At Porter's Lodge? The three of you?" Cole couldn't help but ask.

"My mother was clever. She kept the ghosts at bay. She never wanted to show the Council our secrets, she wanted to plan and plot. And she was good at it. The only thing she didn't bank on was us not managing to be as ruthless as she was about it." She lowered her gaze, eyes shadowed with memories.

"Love is our weakness," Cole muttered.

The sudden grip on his chin made him gasp in shock. "No," Vivienne snarled. "It is strength. It is why your father is free from our curse and why you are free. That was Phineas' greatest gift to both of you. My mother was clever, but she was ruthless. Phineas and I both watched her sacrifice our brother and we swore never to believe as she did. We fought in our way and it almost worked. It could still work. We have never been so close to ridding ourselves of our monsters. You must believe that, Nicolas. We do not need to become monsters to destroy him."

Cole flinched at the name, but said nothing. Instead, he leaned into her touch briefly.

"We fight," she whispered. "You made a mistake,"

Vivienne allowed, glancing down at the bindings, "but we will find a way to fix this, to continue this. To fight for freedom from this. It is what our family does. Always."

He nodded and took a breath.

"Always," he agreed and, for the first time as he pictured his father's determined face, he thought he might actually understand what that meant.

34742259R00204

Printed in Great Britain
by Amazon